CW01461123

MURDER BECOMES MACAU

MURDER BECOMES MACAU

A DALTON LEE MYSTERY

JEFFREY EATON

Book Four of the *Murder Becomes* series

Copyrights & Credits

This book is a work of fiction. Names, characters, businesses, organizations, places, events and incidents either are the product of the author's imagination or are used fictitiously. Any resemblance to actual persons, living or dead, events, or locales is entirely coincidental.

Copyright © 2023 by The Cornet Group LLC
All Rights Reserved

The Cornet Group LLC supports copyright. Copyright fuels creativity, encourages diverse voices, promotes free speech, and creates a vibrant culture. Thank you for buying an authorized version of this book and for complying with copyright laws by not reproducing, scanning or distributing any part of it in any form without permission. You are supporting writers and helping The Cornet Group to continue to publish books for every reader.

Published in the United States of America by The Cornet Group LLC

CORNET

'The Cornet Group' and its logo are trademarks of The Cornet Group LLC

ISBN 978-1-7352092-2-7
First edition, 2023

Cover Design: Randall White
Cover Image: Simon Zhu on Unsplash
Author Photograph: Robin Sachs Photography

Dedications

This book is dedicated to:

Bryan Dunn

Lynne Wingler

Fran Tynan

Val Mellesmoen

Phil Farr

Kirk Rutherford

Steve Owen

Crystal Mayo

Julie Cox Davenport

Joel Choate

Jim Choate

Kathy Choate

Acknowledgments

The following individuals provided invaluable insights that shaped the content of this novel, and they have my most profound gratitude:

Cathay Pacific Airways

Gayle Goodman Lynch

Stella Lam

Bethania Palma

Julian Conway

Randall White

"Before you begin your journey of revenge, dig two graves."
— Confucius

1

For a moment–for one brief, breathtaking moment–it felt as if someone had hit the 'PAUSE' button on some nearby remote control.

Those who had been standing around the edge of the roulette table were now pressing themselves against it, their torsos bent forward, their gazes riveted on the colorful, whirling wheel at one end.

A few minutes earlier, they had all been chatting festively with one another, or chuckling at someone's clever quip. An elegantly coiffed woman in a ruffled white blouse and slim black slacks had been rotating in midair the glass that held her gin and tonic, causing the cubes to clink . . . clink . . . clink . . . clink. Opposite her, a younger man with vaguely Russian features had been rapidly drumming the edge of the table with his fists and whispering a plaintive prayer to some deity above.

But now, no one seemed to be blinking (or even breathing) as the wheel's rotation began to slow, and the nylon ball skittered first toward one pocket, then another, like a hummingbird flitting from one flower to the next.

The expression on every face around the table signaled one thought, and one thought only:

Where is the ball going to drop?

Discreetly seated behind the first row of spectators, Jocelyn Cheng was studying not the ball's trajectory but the looks of anticipation on the faces all around her. Taking in the vibe of one of the seven gaming rooms she oversaw–whatever that vibe happened to be–was one of the greatest pleasures she derived from her job as CEO of the Lucky Fortune Casino Group.

Her predecessor had always been bored by the action on the floor, preferring instead to burrow into the databases and revenue reports that came with being the company's chief executive. But she had always been more energized by the emotion of it all, enough so that she would sneak onto one of the casino floors now and then to bask in the energy of those hoping to hit it big.

The looks worn by the many gamblers around her brought a subtle smile to her lips. She knew, of course, that even if someone standing next to her did beat the dealer, roll a seven, or watch the wheel land on whatever square they'd bet heavily upon, they'd likely lose it all (and then some) within the next twenty-four hours.

She loved knowing the odds were always in her favor. That no matter what, the house always wins.

The room's reverie suddenly broke; the crowd began to murmur and clap. The wheel was about to stop altogether, so the ball was not so much ricocheting now as drifting from the edge of one pocket on the wheel to the next.

She wasn't intrigued with the ball, however, for she knew exactly where it was programmed to land–on number thirty-four, one of the numbers gamblers rarely seemed to bet on.

Tourism was down in Macau, so the house was needing to be more cautious with its payouts.

A hand extended over her right shoulder and set in front of her a chilled martini glass, cleanly accessorized with a tiny lemon twist. "Compliments of the lady in the velvet pantsuit," the server whispered before dashing off as quickly as she'd arrived.

The owner of the casino scanned the perimeter of the table until she noticed a tall blonde (American? Australian?) nodding in her direction. She sorted through her internal contact list, trying to summon up the woman's identity from the vast network she'd assembled over time. She came up blank, nodded back at the blonde to be polite, then took a quick sip of the drink.

Instantly, she could tell it contained a premium Russian vodka with a hint of vermouth. And vanilla. Precisely the way she liked her martinis. *Who is that woman? How do I know her?* she wondered. *Were we on the region's economic development committee together, or on the capital campaign for Macau Mercy Hospital?* She took another, longer sip of the martini, studied the woman more closely.

Maybe she was in one of my MBA classes at Oxford . . .

She tried once more to signal to the woman her appreciation for the cocktail, but the blonde was now locked on the ball's final destination. Any second now, the orb would be completing its journey, breaking more than a few hearts in the process.

"Thirty-six!" the croupier announced. "Number thirty-six!"

Jocelyn Cheng started, then whirled in the direction of her employee, who was casually clearing the board of the chips stacked upon all the other squares.

All the other squares except number thirty-four. The pocket the ball was supposed to land on. The only square that no one usually bet on.

Only this time, someone had.

Something's not right here, she thought. *What's going on?*

Flinging over her shoulder the gold-chain handle of her pink, Chanel purse, she slid off her seat and dashed toward the elevators.

The very last sound Jocelyn Cheng heard before the darkness descended, before her legs went rigid and collapsed beneath her, was the crowd still reacting to the result of the spin. Followed by a woman's voice, shrieking in horror.

But as several bystanders rushed toward Jocelyn Cheng's already stiffening corpse, the blonde woman in the velvet pantsuit casually leaned across the rail and raked in the tall stack of chips the croupier had just pushed her way.

2

"So, Dalton, what's with the fedora?"

Dalton Lee winced, carefully set his pen on the arm of the loveseat. Only one thing irritated him more than being interrupted while buried deep in thought, and that was being interrupted while buried deep in an acrostic.

"You grew up in Northern Europe, Lara, so I would think you would know better," the architect replied with just a wisp of disdain. "This hat is not a fedora. It is a homburg. From Germany."

His executive assistant stared back at him blankly, then frowned.

"Well, excuse me for making such a grievous error. Let me try again. So, Dalton, what's with the homburg? Indoors. In May."

Lee retrieved his pen, tapped it against his thigh, remained thoughtful for several beats. He had been stuck for some time on an especially vexing clue.

M. Causing discomfort.

He counted the number of spaces provided for the answer–there were twelve–studied the ceiling, then exclaimed, "Aha!'

The architect pressed his pen firmly against the puzzle book and deliberately entered the letters:

E -X-A-S-P-E-R-A-T-I-N-G

"Maybe I'm just trying to present a more fashionable image for the firm," he finally replied. "And, speaking of the firm, have we heard any more from the government of Dubai about whether we get to design their new concert hall?"

Lara breathed in and offered a weak smile.

"Well, yes, we have heard more," she began. "But the more we've heard is that . . . we have more bureaucracy to work through before they are willing to finalize a contract with us."

The head of The Lee Group winced, started retracing the letters that comprised his last answer, only with much greater force. He completed the 'G's horizontal shelf with a flamboyant flourish.

"Didn't your mother have some pithy quote about bureaucracy she used to utter?" he asked. "Didn't you tell me that once?"

Lara brightened, gazed off at a distant corner of the room.

"Yes, although if I remember correctly, I believe she lifted it from a Canadian educator in Canada." She stayed in her dream-state for a couple more moments before slowly intoning, "Bureaucracy defends the status quo long after the quo has lost having any status. Or something like that."

Lee chuckled softly and went back to his acrostic.

"And what, if anything, did your father the eminent architect have to say about bureaucracy?"

Lara's smile faded, her gaze descended from the corner of the room to her lap.

"I wouldn't know," she replied curtly. "I've tried to erase from my mind most everything he ever said to me."

He glanced up from the puzzle, analyzed his close friend and colleague for several seconds. Began to reply. Decided not to.

The next acrostic clue swirled in front of him.

N. Form of relief for a couch-potato?

Thanks to Lara's comment, he deduced the seven-letter answer almost immediately, put his pen to paper:

T-H-E-R-A-P-Y

The room remained serene for a while. Lee scanned the upcoming clues, but Lara's silence eventually commanded his attention.

"Did you have any particular purpose when you came into the

room?" he finally asked her. She began to gently massage her hands and pace the floor. Eventually, she cast a forlorn look his way.

"I guess I wanted to tell you I still feel badly about what happened while we were investigating the murder in Mayfair," she said. "I can't believe I fell for such a scam."

Lee pressed his lips together and gently shook his head.

"No need to apologize, Lara," he replied. "We all make . . ." He stopped, chose to recast the sentence. "We all stumble over ourselves at some point."

Lara sniffed, smiled to herself and turned toward her superior.

"I guess that's true. Thank you." She went quiet again, but only for a second. "And that reminds me to ask whether you feel Anisa is integrating well with the rest of the team."

The architect remained focused on his puzzle book but arched both eyebrows dramatically, as if to say, "So you're really going to *go there*, are you?" And he had done such a fine job of forgetting what a fool for love he had proved to be for Anisa after meeting her in London.

At least Lee now knew the real reason why Lara had strolled into his office. Without knocking.

"I take it from your comment you don't think she's being particularly . . . collaborative?"

Lara took a seat in a chair opposite Lee, breathed in and placed the back of one hand into the palm of the other.

"Well, hasn't she seemed a bit . . . stand-offish lately? I mean, I know for certain she's come off that way to Bree and Warren. Even Liam– whom absolutely nobody wants to stand off from–has felt it."

Lee set the acrostic down, convinced he would never be able to finish it while Lara was in the room. He had to admit that Anisa had seemed more distant since they had returned from London, but he had just attributed it to the awkward circumstance they'd experienced with each other while there. This was the first he'd heard that the others on the team had also picked up on her coming across . . . aloof.

The architect crossed his legs and placed his hands in his lap. "Well, I think we need to respect the fact she's under a lot of pressure now, Lara," the architect stated. "The Organization is holding her cousin captive and . . ."

Lara cut him off. "Thanks to them, Dalton, we *all* have people we care about who are in jeopardy. Thanks to them, we are *all* nervous wrecks. Nervous wrecks almost *all* of the time. Yourself included." She paused, pulled back, looked into his eyes. "That should make us more supportive of one another, not more separate from one another."

Dalton returned her gaze and eventually offered a nod of accord. "Okay. Maybe I'll have a word with her about it," he offered. Slowly, he rose from the couch.

"Oh, and, by the way," Lara began, "My sources tell me that The Organization is no longer calling themselves The Organization." He waited for her to finish the thought, but she seemed reluctant to do so.

"And what exactly was the outcome of their little rebranding exercise?" he probed.

She gave him another weak smile.

"*O*," she replied.

"Oh?"

"Yes, *O*. Just, *O*."

Lee squinted some, eventually grasped what she was saying.

"Ohhh. I see. They're going by just the letter *O*," he repeated. "Like the symbol for oxygen."

Lara sniffed. "Or oddballs."

The conversation was interrupted by a distinctive tone from his phone. A tone Lee had tagged to incoming text messages. The tone he had tagged to a certain category of text messages he hoped he'd never receive, but occasionally, periodically, did.

Lara frowned. Peered up at him from her chair.

"Tell me it's not," she said softly.

Lee scanned the message, grimaced a bit, let out a heavy sigh. Using both thumbs, he rapidly tapped a reply, punched 'Send,' returned the phone to his pocket and looked back at Lara.

"*O*, but it is," was all he said.

3

From their expansive veranda just below Mount Nicholson, the three conspirators had a sweeping, unobstructed view of the skyline of Hong Kong Island and the sparkling waters of Victoria Harbor.

Each of them looked like a caricature of the culture they represented. The middle-aged Chinese woman (sipping a sumptuous tea) wore a high-necked red tunic with gold embroidery. The older British male (savoring a pint of lager in a clear, chilled glass) wore gray slacks and a boldly striped business shirt accented with a green bow tie. The thirty-something American male (swigging a bottle of some iconic, name-brand beer) wore cargo shorts, a short-sleeved polo shirt and a faded blue baseball cap.

All three had the letter *O* monogrammed somewhere on their apparel, albeit in different, discreet locations.

The Brit tilted his glass to take another drink of lager, then took a deep breath in.

"What a distinct privilege it is to sit out here on the veranda in May," he announced. The other two offered their agreement.

"You can say that again," the American confirmed. "I've been living here almost five years now and I can't remember a day in May when the sky's been this clear and the humidity's been this low. It almost feels like California."

The Chinese woman turned her head and pointed to a distant spot on the horizon. "In May, I never see that building on the other side of the bus terminal," she said. "Usually, haze make it impossible to see." The others nodded some more at her comment, although neither was sure which building she was referring to, or whether her assessment was really accurate.

After a time, the Chinese woman spoke up again.

"So, the execution in Macau, it was success, yes?"

This time her companions responded enthusiastically. "Yep!" (the American) and "Right-o!" (the Brit).

The latter shook his head and sighed. "Quite unfortunate it had to happen, quite unfortunate," he said. "But decisions have consequences, and the fact is, her decisions had become quite a threat to our plans."

The American took a quick swig of beer. The foot dangling at the end of his crossed leg began shaking vigorously.

"If there's one thing I cannot tolerate," he said, "it's a traitor."

The Chinese woman returned her gaze to the skyscrapers beyond the railing, offered a brief chortle.

"I hope poison did not work too quickly," she said. "Traitors need to suffer. Suffer bad."

The men nodded even more but the American pulled up, cocked his head and assumed a skeptical look.

"No, Yang Li. I actually think it needed to be quick, so she didn't have a chance to tell anyone what we're up to." He turned toward the Chinese woman and smiled.

"But I wouldn't worry. From what I've heard, it was somewhat quick, but she definitely suffered."

She studied the American's smile for a moment then turned back to the view.

Softly, almost imperceptibly, she spat out, "Good!"

The Brit cleared his throat. "I was in receipt of a message this morning saying the architect and his crew will be arriving from America shortly." At the reference to Dalton Lee, the Chinese woman made a hissing sound through her teeth.

"Oh, right, that guy," the American responded. "We need to make absolutely sure he doesn't fuck things up for us again–sorry Yang

Li." She forgave his profanity with a flip of one hand. The American resumed his rant, the timbre of his voice rising as he spoke. "We have way too much invested here to let him stop us from bringing complete personal freedom to every single person in the region. I mean, I'll be damned if we let him do to us what he did to our comrades in Manhattan and Miami."

"And London," the Chinese woman added.

The Brit exhaled. "Well, our agent apparently did a fine job with the assignment in Macau. I'm sure Mr. Lee and his merry band of misfits will be disposed of with the same aplomb when the time is right."

The sun dipped more toward the horizon and the humidity intensified. It became obvious it would soon be time for them to retreat inside. But as twilight began to arrive, and the lights across Hong Kong began to twinkle, an air of solidarity started to seep over the threesome on the veranda.

They did not look at each other or send one another any sort of signal. And yet, in perfect unison, the terrorists raised their left arms, formed fists at shoulder level and chanted, "Power to the cause."

4

"WOW! Is that car for us, Dalton? Seriously? I mean, WOW!"

Warren Jackson jostled his way through the rest of the employees of The Lee Group to peer into the tinted windows of the black Mercedes van that had arrived outside the limousine lounge of Hong Kong International Airport. Lee's senior architect rubbed the palms of his hands together and whistled softly.

"Now *this* is going to be one sweet ride," he added with a grin.

His superior, however, looked unimpressed. Lee removed the baseball cap he had worn on the flight, raked his fingers through his hair, replaced the cap and started plucking some lint that was clinging to the front of his black denim jacket.

"Maybe, but I miss the days when a Rolls Royce pulled up to greet you," he replied. "Since that wasn't an option, I asked them to provide us with an electric vehicle, but apparently those are in short supply right now."

A blanket of clouds made the air turgid and gray, so the team was eager to pile into the air-conditioned interior of the vehicle. Lara and Liam, the firm's tech expert and resident Aussie surfer, entered the van first, squeezing their way into the seat furthest back. Warren gestured to Anisa to access the middle row of seats. Lee climbed in beside

Warren while the firm's other senior architect, Bree Westerman, took the front passenger seat. Their young male driver hopped behind the wheel, adjusted the rear-view mirror and eased the limo away from the curb and onto Airport Road. A separate car would be bringing their luggage to their hotel (in part because Bree had insisted on bringing four suitcases with her on the trip).

"You do realize we're coming here to conduct a murder investigation, not a Vera Wang runway show," Lara had said to her before their departure. Bree just smiled to herself and answered, "Not to worry, Lara. Two of the suitcases are for all the stuff I plan to buy while I'm here."

Lara stared back at her colleague, made a clucking sound. "I pity the customs agent who draws the short stick of processing you back into the United States."

The towering apartment buildings of Lantau Island whizzed past as they sat mostly silent in the van, trying to stave off the sluggishness of jet lag. Warren glanced now and then at Anisa, who seemed preoccupied with a series of texts on her phone; Bree tried to become interested in the local architecture, but dozed off instead, her forehead resting against the passenger window.

After several moments, Liam brought up from the back row an issue that had actually been on the minds of everyone on the team.

"Dalton, why are we staying in Hong Kong rather than Macau?" he posed.

Lee turned his head to one side. "Good question, Liam. For one thing, since my family is from Hong Kong, I have more familiarity with it than I do Macau. Plus, I thought it might do us some good to enjoy a little distance from the actual murder scene–I mean, Macau is only forty-five minutes from the heart of Hong Kong by car or bus, fifteen minutes if we need to get there by helicopter.

"And, before we left the States, I contacted my cousin Samantha, who just emigrated from here, to see if she knew someone in the region who might help us with the investigation in addition to the local authorities. She recommended some former coworker who's semi-retired now but has managed the security details of several business executives and governmental officials across Asia in his career. Apparently, he's situated somewhere on Hong Kong Island.

"So, I guess you could say the decision was mostly one of convenience."

Liam nodded he understood. Meanwhile, Warren made a pretense of nodding off but instead watched Anisa, who made a point of pivoting her torso away from the Canadian as she continued to type away on her phone.

The driver stepped on the brake suddenly, causing Bree to jolt awake. "Are we there?" she blurted before realizing they were still on a freeway and were flanked by the waters of Discovery Bay on one side and by the South China Sea on the other.

"Very sorry, miss" the driver apologized. "The traffic is quite stop-and-start for this time of day." Over time, the procession of cars, limos, trucks and motorcycles began to creep forward. Bree was about to slip into sleep again when Warren brought up the very reason for their trip.

"What do we know about the murder victim, boss?" he asked. Anisa stopped typing on her phone, pulled herself up in her seat to listen to Lee's response.

The architect opened a file he had saved on his phone and cleared his throat. "Well, her name is Jocelyn Cheng. Early fifties, born and raised here, educated overseas like many of those with prominent positions in Hong Kong. She recently became the CEO of one of the larger casino consortiums in the region, not more than two years ago."

"Was she new to the gaming industry?" Lara interjected.

Lee shook his head. "No. She's been with the Lucky Fortune group for almost twenty years. Started in accounting, added some IT skills to her portfolio at some point, then worked her way up the executive ranks. When her predecessor left under some sort of cloud a couple of years ago, she was basically considered the heir apparent."

The van grew quiet again as everyone chewed on the details Lee had shared.

"Any family?" Warren tossed out..

Lee shook head once again. "She never married," he replied. "Has no children. Apparently, she was a woman who was wedded to her career."

"Siblings?" Lara asked.

"Yes, one. A younger sister who lives about sixty-five kilometers away, in Shenzhen. I'm hoping we'll get to talk with her soon." He scrolled through the notes on his phone to see if he had any other details to share with the team.

Bree was now wide awake and relying on the makeup mirror in the visor above her seat to apply some lipstick. "And we know for certain The Organization was behind her murder?" she asked. "We know for a fact that they found . . ."

"Yes, they found a note. *The* note. Curiously, not on the body itself, as is usually the case, but inside her purse. Written like all the others on a page from an original edition of *Wayward Colony*. Claiming, as the note always does, that one of the characters in The Organization's favorite book was responsible for the murder.

"This time, the note stated that Skinny Rockhurst did it. The local police tested the paper the note was written on. It's authentic. Somehow, someway, Jocelyn Cheng got in the way of whatever scheme The Organization has in store, and they once again left behind their little telltale signature just to ridicule us."

Liam scoffed, shook his head. "The Organization . . . what a clown car full of crazies they are."

Lara leaned forward from the back seat. "Everyone! Just a reminder, they're calling themselves *O* now. They're not The Organization anymore. They're just *O*."

Liam shook his head and chuckled. "As I was saying . . ."

"And the cause of death was poisoning?" Warren asked.

Lee nodded. "Well, that seems to be the case, but that has yet to be fully confirmed. She collapsed on the gaming floor of the company's marquis casino while sipping on a martini, but there's no indication she had a heart attack. Therefore . . ."

Lara started to lean back in her seat but then pushed herself forward again.

"Dalton, did you say the note wasn't on her body but in her purse? Doesn't that suggest whoever murdered her wasn't just some random acquaintance but probably someone more intimately involved with her? Involved enough, that is, to have access to her purse right before her murder and when they needed it most?"

Lee glanced into the rear-view mirror and caught Lara's eye.

"I would say it does, Lara," he said softly. "It most certainly, surely does."

***

Nine full hours of sleep had done Dalton Lee a wealth of good. Given the hotel was situated at the very heart of a city with more than seven million people, he was amazed at how tranquil it seemed. And he was thankful for that, for he felt more rested than he had in several weeks.

He decided to indulge in a little nostalgia and have a breakfast not unlike those he remembered having as a child before the family relocated to the United States–a breakfast made up of pineapple buns accompanied by Hong Kong-style French toast that was stuffed with Nutella and drizzled with condensed milk. Then he decided he didn't need to totally ignore his upbringing in America, so he also asked for three slices of bacon on the side.

The order confused room service, since it wasn't breakfast time but a few minutes before noon. They were happy to oblige the world's most prominent architect, however, and the food arrived in less than thirty minutes. Cooked to his satisfaction.

Now, if I can just get them to make a grilled cheese sandwich the way I like it, he told himself.

A quick hot shower had him ready to attack the day. The first order of business: phone the contact his friend back in the States had given him to set up an initial meeting The first ring hadn't finished before someone picked up the other end.

"What?"

Lee was taken aback by the abruptness of the greeting but forged ahead.

"Julian Lao?"

"Yes. What do you want?"

"Um, hello, Julian, my name is Dalton Lee, and I was . . ."

"Where are you RIGHT NOW, Dalton?"

The speaker's sudden increase in volume required Lee to pull the phone back a few inches from his ear.

"Well, um, at my hotel, The Commodore."

"Perfect. Can you meet me at my office in about an hour? It's only about a ten-minute walk from your hotel."

"I . . ." Lee was tempted to postpone the meeting, especially since he didn't have much confidence this person really knew who he was speaking to or why he had called. "I . . . can. I was given your name by a former coworker of yours, Samantha . . ."

"Yes, yes, I know who you are. Samantha told me to expect a call from you. And I'm fairly certain I know why you're calling, too."

"You do . . . ? How . . . ?"

The line was quiet for a few seconds before the former security executive replied, his tone now more genial, his volume more subdued.

"My apologies, Dalton. It's been quite a day here," he said. He took a breath, then, "I know why you're calling because before I went into semi-retirement a couple of years ago, I supervised the personal security of government officials and CEOs from Osaka to Seoul, from Singapore and Bangkok to Jakarta and Mumbai. I'm still kept in the loop on a lot of confidential security issues in the region. I'm very aware of your work in this field, clandestine though it is. And . . ." The speaker's voice lost its bravado, and the line went quiet once more.

"And?" Lee prompted after a moment or two.

"And . . . I knew Jocelyn Cheng personally. We were close buds for a while. Although I didn't see her anywhere near as often once she became the consortium's CEO."

"I see. Well, then, I guess I'll need your office address."

"Certainly. 57 Douglas Street. Just behind Exchange Square. See you at two. If you walk, bring an extra dress shirt. The humidity today is ungodly."

Mortified at the idea of arriving for a business meeting with perspiration stains under both arms, Lee took a hotel car to his contact's office instead. He was thankful he did. Just the short jaunt from the taxi stand to the office building's lobby doors caused several beads of sweat to form on the back of his neck. Fortunately, he was alone in the elevator car, so he was able to pat his neck with the handkerchief he had plucked from a dresser drawer as he was preparing to leave his hotel room.

Note to self, he thought as the elevator began its ascent. *Double the amount of antiperspirant you apply here each morning.*

The security professional was already standing with a broad smile on his face and one hand extended when the doors of the elevator opened onto the building's eighth floor. He was wearing a tan suit, brown shoes, a crisp white dress shirt and a green-and-tan tie accented with diagonal stripes. To Lee, he appeared too young to be even semi-retired, more like someone in his mid-fifties. However, he'd lost much of his hair, a fact he was trying to compensate for with a makeshift combover.

Lee guessed his new adviser to be twenty-five (maybe thirty) pounds overweight. Not really fat, but 'sorta pudgy,' was how he would describe him to Lara when he returned to the hotel that afternoon. But Lee took an instant liking to the gentleman, who seemed completely approachable and eager to please.

"It's such a privilege to meet you, Dalton," he said ushering the architect into his office. "I'm such a fan of your buildings, especially your new hotel in Tokyo. What a jewel that is. Please, please, take a seat." The space seemed much larger, and much more luxuriously furnished, than what someone semi-retired would need. An expansive mahogany desk, and a top-of-the-line, ergonomic chair, commanded a panoramic view of the business towers in Hong Kong's Central district. At one end of the desk was a bulbous, baby-blue lamp base that featured a cloisonne design and was topped by a black shade that filtered the light bulb inside. The result was a warm, twilight glow in the office, despite the fact it was midafternoon, and the window shades were tilted open.

Across from the desk, a tall chrome-and-glass etagere displayed a variety of knickknacks (most likely, gifts from dignitaries across Asia, Lee surmised). His guess was confirmed by a mosaic of framed photographs on the wall next to the shelving, all of which showed the executive smiling at the camera and shaking hands with some government or business official. The pictures had an odd uniformity to them, as if someone had taken another photo of each official, cut them out of that photo, and then pasted them into the photo standing beside the security professional.

It was only the diversity of suits and ties he was wearing from one picture to the next that gave evidence to the fact that the shots were indeed authentic.

"Would you like a cup of jie tea?" His host's right hand gestured to a porcelain canister on a credenza behind his desk. Next to it, an electric tea kettle was plugged into an outlet.

"Really? Jie tea? That would be awesome, Julian," Lee replied. "It's my favorite, but I'm having one hell of a time finding in the United States. Even my favorite tea shop in Manhattan doesn't seem to carry it anymore."

The security professional smiled beneficently. "Oh, I have a contact in the Zhejiang Province where the leaves are grown," he said. "Remind me to put you in touch with him." As he prepared the kettle to boil water, he glanced over his shoulder at his visitor. "Of course, I know the main reason why you are here," he intoned. "But will you be acting as an architect while you're in the region? Do you have any seminars or client meetings lined up as well?"

Lee smiled weakly. "Normally, under these circumstances, I do," he replied. "But not this time. The urgency of the situation doesn't leave me much time for that, I'm afraid."

His host nodded, dropped himself into his leather chair. "Yes, urgency is a good word for it, I'm afraid."

Lee leaned forward slightly. "So, Julian, what do you know about Jocelyn Cheng," he said in a voice just above a whisper.

The security executive tilted back in his chair, placed his hands in front of his face as if he were about to pray, and first pushed his fingers against one another, then released them.

"I guess I met Jocelyn about four years ago," he replied. "I was asked to develop a security strategy for a medical center here, and she was serving on its board of directors at the time. She was impressed with what I came up with, so she asked me to develop something similar for one of the smaller casinos that Lucky Fortune owns.

"I did, but the project fell apart after she assumed the company's reins."

The kettle began to whistle. Julian swiveled toward it, picked it up by its handle and poured the boiling water into a delicate, intricately designed teacup he had previously filled with jie leaves.

Lee took a sip of the tea, closed his eyes, savored its sweet, nutty flavor and fluttered his eyelashes.

"So amazing," he whispered. "So incredibly amazing. Thank you."

Julian leaned over, gripped Lee's upper arm with one hand, said, "You're very welcome, my friend," then returned to his chair.

"So, why do you think the project fell apart?" Lee continued.

Julian dropped his head some, played with the edge of a legal pad sitting on his desk. "Oh, these days, a regional security consultant who's in the process of retiring doesn't command the same sort of cachet as an international security firm with offices on four continents," he replied. "Even if said security firm doesn't really know what the hell it's doing." He glanced up at his guest, who was savoring another sip of the tea. "You'll learn that yourself, Dalton, once you get past fifty-five or so. Both in your role as an architect and as a . . . I don't know, would gumshoe be the right term for this other pursuit of yours?"

Lee was about to partake of the tea again, but at the question, he halted the cup on its way to his lips.

"I prefer the term 'interested party,' " he said before continuing the tea toward its destination.

His host nodded, turned his head some to gaze out the window.

"I was fine with it, really. I somewhat expected it, and I had another project materialize out of nowhere to fill the time that project would have required, so it was all meant to be." Julian's countenance clouded again. This time, however, he looked not at the towers outside his window but deep into Lee's soul.

"I'm not sure which I hate more, Dalton. The fact that they're holding your parents captive, the fact they murdered Jocelyn, the fact they're back to their old tricks, or the fact they've apparently decided to lob their next grenade in the very place in which I've chosen to retire." Lee could tell the security consultant was seething beneath his composed demeanor; he was now bending back the corners of pages of the legal pad he had only been toying with earlier.

Julian sighed heavily, as if to release the tension he held in his body. "They're like those immortal jellyfish in the ocean that revert to a polyp when they die and then repeat their life-cycle all over again," he murmured. "You can injure them—maybe postpone any damage they're about to cause—but you can never, ever eradicate them for good."

Lee considered his host's comparison and deemed it perfectly apt. Carefully, he set his cup on the saucer in front of him and chose to bring the conversation back around to the victim.

"How would you say Jocelyn Cheng was regarded here?" he asked.

The security professional sat up more in his chair. "Very well, for the most part. Of course, she was quite the philanthropist, which usually makes you well-regarded even if you're not well-liked. But honestly, Jocelyn was quite engaging. She wasn't like a lot of the other executives here, who do everything they can to get themselves in the paper, or on the cover of the local business magazines, their fingers glittering with jewels, their foreheads and wattles all snipped and tucked. Quite the opposite. She avoided publicity. People knew about her generosity, but she never advertised it. In fact, . . ."

As he was speaking, Julian leaned toward the credenza and unplugged the kettle, dashing Lee's hopes he'd be offered a second cup of tea.

"In fact, the only time I can remember Jocelyn being photographed in a society setting was when I escorted her to a fund-raiser at the Guia Circuit where the Grand Prix takes place." He let out a laugh and slowly lowered his hands in front of his body to point out his ample physique.

"And let's face it, I'm not really the sort of escort one typically chooses to be photographed with."

Lee smiled, set his tea to one side. As quirky as the guy was, there was something about him Lee found endearing. He wanted to lean over and give his host a great big hug.

"So, we're thinking she may have been poisoned? Any idea as to who might have wanted to do that? Any ideas as to what O might be up to and . . . how she might have gotten in their way?"

Julian assumed a solemn expression.

"Possibly. They're probably just wild, unfounded hunches, but still . . ." He lifted his head and gave Lee a charming smile, but a smile Lee took as one of forced optimism. "By the way, Dalton, who are you going to be working with in Macau? Winston Shi? Jessica Fong?

"No, someone named Raymond Silva?"

"Ah, Ray. I know him very well. Impressive that they've assigned someone of his stature to the case. Yes, he's a good guy. Young. Very bright. His father was a few years ahead of me in the criminology program at the National University of Singapore. You'll enjoy working with him." His host glanced at a clock on the credenza and stood up. Apparently, the meeting was over. "Meanwhile, I'm going to dig a little more into those hunches of mine. I'll let you know what, if anything, I uncover. And, please, don't hesitate to ask me for anything you need. I want to do my best to help, however I can."

There it was again, that urge Lee had to embrace his newfound friend. He stood as well but chose, instead, to just extend his hand.

"Not quite ready to give up the fun of being a detective, Julian?' he asked with a grin.

The security professional returned the question with a sober expression.

"No," he responded. "Just striving to assist in my role as an . . . 'interested party.'"

***

Once Lee stepped outside the building, he was relieved to discover that the humidity had lessened considerably. He thought about walking back to the hotel but decided to take the car he had already summoned.

As he waited for the car to arrive, Lee noticed an odd congruence of five aircraft above him. At first, they did not appear to be synchronized, but suddenly they banked this way, or that, to align in a tight formation about ten thousand feet up. After a few moments, each plane emitted a pillar of smoke which, over time, formed against the hazy, gray-blue sky the words:

WE WELCOME

Aha, Lee thought. *This must be that new skywriting technology I've heard about, where the message is programmed, and then delivered to the plane, via computers. Truly remarkable.*

The planes dispersed, then reconvened and five more plumes of smoke materialized. They hovered in the air and then rearranged themselves to reveal the phrase:

TO HONG KONG & MACAU

Probably a welcome for some convention group that's arrived in town, Lee decided.

The jets regrouped, but this time delivered much more smoke, indicating there were many more characters to whatever it was set to reveal. It took several seconds for the letters to coalesce and when they did, Lee's heartbeat surged.

The message ended with:

DALTON LEE AND
THE REST OF THE LEE GROUP

The convoy beat a retreat toward the horizon. But before they vanished from view, they released five final bursts of smoke. Lee shielded his eyes from the sunlight with his right hand and watched as the white trails gently wafted their way into a distinct, unmistakable shape.

The unmistakable shape of the letter:

O

5

Liam's door was ajar, so Warren sauntered into the room, both hands thrust into his pockets. His eyes bulged when he saw that, in barely more than twenty-four hours, the Australian had managed to make his luxury hotel room look like the party room in a college campus's most partying fraternity house.

An open suitcase sat precariously on one side of the bed, its contents spilling out from every direction. His backpack appeared to have exploded in the corner armchair. Most of the bathroom towels were not hung on their racks but splayed across the granite floor. The top drawer of one of the nightstands was sitting on the floor; meanwhile, all the pillows were crammed between the wall-mounted television and the wall itself.

"Dude, do you realize the picture over your bed is at, like, a sixty-degree angle?" Warren exclaimed. "I mean, how does that even happen?"

Liam tapped a few more keys on his laptop's keyboard, turned toward his colleague and shrugged his shoulders.

"I had a hard time sleeping," was all he said.

Warren sniffed a couple of times. "And what is that smell? Socks? Really dirty socks?"

That's when the Australian assumed his trademark impish grin.

"No, mate. Don't you know quality weed when you smell it?"

The senior architect rolled his eyes, allowed his gaze to float over to Liam's laptop screen. It bore a dark-colored map of the world. In about ten locations, red circles were pulsing, some small, some much larger.

"What's that?"

Liam gave a huge sigh, shifted in his chair.

"Before we left the States, I downloaded this software that picks up pings from fitness devices, smart watches, stuff like that." He looked up, and Warren suddenly found himself looking at a vulnerable young boy rather than the cocky young man who had occupied the seat just a few beats earlier.

"My sister was wearing one of those fitness pedometers when O kidnapped her from the tennis resort near our home," he said. "I have the model number, so I thought I'd see if maybe the software could pick up . . . some sort of . . . blip or something."

Warren peered at the screen over his colleague's shoulder. "Any luck?"

Liam's tightened his lips and shook his head.

"Not really. Maybe something in a rain forest on Java. If that's not the spot, I'm getting a faint ping from the northern coast of Iceland." He sighed again then suddenly swiveled around, forcing Warren to take a few steps back. The firm's tech guru now wore a look of exasperation Warren had never seen him exhibit.

"How long have they had your wife, Warren? For how long have your kiddos been without their mum?"

Warren's response was immediate.

"Three years, ten months, two weeks, two days and . . ." He took a quick peek at his phone "And forty-seven minutes. The kids were about two and three when they grabbed her during her walk."

Liam swiveled back around, swatted the side of his laptop screen with his right hand.

"Damn, this is frustrating, Warren," he exclaimed. "I mean, we stop them here, and they pop up over there. We knock ourselves out to stop them over there, and they start creating chaos someplace else."

Warren pulled in. Since joining the team, he had thought the same thoughts more than once, felt the same surge of futility Liam was feeling right now. He'd grappled with just how hollow their efforts sometimes seemed, yet he'd always found a way to overcome his doubts, rally on to fight the valiant fight.

But seeing Liam now question the point of it all right in front of him only served to remind him of all the hesitation and mistrust he believed he had dispelled for good. Nevertheless, he was the number three person in the firm, behind Dalton and Lara. So, he did his duty and committed to remaining stalwart in front of this relative newcomer to the firm.

"Liam, since I joined The Lee Group, we've rescued three people O had abducted and stopped the group from carrying out horrific plots that would have destroyed the lives of thousands upon thousands of people. To answer your question, it will all end when we've brought home Bree's best friend. Anisa's cousin. Dalton's parents. My lovely wife. And your sister, Caryn.

"Which we will, my friend. And I'm not talking about on some abstract day, way out in the future. But someday soon."

Bree nudged open the door and gingerly entered the room. "I think I heard my name?" she announced, instead of saying what she really wanted to say, which was, "Is it okay if I join you boys?" Her jaw lowered when she saw the anarchy that had taken hold of the room. "Okay, so what tragedy happened in here?"

Warren smiled and pointed toward Liam. "Apparently, surfer boy here did a lot of tossing and turning last night."

She edged further into the room, shoved aside some of Liam's clothing so she could sit on one corner of the bed.

"Bree, when did your friend Carole go missing?" Liam quickly asked her. His directness took her aback, but she steeled herself to answer him.

"Well, Liam, Carole did not 'go missing.' They seized her and threw her into the back of a van. She had delivered a lecture at a college outside L.A. that did not . . . please them. She had passionately advocated for more oversight of negligent eldercare facilities, and they branded her talk as an "overt example of government overreach." Bree's face stiffened as she recounted the memory.

"When I tried to text her the next day, she didn't respond. We were in the middle of developing a major fund-raising campaign for her non-profit and in constant communication then. So, when I still hadn't heard from her forty-eight hours later, I just knew something wasn't right." She toyed with the edge of Liam's bedspread for a moment, bunching up the fabric with one hand, then smoothing it out with the other.

"It was a couple of days later when her daughter received the package."

They waited, knowing the detail would be discomforting.

"It was her upper lip," Bree finally said. "They had packed it in ice and shipped it from some foreign location."

All the oxygen left the room. Warren had heard the details before, but Liam was new to the story.

"Anyway, to answer your question, it's been four, maybe five years ago now. I joined the firm just after Warren did, just before they kidnapped his wife."

Liam jumped up from his chair and moved toward her. "Aw, Bree, I'm such a wanker," he began. "I didn't mean to upset . . ." He placed a hand on her right shoulder, and she placed her left hand on top of his.

Warren decided it might be a good time to shift the focus of their discussion.

"So has anyone had any flashes of wisdom as to who might have murdered Jocelyn Cheng?" Warren asked. "Or what O might be up to here?"

Bree released her hand from Liam's, leaned over and cupped her chin in her hands. "We'll have a lot more to work with after we meet with the local police tomorrow morning," she said. "The problem as I see it is that she was so prominent here. Served on so many committees and boards. Oversaw not one but seven casinos. That means a whole host of people could have easily stepped into her path, embedded themselves into her orbit, so they could easily strike when the time was right."

Warren nodded. "And then there's all the corporate drama to consider, too. Remember, her boss left under 'a cloud.' I'm guessing her ascent to CEO probably ruffled more than a few feathers." Bree began to nod as well.

"I shudder thinking of the number of interviews we may have to sit in on."

"Did you hear the boss say she collapsed on the casino floor after taking a few sips from a cocktail?" Liam said as he returned to his seat. "I'd say few things scorch your public image more than making a face plant in front of all your customers. I mean, talk about spinning 00 on the roulette wheel."

Warren snickered at Liam's joke, regained his composure. "I wouldn't think it would take much to determine what type of poison was in that martini glass," Warren added. "Or who it was that deposited it there."

Bree looked up at her colleague and rolled her eyes.

"Seriously, Warren? Have you not learned over the past five years that absolutely nothing about our work is ever easy?"

Out of the corner of his eye, Warren spied Anisa through the open door, trudging her way down the hallway.

"Hey, Anisa, everything okay?" he asked. "Come on in. We're having a little confab here."

She flashed him a brief smile but did not slow down.

"Yeah, I'm good," she replied over her shoulder. "Thanks."

The senior architect looked back at his coworkers, turned both palms upward.

"And what is that about?" he said.

Bree stood up and strolled toward the door. "I'm not sure," she said quietly. "I asked her earlier if she wanted to go shopping with me and got the same reaction." She hesitated. "It's like she became a completely different person the minute Dalton officially added her to the team."

As she began to exit the room, she leaned back in to finish her thought.

"And I'm going to go ahead and say right now, the person she has become is a person I'm growing increasingly suspicious of."

6

Dalton Lee awoke the next morning with a ringing in his ears.

No, it wasn't quite a ringing, he decided. More like a humming. And not in his ears so much as behind his eyes. At times, it seemed like the humming got interrupted, at which point the humming seemed to be more like a clicking. But over time, it would return to a faint, but continual, hum.

There must be some construction going on nearby, he told himself. *Or maybe housekeeping just flipped the switch on a vacuum.*

Or maybe, it's just another manifestation of . . .

This wasn't how he wanted the very busy day ahead to begin. He was still rattled from the skywriting incident the day before. True, he had come to assume that O was often–if not always–tracking his whereabouts. But he didn't like the aggressive manner of their message. He also didn't like the fact that their subtle little dig had referred to his team.

"Leave them out of this," he said to the bathroom mirror as he lathered his beard for a shave. "This fight is just between you and me."

The architect was eager to connect with the local police contact on Macau who'd be helping with the case. He had grown increasingly impatient over time with the pace of their investigations; too frequently,

36

their success at stopping one of *O*'s acts of terrorism had come 'just in the nick of time.'

And with that, the razor blade nicked his chin.

He dropped his shoulders, winced as he applied styptic to the wound, tried to find humor in the coincidence.

Only, there's no such thing as coincidence, he reminded his reflection in the mirror.

Lee dressed quickly, then glanced at his phone. He was relieved to see there were no emails or texts demanding his immediate attention. And the ringing-humming-clicking in his head seemed to have subsided.

He strode to the closet across from his bed, opened its doors and scanned the array of headwear that lined the shelf above the shirts, slacks and jackets he had fastidiously placed on hangers.

Let's see, he said to himself. *Which hat do I want to wear today?*

***

Everyone in The Lee Group stood on the lower level of the Hong Kong Macau Ferry Pier in Sheung Wan, waiting to board the next watercraft. Everyone, that is, except Bree, who was considering a series of colorful scarves she'd stumbled across in the Shun Tak Shopping Centre just behind the pier.

The day offered more sun than clouds, and the humidity was tolerable despite the fact the wind was dead calm. Everyone had dressed for both the weather and a business meeting, which meant Liam wore khaki slacks, dress shoes and a short-sleeved dress shirt rather than his usual surfer shorts, flip flops and t-shirt. Lara protected herself with gigantic dark sunglasses and a cream-colored poncho over business slacks; Anisa (standing a couple of feet apart from the others and with her arms crossed in front of her) had on a pink blouse and khaki-colored cargo pants tapered at the ankles. Warren looked much the same as Liam.

"I have to say, Dalton, the last thing I expected you to wear to this meeting was a beret," he said to his superior. "I thought Macau used to be a colony of Portugal, not France."

Lee leaned to his right to watch the approach of one of the ferries coming from Macau, chose mostly to ignore Warren's remark.

"You know your history, I see," he replied evenly.

Bree joined the group on the pier, bedecked in an oversized floppy sunhat and–draped around her shoulders–an extra-large scarf from the shopping arcade behind them.

"Lara, you've got to go shopping with me while we're here," she asserted. "Oh, my heavens, the deals here. I'm a little gobsmacked."

Lara gave her the once-over then turned toward the water.

"I was actually thinking of another word to describe you," she said dryly.

Within moments, they were boarding a sleek, bright-red ferry with *TurboCraft* emblazoned on one side.

"This looks like something out of a chase scene in a spy film," Liam said, ducking some as he entered the boat.

They split into two groups. Liam, Bree, Anisa and Warren commandeered four seats in a long row; Lee and Lara took two seats off to themselves. Soon enough the ferry was churning across the water. Everyone settled into their seats and into either silence (Anisa) or muted conversations (Liam and Warren).

After a few moments, Lara leaned toward her seatmate.

"So that you don't think I'm a slacker," she whispered, "I've been doing a little bit of sleuthing into Jocelyn Cheng's financial transactions."

The architect raised both eyebrows.

"And?"

Lara lowered both her head and her voice. "Most everything seems to have been normal up until about three weeks ago. But around then, a significant deposit landed in each of the three offshore accounts of hers that I was able to tap into."

"You mean hack into, don't you?" Lee replied. Lara punched him lightly in the upper arm. He smiled back at his attacker, picked up a nearby newspaper and pretended to read it.

"Sizeable, as in . . .?"

"Each deposit was for something around $3 million."

"Okay. I'd call that sizeable."

Lara squeezed closer to her boss, lowered her voice even more. "But here's the interesting part," she continued. "The day of her murder, the same amounts were withdrawn from her accounts."

"On the very day she was murdered, you say?" Lee contemplated that detail for a moment. "Any indication as to who made the deposits? Or the withdrawals?"

Lara sat back in her seat and breathed out quietly.

"Well, yes. And no."

"Meaning?"

She leaned toward him again, pointed toward the newspaper as if she had been drawn into one of its articles.

"The names of the depositors, and to whom the money was returned, were all identified along with the transactions," she said softly. "But they're obviously shell companies structured to keep the true identities of the owners confidential." She gave her colleague a knowing look. "One was the Oriental Gift Exchange Corporation. Another was Oolong Tea Supplies International. And the third was Ocean Trading and Barter LLC."

Lee nodded hard, once. "Ah, I see. All beginning with the letter O."

He folded his arms and crossed one leg over the other, tried to recall if he'd encountered any of those corporate names before. He decided he hadn't. After a time, he turned toward Lara and nudged her shoulder with his.

"So, you think I consider you a slacker?" he asked, an impish smile crinkling his lips. She didn't return the expression, but instead gazed straight ahead of her.

"Not anymore you don't," she replied.

***

"I'm very sorry, but the superintendent-general is not here at the moment," the receptionist told them upon their arrival. She was no more than thirty, but she looked like a secretary from some previous decade, with a pencil behind one ear and eyeglasses accented with cat eye frames. "Did you have an appointment with him?" She started to tap on the keyboard in front of her.

Lee turned to Lara. "Did we have an appointment?"

His assistant was calling up some information she had stored on her phone when the door behind them swung open and a short, athletically built man in a white polo shirt and gray slacks bounded into the room.

"Dalton Lee, I am very sorry, Raymond Silva here, what a pleasure to finally meet you and your associates," he said, extending one hand. "I got held up by the friend I was playing squash with and lost track of the time. Please, come into my office, all of you. And call me Kip. That's what anybody who knows me well calls me."

He had a perfect smile, tweezed eyebrows and a tan that Dalton Lee coveted. The architect guessed (correctly) that Silva had received his education from one of the Catholic schools in Macau and then graduated from Macau's Academy of Public Security Forces. As they entered his tidy office, Silva rapidly gave his assistant some instructions in Cantonese before once again turning on his megawatt smile for all of his guests.

Lee noticed that Silva's diplomas and awards were expensively framed and neatly arranged on the wall opposite his desk. Liam noticed that Silva had killer calves beneath his slim-fitting slacks, indicating the police official either was a prolific cyclist or played a lot of tennis or squash.

Bree noticed that Silva wasn't wearing any sort of commitment ring.

Their new contact pushed aside a stack of folders so he could sit on the side of his desk, his feet brushing the floor. "Anyone care for a Chupa Chup?" he asked, as he plucked one of the fruit-flavored lollipops from a clear-glass container behind him. "I have cherry, orange, and grape." Lara, Liam, Anisa, Warren and Dalton murmured polite declines.

"I'll take one," Bree said enthusiastically. She quickly added a sweet smile. "Orange, please."

After Silva had obliged her request, he allowed his smile to fade somewhat.

"I can definitely say, Dalton, that, given your renown in the world of architecture, we're honored to have you here." He paused, send a somber look toward his guest. "I'd love to say that I'm *thrilled* to have you here," he began, "but given the real circumstances that have brought you here, the circumstances that bring you and your colleagues anywhere, I suppose . . .'

Lee raised the palm of his left hand.

"Please. I completely understand. I'm used to feeling like the mortuary owner who strolls into the wake of the deceased."

Silva breathed out. "At the same time, I can't say I'm terribly surprised they've targeted us for their next campaign, whatever that may be. Given the . . ." he stopped to select his words with care. "Given the uncertainty the region has been experiencing recently, I've been worried we might become more attractive to them as a target."

Lee chewed on that statement, but decided that for now, he didn't want to explore that. He considered how best to redirect the conversation, led with, "So . . . the cause of death was . . . poison, we assume?"

Silva nodded briskly. "Yes. Fortunately, we were able to retrieve the cocktail glass. We're analyzing it now to determine what type of poison it contained."

"Fingerprints?" Warren interjected.

Silva's brow tightened. "Only Ms. Cheng's," he said. "But are we surprised by that? We all know these aren't amateurs we're dealing with."

Bree removed the lollipop from her mouth. "Wouldn't it be simple to track who made the martini for her and who carried it to her? Seems to me our list of murder suspects is down to two." Silva flashed his smile at Bree, and she returned the lollipop to her mouth.

"I wish it were that simple," he said gently. "Apparently, the casino was packed that night and the bartenders were in the weeds trying to keep up. We can tell who rang up the drink, but that's not necessarily who made it. And, because of the crowd that night, many of the drinks sat unattended at the service station for more than a couple of minutes. It wouldn't have been all that difficult for someone in the crowd to spike hers."

"The casino's cameras would have caught that, though, yes?" The rest of the team pivoted toward Anisa, surprised to hear her speak up.

"One would presume," Silva responded, tossing his now-depleted lollipop stick into a nearby trash bin. "But it's not guaranteed. The casino will be sending us their videos from that night soon, if they haven't done so already. You're welcome to review them once we receive them. And to interview anyone you want, so long as I can join you for those interviews."

"Well, of course you can!" Bree chirped.

Lee turned briefly toward his employee, raised one eyebrow, then turned back to the police official.

"Thank you, Ray . . . I mean, Kip. We may want access to the victim's residence and office, as well."

"You've got it," he responded. His gaze drifted up to the beret resting jauntily atop Lee's head.

"You know, I really should get one of those," he said.

Lee just smiled and began to drum the fingertips of both hands on his thighs. "I assume you know we have some investigative resources of our own," he began.

The superintendent-general nodded again. "Oh, they're renowned."

That made Lee smile. "Well, we recently came across some unusual activity in Ms. Cheng's financial accounts. Large sums deposited a few days before her death, and then withdrawn around the time of her death." Lee stopped to allow the significance of that sink in with Silva. "Would you have any ideas about that?"

Their host allowed his gaze to trail up to one of the corners of the ceiling. It stayed there for several seconds before he looked back at them.

"Well, the amounts don't surprise me all that much," he finally answered. "Given her position, Jocelyn Cheng's compensation was well into seven figures, I'm sure. And her generosity to causes throughout the region often pushed seven figures as well. So . . ."

Lara leaned forward and handed Silva a single sheet of paper.

"The transactions totaled around ten million," she said coolly. "And the entities behind them don't appear to fall into the category of what one might call 'charitable causes.'"

Silva scanned the page, glanced at Lara, then looked back at the page. His lips set firm, and he shook his head.

"I don't recognize the names of any of these companies," he said, as he handed the information back to her. "And I sort of pride myself on knowing most, if not all, of the legitimate businesses in and around the region." He turned his attention back to Lee. "I can have my team dive into that, if you want."

Lee shook his head. "You're probably overwhelmed as it is. Let us handle that." He stood, indicating to his team it was time for them to return to their hotel. "Of course, we all know that a murder like this is just the precursor of something bigger they intend to roll out in the days ahead."

Silva nodded and slid off the side of his desk.

"Yes. And that finding the murderer, finding out why they murdered Jocelyn Cheng, and pressuring the murderer to reveal to us what O has up its sleeve, is our best hope of stopping them."

"Possibly our only hope," Lee added, turning toward the door of Silva's office. "Meanwhile, we'd appreciate it if you could set up some interviews for us with those who were at the casino the night Ms. Cheng passed away."

"Happy to," Silva responded. "And as for the victim's sister, I believe she is coming in from Shenzhen either today or tomorrow." Lee indicated speaking to her would be helpful as well.

They all told Silva goodbye as they filed out of his office. All except Bree, who cupped his forearm tightly with one hand. "Thank you for the lollipop," she said politely. "It was delicious."

Silva's smile grew wider than ever. However, "You're quite welcome," was all he said in reply.

Once his team had filed out of the office in front of him, Lee hung back some and sidled up to the head of the police force. "Kip, I wanted to share with you what happened to me yesterday on Hong Kong Island." Silva listened intently as Lee recounted the skywriting incident from the day before, frowning more and more as the architect relayed the ominous details. At the end of Lee's story, he breathed out heavily.

"I was hoping we could keep your presence here under wraps longer," he apologized. "To get at least a little head start on them." His expression was determined as he clapped Lee solidly on the back. "I'll check with my contacts at the military bases and at the airport to see if they have any records as to who might have been using the air space when that happened."

Lee thanked Silva, then bade him goodbye.

***

As they were heading back to Hong Kong, Anisa raised a concern no one was expecting.

"I'm just wondering," she posited, "has anyone properly vetted this Silva guy? Do we know for sure he isn't a member of O? I mean, if there's anything I've learned about them, it's that they'll stop at nothing to ingratiate themselves with local officials and entice them to their side.

"I mean, I just don't know," she added. "He seemed a little slick to me, is all I'm saying. A little too charming."

Bree cocked her head to one side. "Well, I found him perfectly delightful and incredibly helpful," she said curtly. "Why would the head of security turn on the very region he's entrusted to secure?"

Anisa looked for support from Warren and Liam, who were playing some sort of game on their phones. Liam glanced back at her and shrugged his shoulders.

"Dude seemed bonza to me," he offered, before returning to whatever battle he and Warren were engrossed in.

Across the aisle, Dalton Lee wasn't thinking about Kip Silva, the Organization, lollipops or online games. He was preoccupied with another topic that was of equal, if not greater, concern to him at the moment.

He pulled the beret tighter onto his head and studied the wake being left by the ferry as it chugged its way across the Pearl River Estuary.

When should I tell them, he wondered. *When will I get the courage to tell them?*

Because they most certainly have a right to know . . .

7

Save for the three of them, the beach was completely deserted. The precipitation and blustery winds had made certain of that.

But even if there *had* been another person in the vicinity, it was unlikely they would have noticed the trio huddled behind the craggy rock formation at one far end of the cove. They might have picked up the smell of smoke from the small bonfire the three had built in the center of their circle. But the rocks behind them were tall and broad enough to shield them from direct view.

"Great place for a meeting, Yang Li," the American said. "Nice and private."

"By Jove," the Brit said, "for once, I believe I have to agree with our American friend here. A brilliant choice, Yang Li."

The Chinese woman toiled at a weaving project she had been working on for more than a week, a shawl for a granddaughter living just outside Nanjing, she told them. As she spoke, her needles clicked and clacked with a steady, almost hypnotic rhythm.

"Yes. Hac Sa only beach in all of China with black sand," she said quietly. "Not very lovely, so not so many tourists. Especially when weather like this."

The American pulled the collar of his windbreaker closer around his neck. "So, we're agreed that even with Jocelyn Cheng dead now, we're still committed to moving forward."

The Brit and Yang Li simultaneously uttered, "Hear, hear!' and "*Hai aa nei gong dak aam!*"

Being the largest of the three, the Brit ducked his head behind the rocks even more to prevent anyone strolling by from seeing him.

"I do have one question. Do we intend to aim our assault just on the leadership in the immediate region or . . . "

The American cut him off.

"I think the decision has been made to inflict damage as far across the western Pacific as possible. Our colleagues to the north and in Oceania have spent the last few months secretly installing the equipment that should allow us to accomplish that. The thought is, the wider the assault, the greater the catastrophe to the financial markets and the greater the destabilization to this swath of the world politically. When that happens, within hours we should be able to . . ."

"Take over," Yang Li finished his sentence.

"I prefer the term, 'Liberate,' Yang Li," the Brit said firmly. The woman shrugged her shoulder and continued with her handiwork.

After a moment, the American expanded his chest, inhaled the sea air through his nostrils and cracked a wide grin.

"Imagine how epic it will be when all the worker-bees in those corporate cubicles, and factory uniforms suddenly taste total, unadulterated freedom for the very first time?"

The Brit nodded, dared to peek around the rocks at the tide that was beginning to recede from the beach. "Glorious indeed," he said reverentially.

Yang Li allowed herself only the wisp of a smile and nodded silently. But the clacking of her needles made it perfectly clear that she was in total, ardent agreement.

8

At first, Bree was drawn to the idea of making a shopping expedition to the world-renowned Temple Street Night Market. The chance to snag–at a significant savings–the latest mobile phone, or designer watch, was almost too much for her to resist.

But the more she read about the shopping options in the region, the more she became intrigued with the Ladies' Market along Tung Choi Street. She was especially excited about picking up a pair of silk pajamas or a form-fitting *cheongsam*. Preferably in green, which usually complemented her auburn hair.

Deciphering Hong Kong's subway system was too daunting, she decided, so she chose to cross the harbor on the *Star Ferry* instead. When she learned a first-class ticket cost less than fifty American cents, the transportation decision was sealed.

A bank of cumulus clouds loomed above the harbor, resembling down comforters straight from the dryer. The forecasters were calling for rain to move in within twenty-four hours, but on this particular late afternoon the weather was dry and breezy.

She chose to stand next to a window so she could gaze across the harbor to the hotels and other large edifices on Kowloon. Her work as an architect had her marveling not just at the shapes of the structures but also the engineering that enabled them to occupy what often appeared to be incredibly steep and precarious terrain.

Her more underground work, as a detective, had her pondering who might have slain Jocelyn Cheng. *Surely, we'll be able to identify the murderer through the casino's surveillance films,* she thought. *It's not that easy, these days, to spike a drink in public without it being captured one way or another.* The wind picked up, causing the ferry to rock more than it had been. Bree widened her stance to balance herself as the boat bobbed first this way, then that.

But more important than WHO murdered her, she noted, *is WHY they murdered her. Those huge deposits and withdrawals that Lara found definitely make it seem like she had gotten involved with O somehow.*

For a second, Bree fantasized what it would be like to be the head of a global gambling empire. That life seemed like it would be pretty cushy.

So, why would someone with that sort of wealth and status choose to be involved with a wacko cult like O? What could they possibly do for her when it seemed she already possessed everything she could possibly want?

The ferry started rocking even more, forcing Bree to extend one arm to brace herself against the window. She glanced around, spotted an empty seat near the center of the watercraft and quickly claimed it.

That's when a curious thought hit her.

Maybe Jocelyn Cheng didn't choose to be involved with O after all, she told herself. *Maybe they were coercing her to work with them and, for some reason, paying her exorbitant amounts of money to keep quiet. Or, to execute something for them.*

And then when she didn't deliver what they wanted from her . . . or stopped agreeing to their terms . . .

She turned to study those with whom she was sharing this passage. Most–even the few teenagers who were on board–were sitting still and stoic, wore looks of boredom or sadness (or both) on their faces. She wondered how they'd respond if they knew what she knew–that a group of terrorists was working behind the scenes to steal what few, fragile liberties they had left, even though those terrorists believed they were doing just the opposite. That, for no good reason whatsoever, they'd been chosen to be locked in the crosshairs of some unhinged maniacs who, left unchecked, could bring agony to their lives.

Or something worse.

She wondered how they'd react if she did what she really wanted to do, which was stand up and yell, "We're going to do everything in our power to save you!" But, of course, she couldn't do that, and for perhaps the first time since she had joined The Lee Group, the feeling that she was impotent, at a time of such dangerous urgency, became almost more than she could bear.

And then her thoughts turned to Carole. Who was likely confined in some ramshackle cabin, cloistered convent, unmoored ghost ship or underground dungeon. Unable to preach about the need in the world for more peace, dignity, compassion and faith. She stumbled on that last word, because she was finding it increasingly difficult to tap into the faith that Carole insisted can always see us through even the bleakest times.

But also, because she knew that if the situation were reversed, and Bree were the one imprisoned, Carole would never lose faith that she would somehow, some way, rescue her. Therefore . . .

The ferry had completed its crossing and was edging its way toward the pier next to Tsim Sha Tsui. The sun had made a quick descent; the result was a blue, twilight glow across the harbor behind her, and across the mix of hotels, restaurants and shopping malls spread out before her.

A short taxi ride had her soon standing at the corner of Mong Kok Road and Tung Choi Street, standing somewhat overwhelmed by the bombardment upon the senses it delivered, a raucous world that was many light years from the rural Arizona ranch life she'd grown up with. She had expected the market to be popular but wasn't prepared for the throngs of people who pushed and bumped against her as she edged her way down a narrow street. The merchandise on display also engulfed her; much of what hung from the wire racks on both her left and right were cheap items destined for some tourist's carry-on–t-shirts that read 'I ♥ HK.' Children's backpacks decorated with animé characters she guessed her nieces would recognize. And sunglasses and reading glasses that she could tell would fall apart after a week of wearing them. But then, she'd suddenly come upon a rack of beautiful purses and pocketbooks which—if they were not genuine leather—seemed 'leather enough.' She lingered around one stall that was abundant with handbags and decided to ask the young male staffing it what the price of one or two of the items would be. He scratched the top of his modified bowl cut and feigned a serious contemplation of her question.

His answer still floored her. Only about 40 percent of what she'd pay in the States for a similar bag. And Lara had schooled her that any first price given to her was probably three to five times what she might be able to purchase the item for. She decided to play coy and return to negotiate later. But as she began to move away from the stall, he called out a lower price, adding "CASH!" to his offer. She smiled, kept walking and, over her shoulder, replied, "Maybe."

She sauntered up Tung Choi Street and immediately became enamored with the goldfish market, which brimmed with colorful aquariums and individual goldfish secured in plastic bags pumped full of water. She toyed with buying one or two for her apartment but then considered the obstacles she'd probably face getting them back into the States.

As she was leaving the fish emporium, she spotted a red-and-and-green-striped rep tie, hanging on a rack across the lane.

Oh, wouldn't Kip Silva look terrific in that, she thought. *It would really set off his tan. But, . . . too forward?* She eventually decided it probably was, and to keep shopping just for her.

As she rounded the next corner, lured by several racks of colorful scarves and shawls, a stench suddenly made her stomach churn. On her right was a short row of food counters, and Bree suspected the offending culprit was an item Lara had warned her about—a common Hong Kong dish called stinky tofu. The odor straddled those made by rotten meat and smelly feet. Lara had advised her that the prevailing wisdom was that the more obnoxious the dish's smell, the more flavorful its taste. Another wave of the odor assaulted her nostrils. So rather than stay and test Lara's theory, she did a one-eighty to return to the main street she had veered from.

For such a crowded destination, the market was unusually serene, Bree thought. There was a steady chatter of voices—Chinese, British,

Australian and American accents ebbed and flowed around her, but at a completely tolerable level. Occasionally, the excited voice of a toddler, or the tinkling of a bicycle bell, would rise above the conversations that surrounded her, but only for a few seconds. Then the noise level would return to what one might encounter in a large convention hall during a break in the proceedings.

But as she approached the end of another side street she'd chosen to explore she heard what sounded like a cat mewing for help. The cry had an urgent, desperate tone to it; was most definitely a plea for help or for some form of relief. It seemed to be coming from a stall far up on her right, so she moved to the other side of the narrow street to see from a distance what was causing the clamor.

She was now walking upstream, so she found herself being jostled (or jostling) the shoppers headed in the other direction. But the yowl was so compelling, she felt obliged to learn the cause of it.

Finally, she pulled even with it and spotted what she assumed to be a teenaged girl seated on the ground, one arm extended toward the crowd. As a shopper would approach, the girl would lunge the upper half of her torso forward and utter the cry Bree had heard, a guttural burst of syllables she delivered at a high pitch. Bree guessed the girl was asking passersby for money and, indeed, as she drew closer, she could see that the waif was sitting on a tattered mat littered with a smattering of coins. Although the girl's eyes were almond-shaped, they were a robin's egg blue, and her matted hair was more sandy-brown than dark. The result was an appearance that was more Eurasian than Asian.

What Bree noticed most of all, however, was how filthy the girl was. Dirt was smeared across her forehead, cheeks and chin; her arms and legs were caked with it as well. Even the thin cotton dress she wore had blotches here and there of what appeared to be dried mud.

Bree found the beggar both revolting . . . and mesmerizing.

She watched as scores of shoppers trudged past the girl. Perhaps one or two dropped a coin onto her mat, but most simply ignored her presence. One person even stepped on the girl's ankle, then shot her an indignant look as they moved on.

The entire time, the girl had been focused on those passing in front of her. But for no apparent reason, the girl suddenly took her eyes off all the passersby, rotated her head slowly to her right and centered her attention on the very spot across the street where Bree was standing. Their eyes locked, and Bree felt as though the teenager was not so much looking at her, but into her.

Deep into her.

Deep into her psyche.

As if she were saying to Bree, I know you. And you know that you know me.

Only, Bree didn't know her. *Didn't want to know her, at all.*

Or did she?

A voice suddenly barked out on Bree's left, causing her to lean back to avoid being struck by an older man who was hurtling toward her on a rickety bicycle. When he passed, a gaggle of shoppers who'd been stuck behind him surged forward in front of Bree, temporarily blocking her view of the beggar across the street.

When the crowd cleared, however, the girl was nowhere to be seen, and her plaintive cry could no longer be heard.

Bree felt a distinct tingle traverse the entire length of her backbone. "Something about her," she said softly.

It had moved from twilight into evening, so Bree decided she needed to forgo any more sightseeing and finalize whatever purchases she was going to make. She pulled a piece of wintergreen chewing gum out of her pocket, plopped it into her mouth and strolled back to Mong Kok Road, where she had noticed the rep tie she believed Kip Silva might like. She gave it one more once-over but slowly turned away and continued up the street.

I can always come back for it if I want to, she reminded herself.

Moments later, she was back at the stall that was selling the leather goods she'd found alluring. The vendor with the bowl cut was helping another customer, but he brightened when he saw her approaching.

"You still want those calfskin leather pocketbooks?" he asked in perfect American English. "I can give you a great deal if you buy two of them."

Bree gave the offer some consideration but decided to take just one, a tan pocketbook that, from afar, looked exactly like one crafted by one of Italy's more renowned designers. The suppleness of its leather made her think the item might actually be the real deal.

They agreed on a price that was still far less than what Bree had expected to pay. She started to drop it in the large tote she'd brought with her, but the owner of the stall interrupted her.

"Here, let me get you one that hasn't been handled by everybody," he said, bending behind a table to pluck a more pristine pocketbook from an open cardboard box. Bree checked to ensure it was of the same quality as the one she had just inspected and, satisfied that it was, thanked the vendor and scooted on toward the pier to catch the next ferry back to the hotel.

The approaching rain clouds had lowered, casting a dark, foreboding filter across the skyscrapers that towered side by side on Hong Kong Island, their lights shimmering in the water below. Bree found the montage both stupendous . . . and more than a little ominous.

The flavor had left her chewing gum, but she couldn't find a bin to toss it into. She fumbled around for a few seconds; she supposed she could drop it inconspicuously on the pavement next to the pier, or even toss it into the harbor when no one was looking.

She decided instead to secure it inside her new pocketbook until she could locate a rubbish bin at the hotel. The clasp of the clutch unlocked easily, but she stopped short when she found inside a small piece of paper folded onto itself.

Carefully, Bree unfolded the sheet and tucked her gum inside it, but stopped short when she noticed what appeared to be a handwritten message on the page. She unfolded the paper completely and took in a breath when she saw the sentence it spelled out in small block letters:

GET OUT OF MACAU, LEE GROUP, OR SUFFER THE CONSEQUENCES

9

The tapping at Dalton Lee's hotel room door came so softly, he almost didn't hear it. As if the caller was, in fact, reluctant to connect with the architect.

He exhaled, squinted once more at the acrostic clue in the puzzle book.

T. Limits to respect?

The answer contained ten letters. When the tapping on his door returned, this time with greater force, he raised his head a few inches and went, "Oh. Of course."

Putting pencil to paper, he entered the letters:

B-O-U-N-D-A-R-I-E-S

"Dalton, It's Anisa," she whispered through the door. "You wanted to talk?"

At that, he sat up, began to sweep away the crumbs from the grilled cheese sandwich he'd just finished.

"Yes. Give me a moment," he called back to her. He scrambled out of the armchair and dashed to the mirror hanging above the bedroom dresser to make sure he was presentable. Assuring himself that he was, he trotted to the front door and casually opened it.

Even in a t-shirt and blue jeans, Anisa looked radiant. Her makeup was minimal, but he was still taken by her compelling eyes, her full lips, her prominent cheekbones. Her shortish haircut was swept up into an intentional bird's nest of tangles and curls, and she wore a perfume that gently combined the fragrances of jasmine and rose.

Only, instead of an ingratiating smile, she wore a look of befuddlement.

"Is something wrong?" he asked.

"Um . . . no . . . it's just . . . I can't remember the last time I saw a . . . porkpie hat on someone."

Lee's eyes trailed upward and the fingers on his right hand automatically flew up to caress the hat's brim as if to confirm it was truly there.

"Oh, right, I forgot I was wearing it." He smiled meekly, then added. "Please, come in." She strolled into the room, hands clasped in front, her look of confusion replaced by one of sheepishness. Her eyes traveled back to the hat. She began to make a comment, chose not to.

"I'm sorry if I'm disturbing you."

"No, no, not at all. I just finished dinner and I was trying to make some headway with this acrostic I've been fiddling with."

She glanced at the plate that rested on the top of the leather footstool in front of his chair.

"You had a grilled cheese sandwich? For dinner?" Her trademark look of bemusement swept away all of her previous expressions.

"Yes. I did. Your point?" Soon, he was smiling along with her. "Actually, it was an outstanding grilled cheese sandwich if I do say so myself. They used the shokupan bread from Japan I'm so fond of, and they didn't put too little butter, or too much, on each slice. Or a sweet pickle. If they put a sweet pickle on it, I can't eat it."

Her smile widened. "So, no need for you to put on an apron, barge into the kitchen and give the chef a lesson in the art of making a grilled cheese sandwich to Dalton's liking?"

Lee just chuckled, shook his head at her remark and strolled to his armchair. He gestured for her to take the one across from it.

"Oh, I suppose I could find some way to improve it, if I thought long enough about it," he answered.

They lapsed into an awkward silence, until Anisa decided to break it.

"Well, you texted that you wanted to see me? I was hoping this might be a good time for us to talk, but if not, I can come back some other . . ."

"No, this is fine, Anisa. It's just . . . I wanted to bring up . . ." It was at times like this that Lee recognized how much he relied on Lara. People skills were more her forte. People, in general, were more her forte.

Finally, he locked on those exquisite eyes that had transfixed him so in London.

"I think . . . I think the team thinks . . . that you don't . . . like them very much."

Her exquisite eyes expanded and subtly took on a steely quality.

Uh oh, she's shutting down on me, Lee worried.

"Don't like *them*? Oh, my gosh, Dalton, I was thinking it was the other way around."

It was now time for the head of The Lee Group to express his amazement.

"How could anyone not . . . I mean . . . um . . . why would you think *that*, Anisa?"

She studied the carpet for a couple of minutes.

"It's just that, all of you have been together for some time now, working on these investigations long before I arrived on the scene. You all have this sort of . . . rhythm to what you do, and I don't know that I'm getting into that rhythm very well."

Lee analyzed his associate closely. Something about her body language didn't seem to match up with her words. Besides, hadn't she meshed extremely well with the team while they were working in Mayfair? Hadn't it been her contact with an old college friend that had enabled them to prevent widespread catastrophe across London?

Her assertion that she didn't feel like she meshed well with the others was most definitely breaking news to him.

"Well, that's very interesting," he said, his tone becoming a bit more cathedral. "Because they seem to feel you've been detached from them. 'Not very engaged,' is the precise phrase I think I've heard them use, more than once."

A grin slowly crossed her face. "I guess I can understand that,

Dalton. It's just that I'm a little preoccupied right now with a . . . side project, I guess you'd call it."

The architect pulled up in his chair.

"A side project? What kind of side project?"

She breathed out heavily and went back to scrutinizing the carpet.

"I can't tell you right now, Dalton," she answered. "I want to, I really do, but I just can't. Not right now. The time isn't right."

There was a vulnerability in her reply that tugged at Lee. However, he'd pushed all of that aside while they were in Mayfair.

Or he was under the impression he had.

"Does this have something to do with your fiancé in South Africa?" he asked.

She glanced up at him. Her eyes were dewy now, her lips set tight. "There's no fiancé in South Africa anymore. We broke things off about three weeks ago."

Oh, that doesn't help the situation AT ALL, he thought to himself. He was resolved, however, not to let his bent toward romanticism shove his good judgment out the window.

"Well, Anisa, I'm sorry about that," he said to her. "I truly am." (Could she tell he was lying)? "But we don't have the time to be working on side projects. I certainly don't need one of my associates charging off on some secret mission I don't know about. They're watching our every move." He softened the harshness he suddenly heard in his tone.

"I couldn't live with myself if they abducted you, as well."

That seemed to register. She nodded almost imperceptibly, then locked her eyes on her superior with the same intensity he had shown her just a few moments earlier.

"And I couldn't live with myself, Dalton, if I found out you didn't trust me." There was almost a whimper in her voice now. "I need you to trust me, and I need you to trust that whatever it is I'm up to is for the greater good.

"Even if I can't tell you what that greater good is just yet."

They remained quiet for a time. Somehow, the ticking of a clock that had been almost imperceptible suddenly became almost deafening.

"Okay then," Lee countered quietly. "So long as it doesn't interfere with the work I need you to do on this case. I assume I don't need to remind you that millions of lives might be at stake?"

She issued a smile (*A little forced?* he wondered), leaned over to him and gripped him at the wrist. "I promise I'll make more of an effort to be . . . engaged, is that the word?"

He returned her (forced?) smile, but only nodded his assent to their compromise.

After she showed herself out, Lee sat in the chair and sorted through everything he'd just learned. That she was convinced the rest of the team didn't like her. That she was involved in some important mission, the nature of which she couldn't (make that, wouldn't) reveal to him.

That she was single again.

Or perhaps it was just some clever compilation of false facts, a mirage she had manifested to stay in his good graces while she pursued whatever true agenda she had in mind. If Mayfair had taught him anything, it was that Anisa had a magical way of communicating 'X' when what she really had in mind was 'Y' or 'Z.'

Or possibly even, 'O.'

He shifted in his chair and as he did so, his elbow jostled the manila folder full of charts and reports he had been reviewing right before room service brought him his meal. *You probably shouldn't have printed this out,* he chided himself. *You wouldn't want anyone on the team to stumble on them.* But there was something comforting about holding the pages firmly in his hands instead of staring at them on some cold computer screen.

He sauntered through the pages first from front to back, then from back to front, pausing now and then to consider some scientific term or compare one chart to the next. The medical staff in London who had prepared the report were as conscientious and professional as the nurse there who had administered his scan. There was a section that outlined what they called 'Potential Positive Outcomes' and another that had the heading 'Common Risks.'

But the one word in the report he kept trying to avoid hunted him down and tackled him, nonetheless.

Malignant.

Rain began to splatter against the window beside him; somewhere in the hallway, the wheels of a food cart began to squeak.

He returned the folder to the top of the table beside his chair. As he was about to refocus his attention on the acrostic in his lap, his phone buzzed. It was a text from Kip Silva: 'Dalton, we have approval from Lucky Fortune to interview the casino's employees. Meet me there at 10 a.m. if you can.'

The architect quickly confirmed the appointment, then picked up the puzzle book and considered the next clue.

W. In a sweat?

As was the case with the previous clue, the answer had ten letters in it.

He once again ran his fingers along the edge of his porkpie hat, then vigorously penciled in what seemed to him to be the perfect answer:

F-R-I-G-H-T-E-N-E-D

10

"Did anyone else get a ringing in their ears overnight? Like somebody in the hotel turned on a high-speed blender? Only, a little louder than that?"

The car transporting The Lee Group to the Lucky Fortune Grand Casino on Macau's Cotai Peninsula had been eerily silent until Liam broke the spell with his question. Dalton Lee craned his neck to listen to the responses, but there were none, other than the occasional mumbles of 'not me' and 'nope.'

The CEO of The Lee Group adjusted the herringbone deerstalker hat he'd put on that morning, leaned back into the limo's plush leather seat and relaxed.

So maybe that wasn't something I was imagining after all, he thought.

The sky was dark and as they headed toward their destination, plump raindrops began to hit the car's windshield and side windows. But as quickly as they had arrived, the raindrops retreated, only to be replaced with the occasional shower. Their driver activated the wipers, then turned them off, then activated them again as the rain became intermittent and irritating.

The passengers in the vehicle turned their attention to the casinos lining the Cotai Strip, and everyone agreed they took their breath away. The assembly of architecture on display was not as expansive or impressive as what one found on the strip in Las Vegas, but of all the team members, only Liam had spent any time in that gambling mecca, and that was for a bachelor party the details of which he could barely remember.

They first drove past the Parisian Macao (with its faux Eiffel Tower) then the Londoner Macao (with a façade resembling that of Buckingham Palace) and then the MGM Cotai (featuring the world's largest art garden). Even with the gloomy skies and the occasional passing shower, the structures seemed monumental, if not original.

Kip Silva was waiting for them at the casino's front door. When Lee exited the car, he clapped his hands and chuckled broadly.

"Well, if it isn't Sherlock Holmes," he said, bending over at the waist. The others on the team snickered some, for Lee did indeed resemble the renowned sleuth, sans the pipe and inverness cape.

Lee, however, was not amused.

"Exactly how many form-fitting polo shirts do you own, Kip?" he countered.

The lobby of the Lucky Fortune Grand instantly made the architects swoon. They squinted and animatedly argued with one another as to which luxurious materials had been used in the building's floors, banisters and ceilings.

"Is that Brazilian granite I see, or Italian granite?" Warren wondered aloud, his jaw agape.

"It sort of looks Italian," Bree countered, "but given our location, I'm going to guess it's either from the Fujian or Shandong province of China."

"Wherever it's from, the craftsmanship is impeccable," Lara added.

Then the team strolled into the casino's primary gaming room, where all discussion stopped, and all jaws dropped. The magnificence of the interior–a palace of gold and crimson–was far more majestic than even Dalton had expected. The vaulted ceiling ascended toward a circular viewing platform on the second floor that was brightened from above by multiple, oval skylights. The gaming tables below were in military formation; an egg-shaped, azure blue sculpture commanded the center of the room.

Almost in unison, Warren and Liam let out long, slow whistles.

"No pun intended, but I'm betting you were expecting something tackier," their host ventured. Lee was sure that Silva's tan had gone a shade darker and his smile a shade whiter, than when they'd last seen him.

"Well, I certainly wasn't," Bree responded merrily.

Given it was midmorning, the casino's vibe was subdued. Chirpy music filtered softly from the expansive room's numerous speakers but only a couple of tables were open, and each of those hosted a handful of gamblers at most. Silva led the group to one end of the gaming room and raised an index finger to indicate they should wait while he ducked behind a series of walnut-colored panels.

"Crikey, and to think we could be staying here," Liam offered, his head tilted back to take in all of the room's grandeur.

"Not on the budget Lara sets for us," Lee shot back. She glared at him in return for several seconds but said nothing.

Silva reappeared, with a short Chinese woman in tow. Lee pegged her to be in her fifties, and her white shirt topped by a dark vest indicated she was probably one of the casino's croupiers. He surmised she was probably the croupier who was overseeing the roulette table Jocelyn Cheng had been seated at moments before her demise.

"This is Jun Li. She was working on the floor the night Jocelyn Cheng died," Silva said. "She speaks some English, but I will help translate." He then pivoted and explained to her what he had just told the group. She nodded once and turned her attention to Lee and the others.

"Thank her for us, Kip, and ask her if she remembers seeing Jocelyn Cheng on the night in question," Lee said to him.

Silva swiveled toward the architect. "Dalton, I suggest you direct your questions to her, not me," he said politely. "I'll translate for her what you said, she'll reply directly to you, and then I'll translate for you what she said."

Lee found the protocol a little cumbersome but went along with it anyway. He repeated the question, this time looking directly at Jun Li with a tight smile.

She nodded vigorously and replied, *"Hai. Hai!"*

"And how did she look, Jun Li?"

Silva translated. The woman spit out a string of words, her hands flying in front of her, then stopped and blinked a few times. "She looked . . . very confused," she added, more as a question than a statement.

"Confused? Why is that?" Silva asked her. The croupier shook her head a few times then shrugged her shoulders.

The police officer turned toward the team. "She says that when Jocelyn first sat down, she seemed composed and enjoying herself. But that after her drink arrived, she seemed confused and was looking into the crowd, as if she were trying to locate or identify someone."

Warren spoke up. "I wonder, Jun Li, if you noticed anything odd going on in the casino that night. Anything unusual or suspicious? Anything that might have upset Ms. Cheng . . . ?"

Silva reiterated what Warren had said. The woman considered the query, tilted her head one way and shook it some as if to say 'no.' Lee could tell, however, that she seemed more inclined to fear the question than reject it, for she kept glancing back at Silva timidly. He noticed her behavior as well, which prompted him to send out a flurry of Cantonese that caused the croupier to wring her hands and frown. She hesitated, glanced back at Silva, then replied to him quietly but fervently.

Something Jun Li said made the policeman pull up. "What do you mean they weren't going where they should?" he said. She quickly answered, now with a tone of exasperation and impatience. When she was finished, Silva breathed deeply, shoved his hands into his pockets and swiveled back to the team.

"She was saying the pills–the roulette balls–weren't always dropping into the pockets they were supposed to."

"So . . . is she saying . . . the game was rigged somehow?" Bree asked.

Silva gave her a sheepish grin, which soon blossomed into a broad smile. "Sometimes it can be," he answered. "Not most of the time. And certainly not all the time. But if the casino is experiencing some, you know, cash flow issues . . . that can be one way for management to mitigate that." He paused, then added, "Jun Li just said the pills weren't always falling into the number slots they should have. But she doesn't know why."

"Wouldn't she be the one responsible for that?" Liam questioned.

Silva shook his head. "Not necessarily. Sometimes, gamblers can influence where the ball lands by secretly putting a trip pin in the ball track. But I'm sure the Lucky Fortune has installed plastic security shields around its wheels to prevent anyone at the table from doing that.

However, a casino can use trip pins to influence a ball's trajectory as well if they want to. In the past, the croupier might use a lever beneath the table to trigger the trip pin. These days, however, it's more likely that would be done electronically by remote. Which could mean that . . ."

Lee chose to finish Silva's sentence for him. "There was someone in the back room who was influencing the results somehow." The superintendent-general confirmed Lee's deduction with a quick nod.

All the discussion from one person to another in English had caused Jun Li to whip her head back and forth like a spectator at a torrid tennis match, and she became increasingly agitated as the dialogue dragged on. Noting that, Silva thanked her several times and patted her once on the upper back to let her know she could return to the employee lounge where he had found her.

She trudged toward the entrance leading to the back of the house. But rather than smile to the group as she rounded the corner, she shot them what Lee perceived to be a look of profound distrust.

Or was it one of downright deception?

Just then, the architect felt his phone vibrate. He was inclined to ignore it, but the zzzzzzz was unusually persistent: 'I see you and your cronies are already trying to undermine what we're up to. Ha! Good luck with that, Dalton. Urgent news to discuss. Soon?'

He wanted to reply 'No,' but the phrase, 'urgent news to discuss' piqued his interest. So, he quickly typed out: 'Tell me where and when' and then returned his attention to Kip Silva.

"The casino manager should connect us here shortly with the woman who brought Jocelyn Cheng her drink that night," Silva told the group. "Might be a few minutes." He began to twist at the waist, first to the left and then to the right. He followed that by raising his right arm above and behind his head and pulling his dangling hand away from his body. He then repeated the maneuver with his other arm.

"You look like you need a serious massage," Bree said matter-of-factly. "All those sports you play, I assume?"

Silva dropped his left arm and revealed his killer smile once again.

"You are so right . . . it's Bree, right?" She nodded enthusiastically. "You are so right, Bree. You'd be surprised how strenuous a badminton or squash match can get." He paused as he tilted his head down toward one shoulder and then the other. "As a matter of fact, I'm going to make an appointment with my masseur right after we're done here. By the way, he's over in Central, not far from your hotel, so if any of you are looking for someone to help you de-stress, I highly recommend him."

He snapped his fingers. "Oh, that reminds me, Dalton, I looked into that little air show you witnessed in Central a couple of days ago."

"And?"

Silva winced a bit. "It seems they reserved the air space for what they claimed would be some sort of aerial advertising for a yacht show. Used one of those fake corporate names you showed me earlier. I guess they delivered that advertising, didn't they, only they ended up advertising themselves, not the yacht show they had promised."

Lee felt the buzz in his pocket again and assumed it was the information he had requested from the person on the other end of the text conversation.

I'll deal with you later, he thought.

If Jun Li had been a pleasant and cooperative interview, the server who had brought Jocelyn Cheng her martini was anything but that. Her name was Regina Bauer, and she was an American, born and raised in Nebraska, who was in Macau on a temporary work permit. She entered the room as if she were primed to wrestle someone, and she kept glancing at Silva with an expression that said, "Can I go now?" She wore a tiny stud earring on her left earlobe and Lee made out a small tattoo on the back of her right hand that appeared to read, 'Outlaw Biker.'

The first words out of her mouth were, "Do I need a lawyer here?"

Silva smiled and did what he could to calm the server down, but to little avail.

"Look, I didn't do anything," she added before Silva, or anyone else in the room, could respond to her first question. "All I did was deliver the martini. Next thing I know, she's taking a header onto the carpet. Everybody starts rushing toward the body and I just calmly walked back to the well and told the bartender to call hotel security. That's it. That's the whole story."

She gave them a defiant look, then added, "Can I go now?"

Silva smiled again, but for only a half-second.

"Um, no, we need to ask you a few questions. First of all, when did Ms. Cheng order the martini? Before she came into the casino or after she arrived?" The employee pulled back a few inches and scoffed.

"She didn't order the martini. Some lady at the roulette table ordered it and had it sent to her. I just carried it from the bar to Ms. Cheng like I'm supposed to. Followed my instructions. To the letter."

At the mention of the drink being sent to the victim, everyone on the team exchanged glances, their suspicion of the person sent to high alert.

Silva took a step forward. "Can you describe this woman . . . the lady who sent the drink to Ms. Cheng?"

The server rolled her eyes toward the ceiling and took a breath in. "I only saw her out of the corner of my eye after Kai–he was working the bar that night–pointed her out to me. She was tall, but not the tall and skinny type–big-boned. Big hips. Big hair, too. Blonde." She shrugged her shoulders. "That's all I remember.

"Can I go . . ."

"No," Silva interrupted, more forcefully this time. "Not yet, that is. Really, we don't intend on keeping you very long, Miss Bauer, but we need to collect as much information as we can."

The server bristled. "It's *Mrs.* Bauer," she replied, elongating the 'M' in Missus. "I may not look like one of the Kardashians, but I've been happily married to my faithful husband for twenty-nine years now. Faithful, that is, except for that summer when I was laid up with the shingles and that bitch of a next-door neighbor of ours hit on him because she knew he probably wasn't getting any."

Silva's eyebrows leapt skyward, and he rushed to regain control of the conversation.

"Yes, yes, of course. *Mrs.* Bauer, of course, I am very sorry for that, I should have known." The server squinted at him, and the policeman became even more flustered. "I meant I should have known that you were married, not that I should have known your husband was unfaithful to you."

Lee decided to step in and rescue Silva. "I'm curious . . . *Regina* . . . did this big-haired blonde woman pay for the drink with a credit card or did she charge it to her room?"

The server looked Lee down and up then pivoted back to Silva.

"Who's he?" she asked, tipping her head in the architect's direction.

"Oh, Mr. Lee, he's an American architect who was . . . going to be . . . doing some work for Ms. Cheng. I told him it would be all right if he and his staff accompanied me on our interviews."
She turned toward Lee once more and squinted.

"You're American? You sure don't look American," she said with a huff. Lee extended his right arm to block Liam from charging the woman, then sent her way a smile even bigger than the best smile Silva had ever shown them.

"Well, I assure you, Regina, that I am American. But I was born and raised in Hong Kong before we immigrated to California about the time I turned six."

That seemed to satisfy her. After a moment she shook her head, decided to answer his question. "Cash. She paid cash for the drink. And tipped pretty well, too, I have to admit." Lee's shoulders slumped, for he had hoped they could locate the woman through her method of payment.

Warren chimed in. "Have you ever seen her before?"

Regina studied him for a moment before nodding slowly. "Yeah, she looked sort of familiar. Then I remembered I'd seen her riding around the peninsula on one of those bicycles you can rent over in Taipa Village."

"So maybe she lives somewhere nearby?" Bree posed. The server squinted again.

"Wouldn't know. Seems like I've only noticed her around over the past few days or so."

Again, the team exchanged glances. They knew that *O's* classic strategy was to embed their operative into the circle of their intended victim a few weeks or months in advance of the kill. That way, their target would be more comfortable–and less suspecting–of the toll the person was about to inflict.

The server sighed heavily, took a look at the plain black watch she wore on her wrist.

Lee cleared his throat to gain her attention. "One last thing. And by the way, Regina, you've been very helpful." She relaxed her wrestling stance some and issued a brief smile. "The drink, the martini. Did you watch the bartender make it?"

"Nope," she replied. "It was sitting at the well when I walked up there. That's when Kai told me it was for Ms. Cheng. She placed the order with him, not me."

"I see. And do you have any idea how long it had been sitting there?" Lee thought the server's expression shifted some at that.

"Not really. It may have been a while. See, I had to run to the can right before I delivered it. And I was in there longer than I intended to be, because . . ."

"Thank you, Regina!" Silva blurted. "You've really been a significant help to us. We'll probably follow up with the bartender later today."

She swung her head back to Silva. "Um, no, you won't," she said defiantly.

The superintendent-general looked one-half upset, one-half perplexed. "I'm sorry?"

The server stood there, shaking her head back and forth.

"I said you won't be talking to Kai later. Apparently, you haven't heard. They found his body in the estuary this morning. The poor guy is deader than dead."

11

Making a trek out to the farthest corner of the New Territories was the last thing Dalton Lee wanted to do on this night. Especially with the rain, which had become increasingly steady as the day wore on.

He'd even considered cancelling, but the mention of 'urgent news' caused him to reconsider. He usually gleaned some important news at these rendezvous, but rarely (if ever) information he would call urgent. Of course, he also had some urgent news to share, but he presumed his confidant would want to do all the talking. As usual.

Which was fine with him.

When Lee announced to the driver of the vehicle the hotel had provided him that he wanted to be taken to So Lo Pun village, the driver jerked his head around and bulged his eyes.

"Aiya, there?" he exclaimed. "Tonight? Are you sure?"

The architect narrowed his eyes and waited a beat before responding to the driver.

"Yes," he emphasized. "I want you to take me *there.*"

Lee understood the chauffeur's reaction. When he was a boy, So Lo Pun village had been the setting for many of the ghost stories his father would regale him with late at night. Its reputation as a haunted locale may have been exaggerated, but it was meaningly embedded nonetheless in the culture of the region. Like most places mentioned in a tale of horror, So Lo Pun had been abandoned decades earlier. Not just abandoned, however, but inexplicably abandoned by its villagers *overnight*. Nevertheless, hikers had claimed (more than once) that they had come upon untouched food sitting on the dining tables inside the vacant dwellings.

Then there was the eerie assertion by many that compasses failed to work in the village, a myth likely born from the fact that 'So Lo Pun' literally means 'compass-locked.' Lee knew from his own research that the town's name was likely a recent mistranslation of 'So NO Pun,' meaning 'valley surrounded by mountains.' Which made more sense.

Semantics aside, Lee respected the fact the village was creepy beyond belief. Especially on a night like this. Decades-old playground equipment, barely visible in the dark, was sheathed in layers of green algae, and the brick facades of the village homes (all that remained of the homes) were cracked and darkened by mold. Many of the facades sported crimson-colored scrolls on either side of the doorway, their bright-red backgrounds accented with jet-black characters that were actually lines of poetry extolling an upcoming spring festival. Beyond the facades, overgrown banyan trees thrust spiny tendrils into the darkened sky.

Meanwhile, the only sound was that of the rain pelting the foliage and the roofs of the few buildings still left standing.

The limo pulled up alongside one of the rows of structures. "Let me out here, please," Lee instructed the driver, "and take the car a couple hundred meters down the road." His chauffeur shot him another 'you must be kidding' look, but Lee was out of the back seat and heading toward the nearest row of houses before he could see how the driver had reacted. He slid twice on the wet, moss-covered entryway; his second mishap required him to balance himself against the remnants of a stone pillar that happened to be on his right.

Meanwhile, a large bird nearby emitted a menacing and piercing squawk. Lee assumed it was a dire warning from some falcon, raven or stork.

Once his car was down the road and around a corner, a spectral image munching on an apple stepped into view from behind one of the facades. Lee sniffed. "Tempting me, are you?" he said quietly.

"No, Dalton," the figure replied. "Just trying to get my daily dose of fiber, that's all."

The rain began to let up, but the branches that arced above them continued to drip from the previous downpour. They sought refuge behind another façade, but with little success.

"Nice rain hat," Lee's confidant said. "Did you buy it here?"

Lee merely shook his head and sent a grim look his friend's way.

"You said you had urgent news to share. Given what I went through to get here, it had better be super- urgent."

His companion took another bite from the apple, then tossed what was left into the brush behind them.

"Well, it's urgent to me, anyway." The figure paused a moment, took a few steps to the right before continuing. Then, Dalton heard a heavy exhale, a lamentation of sorts that took him somewhat aback.

"The fact is, I've decided to retire, Dalton. I'm getting too old for all of this. These campaigns . . . of ours are becoming too onerous for me. I can't . . . I don't want to . . . keep up this charade any longer."

Dalton raised his eyebrows–this truly was unexpected. "So, no more 'Power to the Cause' for you, is that what you're saying?"

A chuckle. "Oh, nothing so extreme as that. I still believe in the cause. I still believe governments oppress their people and that the world would be a much better place if everyone were left to make their own decisions on most every aspect of their lives." A pause. "But both my health and my mobility are declining. My power for pursuing the cause is waning. And . . ."

The rain intensified again, but they decided to stay where they were.

"And . . .?"

"And . . . I feel the need to reconnect with Lara. Reconcile, even, if possible."

Lee shook his head more to indicate futility than outright disagreement. "What if she doesn't want to reconcile with you? You lied to her, have caused her substantial grief for many years now."

The figure took a long breath in. "There's no need for you to remind me of that."

They were both quiet for some time. The rain was making the gravel beneath Lee's feet slick in spots; when he extended one arm to brace against the nearest façade, it felt mossy and moist. To maintain his balance, he returned to the more erect, wide-legged stance he'd held before.

"So, tell me, how exactly does one leave *O* after several years of service?" Dalton finally asked. "Does one just up and . . . go? Is there a formal retirement ceremony of some sort? Do they give you a gold watch, or a plaque? Or just a pat–make that a shove–from behind?"

His companion sniffed again.

"Don't be ridiculous, Dalton. One doesn't *retire* from 'O.' At least, not without their permission which, as best I can recall, has never been officially granted."

The figure moved closer, then Lee felt a hand on his upper arm. "That's why I said the news was urgent. I need to defect. I want you to help me defect."

Lee felt simultaneous rushes of excitement, anger, jubilation and distrust. He considered the request for a minute, found himself dubious of its validity.

"So . . . let me get this straight. We help you reunite with your loved one while our loved ones remain in captivity, is that it?"

The grip on his arm released; the figure took a few steps back.

"I'll do whatever I can to help, Dalton," came the reply. "I have a lot of institutional knowledge about what they're planning to do here, and what they're doing right now with your parents. And what they're doing with all the others, for that matter.

"But you need to understand there are no guarantees. *O* doesn't operate in a linear fashion. It's more like a kaleidoscope. How things are today, where people are today, are not necessarily how and where they'll be a few hours from now, much less a few weeks, or months, from now. That 'freedom' thing we cherish, you know."

Lee kicked at the dirt with one foot. "Why don't you just tell me everything right here, right now? Reveal to me what the plot is. Who it is they plan to harm and how they plan to harm them. Just get in the car and come back to the hotel with me tonight. Poof! Defection done. Lives saved. Retirement underway."

In the dimness, the architect could barely make out the figure shaking its head forlornly, like some parent disappointed with a child's naivete.

"Oh, Dalton, if I did that right now, they would know. They would most certainly know. I want to come out of my relationship with them . . . alive." A pause, then, "I want you and Lara to come out of this alive."

Lee bristled. "What benefit would they derive from killing Lara, of all people? I can understand their being upset with me. But Lara is an accomplished architect and a consummate executive assistant. What has she done to deserve their wrath?"

Although Lee could not make out his colleague's facial features in the dark, he could tell the person was displaying a supercilious smirk.

"She helped you thwart our plans in three different cities," came the reply. "There is that to consider."

Lee heard knuckles being cracked, then a throat being cleared. "Well, give it some consideration anyway, Dalton. I think your helping me defect could lead to a lot of healing all around." There was another pause, followed by, "And as for what the plot is, it is something that will certainly be devastating to this part of this world, and could very likely wreak significant distress throughout the rest of the world. The most successful revolutions usually result in that, in the short term anyway.

"As always, I cannot share specifics with you. But I can say this: when it comes to one of our initiatives, I have usually told you what it is you need to be on the lookout for."

The figure paused again for only a moment, then added, "This time, Dalton, I'm telling you that you and your team need to keep your ears attuned to what's happening around you."

Lee laughed with derision. "What in the hell is that supposed to mean?"

No answer. Then, "Give it some meaningful consideration, Dalton, and you'll probably figure it out."

There was another scrape of gravel, followed by a chilling breeze sweeping past him. Then, from several feet away, he heard the voice call back, "I must go. Tick tock, tick tock."

12

"What's that smell? Wait! Is that what I think it is?"

Within moments of entering Liam's room, Bree had twisted both her nose and mouth into more than one contortion. Warren and Anisa were already in the room and seemed nonchalant about the aroma that had rankled their colleague. In fact, they exchanged conspiratorial smiles with one another since they were both very well aware what the smell was.

Bree took a position against a wall, once again thwarted from taking a seat on the bed by two large piles of clothing. "Lara's on her way," she added, "and I don't think she'd approve of whatever it is you've been smoking." She pointed toward the clothing on the bed. "And you do know don't you that you're allowed to use the very nice dresser the hotel has provided for you?"

Liam leaped from his desk chair. "*Streuth!* I totally forgot Lara was coming to this meeting." He dove toward a duffel bag on the floor next to his chair and emerged with a large can of room deodorizer that he began to wildly spray throughout the room. Its treacly fragrance made everyone in the room cringe.

Moments later, the executive assistant stepped into the room. She stopped short, breathed in through her nose. Liam shut his eyes and

Bree snickered.

"Ah, takes me back to my days in university and attending a Montreux Jazz Festival with a German boy I had my eye on at the time," she declared wistfully. She breathed in once more. "Only this is far more aromatic than the cheap versions we used to enjoy." She turned toward Liam. "Must be from the Netherlands. Afghanistan, maybe?"

Liam's lower jaw remained ajar for a few seconds before he found the wits to reply to her.

"Nah, Lara, straight out of good old Oz," he said. He chuckled some, then added, "I knew there was a reason why I liked you."

She smiled back at him. "Yes, and I like you too, Liam. So much so I'm going to go out first thing tomorrow morning and buy you a much better room freshener."

The surfer swiveled back to his computer, which displayed the map with pulsating lights that he had been studying when Warren entered his room earlier in the week. "Anything, mate?" Warren asked as he moved up behind his colleague and peered over his shoulder. His coworker just shook his head.

"The blips keep moving around," Liam replied. "I'm not sure what to make of that."

Lara cleared her throat, her usual hint that she was ready to conduct business. "So, with Dalton away this evening, and with it raining outside, I thought this would be the perfect time for us to convene here and review our strategy for finding out just who poisoned Jocelyn Cheng."

Bree pushed away from the wall. "Well, we know who poisoned her, don't we? It's obvious it was O."

Anisa looked up from her phone and took on a troubled look.

"Not necessarily," she stated with more than a little attitude. "I mean, we assume it was someone associated with 'O,' but there could be copycats out there. Maybe someone she swindled in the past planted that note on her body to make us think it was O who killed her." Her fervor had left her a little out of breath, so she paused to catch it.

"Or maybe," she continued, "she faked her own murder. To get out of paying some debts she owed. To escape someone who was harassing her. Or, to avoid some type of prosecution that was coming her way. I think it's very possible *O* had nothing whatsoever to do with her murder."

Lara cocked her head to one side and studied the team's newest member intently. "Well, Anisa, first of all, we know she didn't fake her murder because she is, most definitely, dead. And given the authenticity of the note left on her body, and the skywriting episode Dalton experienced the other day AND the message Bree found in the pocketbook she bought in Ladies' Market, I think it's safe to say it's clear that *O* was involved." She paused for a moment to consider her next sentence. When she resumed, however, her demeanor was less that of boss and more that of a mentor. "But since you brought it up, you have a law background, as I recall? You might be just the right person on the team to look into Jocelyn Cheng's legal affairs. Find out if there's anything from that standpoint that might connect her to 'O,' or, whether she has any legal skeletons in her closet that might have some relevance to the case?

"Would you be at all interested in that?"

Anisa considered the offer for a while. Her look shifted from suspicious to sly.

"Sure, I can do that," she responded. "I'm on it. Only . . ." She tilted her chin up and allowed a sneaky smile to materialize. "Only . . . don't be surprised if I find out that *O* wasn't responsible for her murder after all."

Lara studied her a bit more, a cloudy expression on her face. Then she nodded once and said, "Good. And I am going to continue to look into Ms. Cheng's financial affairs. I could probably use your help with that, Liam?"

"Of course," he replied smiling broadly. "Maybe I can introduce you to some of the other . . . um . . . herbs Australia produces, and we can enjoy them together."

Lara emitted a quick laugh, glanced at her lap then back at Liam.

"Likely not," she replied, "but I do appreciate the invitation."

Warren raised his hand.

"Can I pick my own assignment?"

"Of course, Warren. What do you want to focus on?"

"Security tapes and surveillance videos, from Macau and anywhere else she may have gone in the days before the murder. I'll study anything I can get my hands on."

Lara nodded. "Excellent." She pivoted toward Bree. "That leaves you, my dear. What angle would you like to tackle?"

Bree studied the ceiling for a couple of moments. "Well . . . I was thinking it might be worthwhile to dig into her personal and philanthropic relationships. Who were the people she connected with in the weeks prior, who did she have lunch with? Those sorts of things.

"I'm betting Kip Silva would have loads of information about that, and . . ."

Lara quickly interrupted her. "I'm thinking Mr. Silva is going to be quite busy as it is, and that we should probably allow him and the rest of his colleagues to focus on the aspects of the case they're already pursuing."

Bree nodded, but her mouth turned downward.

Lara exhaled. "Well, I guess we all have our little threads to pursue. Does anyone have any other questions?" She scanned the faces in the room.

"I do," Liam announced. "What's up with Dalton and all of his hats?"

The rest of the team looked off in different directions, waited for Lara to respond. The executive assistant looked down at her lap before answering.

"I'm not sure," she finally replied. "It's not the first time Dalton has been into headgear, but I have to admit, his choices have never been quite so . . . unique . . . as they have been on this trip.

"What I do know is, Dalton has always gravitated to wearing a hat when he's stressed about something. But given everything that's been happening recently, and everything we're grappling with right now, what the particular stressor is that's triggering him at present is totally beyond me."

＊＊＊

"Dalton, where are you RIGHT NOW?"

In fact, when the phone shimmied, the architect had just stepped out of the hot shower he'd decided to take upon returning to his hotel and had been examining his appearance in the full-length mirror that hung on the back of the bathroom door.

He was disheartened to see that more gray had sprouted around his temples and a bit more skin was sagging just below the jawline. His upper torso still looked reasonably fit thanks to all the exercises he had performed in the weeks leading up to their departure from the States. But he didn't have much confidence his bulk and tone would last much longer, given that the hotel's gym was not much more than a large closet cluttered with miscellaneous dumbbells and the case before them was going to occupy far more time than he had hoped.

And now there was the reunion of sorts he had just been asked to somehow orchestrate.

"I'm . . . having a late dinner in the hotel's cafe," he lied. "What's up, Julian?"

The former security official sounded as though he were munching on a piece of fruit. "I told you . . . I had some . . . hunches I wanted to follow up on," he said between bites. "I remember . . . the last time I saw Jocelyn, she said she . . . had a couple of sorority sisters coming to visit. Sorority sisters that had just sort of . . . contacted her from out of . . . the blue."

"Interesting," Lee said, wrapping a towel around his waist and strolling into the bedroom of his suite.

"Yes, I thought so. I recalled the name of one of them–it was so unusual–and I was able to . . . track them both down through that. One is back in the States now and . . . the other is in Shanghai. Might be worth pursuing."

Lee struggled to locate a pen to write with and keep his towel secured to his waist. When he leaned across the armchair to pluck a pencil from the table on the other side, the towel came completely unraveled and dropped to the floor. He froze, moved the phone to his other ear, bent over to pick up the towel, then decided to give up on being modest and prayed the housekeeper wouldn't waltz into the room unannounced.

"Are you still there, Dalton?"

"Yes, yes, sorry I . . . dropped my . . . pen on the floor. On the floor of the café." He snatched from the side table a piece of paper and said, "OK, shoot."

One of the sorority friends–the one Julian had tracked down first–was a venture capitalist by the name of Poppy Considine. "Not a name you easily forget," he emphasized to Lee. The friend in Shanghai was a Victoria Vo, an investment banker.

"A banker, you say." Lee offered.

"A banker," Julian confirmed.

Lee decided it might be wise for Lara and Liam to follow up on this lead, since they were looking into Jocelyn Cheng's finances.

"Okay, Julian, thanks. I really appreciate it. We never know if anything will come from these leads, but these women do sound more than a little . . . suspect, dropping in on their old friend after several years and all."

"I agree, and you're welcome. Oh, I also have the name of the purveyor of jie tea I promised to get to you. I'll text it to you shortly."

"And one more thing. I wondered if you might like to take a little stroll soon around your old stomping grounds here. Around the old 'hood. It's changed quite a bit since you were six, of course. But I imagine there are enough landmarks remaining to trigger some positive memories."

Lee momentarily floated off on a cloud of nostalgia. He had adored his early days in Hong Kong's North Point neighborhood. Its culture and character–from the diverse population of expats and locals to the numerous wet markets–was something he continued to cherish to this day.

"Yes, yes, I would love to do that, Julian," the architect finally said as he retrieved his towel from the carpet. "But it may need to wait a couple of days at least. We have a lot of investigating to do and a lot of interviews to conduct."

"I understand, my dear. Just let me know when you can get away and I'll slot it on my calendar. I even have another hunch I'm going to follow up on. But more about that later. *Haa ci gin.*"

It was only after Lee had properly armed himself with antiperspirant, was back in his bedroom and mostly dressed for the day that two revelations hit him almost simultaneously.

One was that Julian had just referred to him as 'my dear.'

The other was that it had felt perfectly natural.

13

For more than a few days, Warren had fully expected Anisa to sneak out of the hotel late some night. He'd set his black jeans, hoodie and sneakers on the armchair across from his bed, so they'd be ready when needed. He'd even counted how many steps it might take her to get to the elevators on their floor, so he wouldn't come upon her from behind too quickly.

He knew it was going to happen, sensed it at some cellular level. In his mind, it wasn't a matter of whether she was going to slink out of the hotel, but when.

And then, when he detected the almost imperceptible click of the lock on her door just before midnight, he realized that the 'when' he had been anticipating was going to be 'tonight.'

He was into his clothing and out the door in seconds. Stayed close to the wall and took his time advancing along the hallway. But he did what he could not to look like a stalker to whoever downstairs might be watching that floor's security cameras. At one point, he made a brief squeak when he accidentally scuffed the toe of one sneaker against the carpet. That prompted him to wait a couple of seconds before continuing on, stealthily moving forward until he reached that point where the hallway wall ended, and the elevator alcove began.

The doors to the lift she had entered were closing and, just as he had hoped, her head was down into her cell phone as she furiously thumbed a message to . . . someone.

Warren tilted his head upward and waited for the number of the floor below theirs to illuminate before he dashed to the stairwell door and sprinted several steps at a time to the hotel lobby. Before opening the door, he pulled up. Here, he'd have to be cautious. It was after midnight. He'd be exiting from a rarely used stairwell, perhaps in full view of a security guard or someone working the front desk. He was a Black man dressed in a black hoodie and black sneakers. Somehow, someway, he'd have to make it all seem . . . perfectly natural.

As he opened the door to the lobby, he was relieved to see Anisa striding through the automatic doors to the sidewalk beyond and the front desk clerk staring at a sheaf of papers that lay on the counter in front of her. He adopted a moderate gait–something that was more than a saunter but less than a trot.

"Can I help you sir? Do you need something?" The front desk clerk was now peering over the counter, staring at him with concern in her eyes.

He didn't slow down, much less stop.

"*Siu mai*," he replied, referring to the aromatic pork and shrimp dumplings that were a staple of late-night Hong Kong dining. He pointed toward the door and smiled broadly. "Totally jonesin' for some *siu mai*."

He was through the doors before she could respond. But once outside, he quickly checked himself–what if Anisa was sitting in one of the taxis in the short queue immediately to his right? He relaxed when he instead spotted her on the other side of the street, leaning against a wall on the left side of one of the region's major banks.

A taxi flew past, blocking his view of her temporarily and sending a small spray of puddle water his way. Once the taxi was down the street, he saw that Anisa was now chatting on her phone and skittering around the left side of the bank.

Time to move, he told himself.

He jogged across the street but veered to the right of the base of the financial institution. Eventually, he slowed to a stroll and hopped over a couple more standing puddles on the concrete plaza before sidling into the darkness cast by the base of the building. As he approached the bank, he breathed in once more–he had no idea at this point exactly where, and how, Anisa might be positioned. But when he craned his neck around the corner, he was elated to see her at least thirty meters away, her back turned toward him.

He could hear her voice now, but her sentences were in shards. (The whirr of some industrial HVAC unit nearby didn't help.) What was comprehensible came to him in one or two-word blasts: "I can't." "Later." "More time." "Not ready."

Suddenly, the moon emerged from behind a bank of clouds, bathing the plaza temporarily in a wide swath of light. It was when Warren glanced up at the moon that he noticed the long open balcony that stretched along the back of the bank's second floor. It was empty save for a potted plant and a couple of long banquet tables topped by white tablecloths whose corners flapped when a breeze came through. He studied the balcony for a few moments, took breaks now and then to check on Anisa's status.

If I can just get up there, he told himself, *I can skulk down to a spot just above where she's standing and probably hear everything she's saying.*

Good thing I once had excellent cat burglar skills.

The ascent wasn't easy. The surfaces were slick, and footholds were few. But the noise of the HVAC unit drowned out both the sound of his shoes scraping against concrete and his increasingly belabored breathing.

After this assignment, I'm going to get back into shape, he promised himself.

With one arm, he strained to reach the bottom of the balcony railing and used every muscle he had to hoist his body up to its level. Fortunately, the railing wasn't very tall, so once he had a strong handhold upon it, he was able to swing his right leg over it with little difficulty.

Making as little noise as possible, he planted his feet on the concrete floor of the balcony and immediately dropped to his haunches. Hoped Anisa would remain precisely where she was and maintain her level of volume on the call. When the moon retreated behind the clouds again, he scooted to a position on the balcony that was almost directly above her. He could decipher more of what she was saying, but the rumble from the HVAC unit continued to prevent him from hearing every word with clarity.

Surely my hearing isn't also going, he worried.

He directed all of his mental energy to calming himself and his surroundings. He stopped panting by taking in longer and deeper breaths. He became more conscientious about staying still, to calm his heartbeat. Finally, he performed a little visioning exercise in which he imagined the HVAC system going quiet and Anisa's conversation becoming much more intelligible.

And then, suddenly, the unit actually did shut off.

Well, what do you know, he said to himself.

At first, the sudden gift of silence seemed all for naught–Anisa was not speaking now, only listening to whoever was on the other end of the phone. He was growing impatient and increasingly concerned she might dart off once again to another location well out of earshot.

But finally, she cleared her throat and a full sentence emerged, a sentence that sent a chill throughout Warren's system.

"The bottom line is, I think Dalton may suspect something," she told the other person on the line, "so you're going to have to be patient and I'm just going to have to stay under the radar a little while longer before we move forward with our plan."

14

Overnight, the steady rain had finally come to an end, but the humidity had returned in spades.

Bree stood in the center of the ferry to Macau, fervently cooling herself with a red and gold fan she'd bought in a shop alongside the pier. Lara kept pulling out the collar to her white silk blouse; Liam could already feel perspiration beads forming under both arms (even though he'd applied a substantial amount of antiperspirant that morning).

"I hope everyone took my advice and wore the lightest fabrics possible," Lee stated, looking cool as a penguin in his white seersucker slacks and his short-sleeve linen shirt.

All topped by a wide-brimmed, Panama hat.

When he'd arrived in the hotel lobby that morning, everyone else had cast furtive glances at one another. They chose not to say anything.

The architect had expected Kip Silva to brief them on developments upon their arrival. Instead, they were escorted into a large conference room on the second floor of the headquarters. Inside, they found Silva seated at one end of a long, mahogany conference table.

Sitting next to him was a tall, blonde woman wearing a dark velvet pantsuit. Silva stood as the members of The Lee Group filed in.

"Dalton, hello, welcome all of you, please take a seat," he said, his smile turned on ultra-bright. "Let me introduce you to Alexandra Wentworth. Ms. Wentworth is a former friend of Jocelyn Cheng's and was at the same roulette table as Ms. Cheng just before she . . ." Silva's smile fell as he stumbled to complete the sentence. "Before she suffered the fate she did," he concluded. "Ms. Wentworth, these are the associates of ours I was telling you about."

The woman smiled briefly, then returned to her repose. Bree picked up her pace some, darted around Dalton and slid into the seat next to Kip Silva.

Silva turned to the blonde. "So, Ms. Wentworth was just . . ."

"Please, call me Alex," she interrupted.

Silva nodded at her, resumed his monologue. "So, Alex here was just telling me about her connection to Ms. Cheng."

Lara held up a small steno notebook. "Excuse me. Is it all right if I take some notes?"

The pair at the opposite end of the table both nodded their consent. Alex Wentworth shifted in her chair.

"Yes, as I was telling the superintendent-general here, I met Jocelyn on a cruise a few years ago. A cruise through the Baltics. We were both singles on the trip and we just sort of hit it off. I was in the process of how to play mah-jongg, and she started sharing some of her strategies with me. We started dining together every other night or so, had drinks in the bar once, etc."

"How long was the cruise?" Lee interjected. The woman looked up at the ceiling and silently counted.

"About ten days," she replied, barely hiding the fact that the question made little sense to her. "Anyway, we didn't keep in touch much afterward, just an email or two, that's all."

"Do you live in Hong Kong?" Lee asked.

"No. I live in Canada . . . Toronto . . . but I come to Asia three or four times a year on business. I'm a wholesale buyer. I scout out items manufactured in the region . . . toys, handbags, household gifts, those sorts of things, for several retail clients of mine."

Lara scribbled in her notebook but surreptitiously sent looks of concern toward her boss, who had carefully set his Panama hat on the table in front of him. She knew the woman's 'serendipitous' meeting with the victim was precisely the way *O* would embed their agents into the lives of those they sought to eliminate.

"My flight back to Toronto this week got canceled," the woman continued, "so I decided to ferry over here and do a little gambling. Truthfully, I was stunned to see Jocelyn not only walk into the casino but also sit at the opposite end of the very roulette table where I was playing.

"I planned to head right over and give her a hug afterward, but then . . . everything went . . ."

"Did you send a martini over to Ms. Cheng?" Lee asked abruptly.

Alexandra Wentworth sat back, stiffened some. "Well, yes, I did. It's what we would drink together when we were on the cruise." She hesitated, sat back even more. "You're not implying that I . . ."

Kip Silva put his hands up to intervene.

"Not implying anything at all, Ms. Wentworth . . . sorry, Alex, I mean. No implication. We're just trying to confirm every possible detail of what happened that evening."

Dalton leaned forward. "Did you notice anything odd happen at the table while you were there? Did anyone interact with, or distract, Ms. Cheng? Did she seem agitated at all, or withdrawn?"

She considered the question for a time, then shook her head. "No, not really. In fact, from what I saw, she seemed quite content, basking in all the energy around the table. She tipped her glass in my direction to thank me, I do remember that, although I'm not entirely convinced she recognized me."

"And you never did connect with her, is that what I heard you say?" Kip Silva was now scribbling some notes of his own.

"That's . . . that's right," she responded. The woman wrapped one arm around her midsection and began to breathe rapidly and deeply. "I'm sorry, I'm just more than a little emotional about all this. On the trip, Jocelyn sort of took me under her wing, became like a mentor to me. She gave me some advice on how to expand my business, some relationship advice, investment tips, that sort of thing.

"Over those ten days, I came to feel like she was the big sister I had always wanted, but never had." The woman was now profoundly morose, holding onto the edge of the table tightly with the fingertips of her right hand. Silva looked over at Lee who indicated it might be best to let her depart.

"You've agreed to stay in the area for another couple of days, is that right?" Silva asked her.

"Yes," she responded. "I'm going to use the time to visit with a couple of suppliers nearby. But I do have to fly back to Toronto this weekend."

"All right . . . Alex. Thank you. We'll be in touch if and when we need anything else."

They all rose and watched her stride across the room. But just before she reached the door, Dalton Lee added, "By the way, Ms. Wentworth, congratulations. I'm told you did quite well at the roulette table that night."

The blonde in the velvet pantsuit took on an expression that conveyed both bemusement and amusement.

"Thanks!" she trilled, her sorrow seeming to have suddenly evaporated. "Just lucky, I guess."

***

"Well, that was certainly an interesting exit," Lee announced after they had all reseated themselves.

"We're having her closely monitored," Silva replied. "At the end of the day, she's the one who had the martini sent to Ms. Cheng. And, after fifteen years in this business, I tend to be the most suspicious of the person who comes off the most bereaved."

Bree pushed her chair back and reached into her tote bag, which was sitting on the floor. She came up with a medium-sized brown paper bag, the top of which was folded over and secured with a piece of Scotch tape.

"Here, Kip, these are for you," she said. The police officer looked at her quizzically, ran one finger behind the seal, opened the bag and pulled out two packages of Chupa Chups.

"Wow! Orange and watermelon? I love these flavors, but they're not that easy to find around here. Thank you, Bree. That's very kind of you!"

She responded with a sheepish grin. "Nothing but the best for the superintendent-general," she quipped.

Warren scooted his chair a bit. "So . . . back to the case . . . I was wondering . . . have we learned any more about the death of the bartender? The one who was working in the casino that night."

"Ah, we have!" Silva exclaimed. "It seems we can rule out foul play there. Poor guy apparently had a massive heart attack while riding his bike alongside the estuary. At thirty-six, no less." The policeman leaned back in his chair, extended his arms on either side and cocked back his head to stretch his neck. "One of the reasons I work out as much as I do," he continued. "To keep Father Time as far away as I can for as long as I can.

"If that bartender was the murderer–which I strongly doubt–he's forever eluded our grasp, it seems."

Someone tapped lightly on the conference room door, then opened it a few inches. Through the gap, Lee could see it was the receptionist who had welcomed them on their first visit.

"Very sorry," the young woman said in a meek voice. "Jocelyn Cheng's sister is here?" Silva nodded for the assistant to deliver her to the room. While they waited for her to arrive, Silva unwrapped an orange Chupa Chup and began to suck on it.

"That looks really good," Bree offered. "Is it sweet . . . or is it tart?"

"You want one?" Silva replied. He picked up one of the bags she had given him and held it out to her.

Bree shook her head, looked at him demurely. "Thank you, but no. I really need to start watching my figure. SO much good food here to eat. But I have no idea which restaurant I should start with. Do you have any suggestions, Kip?" Lara turned toward Warren and Anisa and discreetly rolled her eyes.

Silva thought for a moment, then snapped his finger and gave his trademark smile. "I know exactly what to do!"

Bree looked at him in anticipation.

"I'll have my receptionist send a list of my favorite places over to your hotel. I'm sure you'll be happy with any of them."

The door opened before Bree had a chance to respond. In crept

Jocelyn Cheng's sister, Jacquelyn, who looked just like her older sibling, only five years younger. However, the impression she made upon entering a room was quite different. Her hair, makeup and dress were less polished than those of her sister's. She also lacked the casino executive's rocklike strength and compelling personality.

As she tentatively entered the room, Silva jumped from his seat and rounded the table, one hand extended. "Ms. Cheng, I'm so sorry for your . . ."

She cut him off. "Please, don't say it. It's become such a cliché in my life these past few days. To be honest, I view Jocelyn's death more as a passing than a loss."

With that, Lara and Dalton gave each other a look that said, *What the hell?*

"I don't mean to be rude. I'm still trying to process it all. I'm happy to answer whatever questions you have for me. Jocelyn was truly a . . . force, I can tell you that."

Silva had returned to his seat. "May we call you Jacquelyn?" he asked the woman.

"Yes," she replied. "Please do."

"I hope your trip in from Shenzhen was comfortable."

"Yes. It's only twenty minutes by train, so it goes by quickly."

As different as the woman's demeanor was from that of her sister, Lee was struck by how many similarities they shared. He noticed that Jacquelyn's haircut was almost a replica of her sister's. Her makeup was not as expertly applied, but it was the same type of makeup in the same hue and in the same amount. Even her handbag looked similar, if not identical, to the one Jocelyn was carrying with her when she died.

There were some eerie dynamics playing out in this family, Lee noted.

Silva introduced the team and explained their reason for being in the room. He then reviewed a square of paper on the table in front of him before giving the woman a long, serious stare.

"So, where were you, Ms. Cheng, when you learned of your sister's death? For that matter, where were you in the day or so leading up to it?"

She hesitated, aware of the implication embedded in the last half of his request. She took a few beats before answering him.

"Actually, I was working with a client in Shenzhen. Both in the week leading up to her death and on the day she . . ." She lowered her head, gazed at her lap for several seconds. "To be precise, I was in my garden when I received the message on my phone about her passing."

"I see. And how would you describe your relationship with your sister, Jacquelyn?"

She flashed a short smile, tilted her head.

"Complicated," was her reply. "I mean, we got along fine. I always admired Jocelyn even if I couldn't . . ." Her focus turned to the wall of windows to her left and the montage of images beyond it.

"You couldn't . . .?" Silva prompted.

She shifted her focus from outside the windows to the tabletop.

"As I mentioned, Jocelyn was a force. For as long as I can remember. Number one in her class from the day she entered kindergarten. Raising money for local charities by the time she was seven. While I was struggling to make C's in my classes at Wuhan University, she was being offered full rides by top schools around the world before she'd completed her secondary education and breezing through an MBA before everyone else her age, and even some who started before she did."

She paused, lifted her chin, smiled broadly (a bit too broadly, in Lee's estimation).

"That wasn't me," she finally said, with more emphasis than anyone expected.

The quiet that pervaded the room after that eventually became awkward. Lee chose to resume the conversation.

"Would you say you and your sister were competitive?"

Jacquelyn Cheng raised her chin even more and breathed in through her nostrils.

"No. Not at all. We had different interests, different . . . strengths. Jocelyn knew how to read and interpret a financial statement or annual report, I know how to create a beautiful centerpiece. Jocelyn mastered the art of negotiation. I excel at glassware and place settings. I have always been someone fascinated by beauty where Jocelyn was always someone consumed with . . . commerce.

"We were never really competitive because I discovered early on

91

that there was absolutely no point in my trying to compete with her."

Lara was scribbling forcefully in her notebook. Lee deftly placed a palm on her wrist, shook his head at her when she turned to look at him.

"Can you think of anyone, anyone in particular that is, who would want to poison your sister?" Silva was leaning forward again in his chair, staring even more intently at the woman he'd posed the question to.

She turned and began once again to study the movement and shadows just beyond the window to her left. When she finally spoke, she suddenly embodied all the bravado of the sister who was now departed.

"Mr. Silva, when you succeed in the world of big business, you learn everyone around you is trying to poison you one way or another."

No one said anything for several moments. Eventually, Silva shifted his weight in Lee's direction.

"Any other questions you'd like to pose?"

Lee tapped the brim of his hat with a pen a few times before answering.

"Only one," he finally replied. "I'm just curious, Ms. Cheng, how did Jocelyn interact with you? Was she the typical big sister? Was she the mother hen type? Did she ever try to mentor you?"

Jacquelyn Cheng gave a short laugh. "Jocelyn? No. Not at all. She was much too focused on ticking off her next achievement to expend her energy on anything like that. I'm not saying she was ever mean or belligerent toward me. She wasn't.

"But a big sister type? A mentor? No, if Jocelyn thought of me at all, she probably thought of me as little more than . . . a curiosity."

***

On the ferry back to Hong Kong Island, Anisa immediately made her feelings known.

"I think the younger sister did it," she declared. "And I don't think she's involved with O at all."

Warren moved closer to her. "Why do you think that?"

Anisa gave him an almost defiant look. "She doesn't have what *O* looks for in their recruits. She doesn't have the grit. She might have killed her sister out of some sort of sibling jealousy but all she cares about is flowers and napkins and beautiful place settings.

"She doesn't have the spine of a terrorist. She doesn't have the anarchist's soul."

Lee felt his phone shimmy in his pocket. He extracted it, read the text Kip Silva had just sent him.

"Well, I certainly wasn't expecting that," he said in a listless monotone.

Lara turned toward him. "What is it?"

He exhaled, began to read the text to his associates, all of whom edged closer to hear the news.

"Dalton. Toxicology reports just came back. The glass and the remaining traces of alcohol inside all came back clean. No poison found."

15

It was the best of mornings; it was the worst of mornings.

On the positive front, Lara informed Dalton that the emirate of Dubai had narrowed to two the number of firms in the running for their concert hall commission–and The Lee Group was one of the remaining finalists. Even better, the governing body overseeing the selection had decided to trim some of the bureaucracy attached to the competition.

The bad news was that Lee's head had been buzzing all night long. Buzzing or throbbing. Maybe, it was more like a pulsing, he decided. Anyway, whatever it was, it had interfered with his sleep–and his sense of well-being–once again.

Then came the call from Kip Silva.

"Rat poison?" Lee blurted upon hearing the news. "She died from ingesting rat poison? How does someone of her stature swallow rat poison? And wouldn't someone taste the rat poison immediately and . . . stop ingesting it?"

"Well, I assume she didn't ingest it intentionally," Silva responded. "And apparently, manufacturers these days lace their poison with sweet flavors like vanilla or maple to make it more appealing to the rats." In the background, Lee heard what sounded like a ball being slammed against a wall.

"If I remember correctly, it takes a while for rat poison to . . . do its thing," Lee added. There again was the slam of a ball against some solid surface.

"You're right. Up to two or three days. Which complicates things for us. The window of opportunity isn't as narrow as we had hoped."

"And neither is our list of potential suspects," Lee added. He could now hear Silva breathing more heavily than before.

"Are you playing some sort of game, Kip?" he asked.

The breathing slowed some. "With you, Dalton? No! Never!"

"No, I mean are you playing some type of sport?"

Kip's breathing seemed to return to normal, and he suddenly sounded much clearer over the line.

"Sorry, yes, I was in the middle of a squash match. Do you play?"

Lee winced as he recalled being bashed on the side of a head by a squash ball while watching friends play a match in middle school.

"I do not," he replied emphatically.

"Okay, too bad. Anyway, my staff is scouring Jocelyn Cheng's apartment and office to see if we can find any evidence of where the rat poison might have come from. You and your team probably want to take a look around there as well, I imagine?"

Lee nodded. "Definitely."

"Fine. We'll make the arrangements. Oh, and we're still keeping tabs on Alex Wentworth, the blonde from the casino. But everything about the story she gave us seems to check out. The cruise line confirms they were on a ship together a few years ago. And the airline says her flight back to Canada earlier this week was canceled but that she's booked on another flight this weekend."

"Doesn't mean we can rule her out," Lee offered.

"Agreed. But detaining her at this point is going to be difficult, if not impossible. We really have nothing to hold her on."

Lee pulled the phone back from his ear and looked at the time. "Sorry, I need to run, Kip. I have plans with a friend. I'll check back in with you later."

***

Lee was standing at the intersection where Julian had suggested they meet. He tugged at the golf cap he was wearing to secure it against the brisk breeze that had sprung up that morning.

The view across the intersection became obstructed when a double-decker bus pulled up and stopped next to the curb in front of him. Most of the cherry-red conveyance was plastered with Hanzi writing in bright gold that he assumed was advertising some nearby shop or a particular brand of cigarettes. However, facing him on the side of the bus was a cartoon figure that Westerners would recognize as a mash-up of Dora the Explorer and any of the characters from the animated series, "South Park." The character clutched a pair of chopsticks in her hands, leading Lee to believe the ad was actually promoting some nearby restaurant.

He was drawn to the character's goofy face and particularly its crudely drawn eyes . . . which began to slowly blink at him.

"Why are you looking at me like that, Dalton?" the character asked.

Oh, no, Lee said to himself, pressing his eyes closed. *I was hoping we were done with this.*

"Well, you're not," the character replied, its stern tone out of sync with the happy-dopey expression it wore. "Not by a longshot."

Lee opened his eyes, hoping either that the bus had moved on or that the character had decided to stop engaging with him.

He was wrong on both counts.

"You do know you're going to have the tell the team at some point, don't you?" it continued, presenting the comment more as a declaration than a question. The character then offered another long, slow blink.

"Maybe," the architect replied. "Not necessarily."

The brakes of the bus released, and the vehicle began to inch forward. As it did, the character discreetly shook its head at Lee. He wasn't sure whether it was displaying displeasure with him, pity, or both.

Seconds later, the bus was lumbering out of view. And Julian was coming into view. On a 1961 Maicoletta scooter that looked just like Dalton's only with a seat that could accommodate two riders.

"OMG, Julian! You have a Maicoletta too? It was going to cost me a major commission to ship mine over here from the States. And it's in such great shape, too!"

The security professional wore a broad smile and nodded. Slowly, however, his eyes trailed upward some.

"My dear, Dalton," he said. "You didn't tell me you had a tee time this afternoon."

It took a moment for Lee to understand what had prompted the comment.

"Oh, this," he said, tugging again at the cap. "No . . . it was just . . . the closest thing near the door, really." The architect swung one leg over the seat of the scooter and embraced the driver's waist. Julian looked over his shoulder before pulling away from the curb and into traffic.

"So good to see you again, my friend, did you get the name of the purveyor of jie tea I sent you?"

Lee acknowledged that he had. He also acknowledged to himself that it felt unusually comfortable to be so physically intimate with Julian.

"So, tell me, Julian, what else I should know about Jocelyn Cheng?" he asked as he tilted his head back to let a steady breeze sweep across his face. "Besides the fact she liked martinis, played mah-jongg and was a renowned philanthropist."

Julian kept his eyes on the road, but Lee could tell his chauffeur of sorts was smiling.

"Well, let's see. She had a secret interest in standard poodles but was afraid if she got one, people would ridicule her for being so pretentious." He chuckled once, then added, "And, she couldn't cook worth a damn, but at least she owned it. Any get-together at her home–and I mean, even a simple lunch for two–was brought in. She was much too private to hire a full-time chef."

Julian had to slam on the brakes to keep from driving them into the path of a teenager who was flying his bicycle across the center of the road without looking. Once the cyclist had rushed beyond them, however, they resumed their trip and the conversation.

"Oh, and she was a huge devotee of feng shui. Being an architect and all, that might be of some interest to you. She'd often have someone come into her home or office and reposition the furniture because she wasn't comfortable with the current arrangement. She believed something different might improve the business, her personal relationships, those sorts of things."

Julian carefully guided the Maicoletta around a corner and looked back at his passenger. "I don't really believe in such nonsense, do you?" he shouted.

Lee shrugged some, smiled weakly, moved his hands from Julian's abdomen to his shoulders.

"Well, Julian, I've never really been fond of superstitions. Generally, I think they do more harm than good." He turned to study a young woman they were gliding past who was clutching several balloons and frowning intently at no one in particular. "But, well, I did grow up here, and I have to admit I'm sort of drawn at some cellular level to the mysticism of it. To be honest, I've incorporated the tenets of feng shui into some of my buildings.

"Do I actually believe the tenants of structures facing the sea experience bad luck just because the architect failed to incorporate a dragon's gate into the building's design? Of course not. Still, I sort of like the fantasy that says one must offer flying dragons a way to pass through the building as they head toward the sea. It's magical. Even romantic, in its own way."

He heard Julian scoff in return.

"Feng shui? Romantic? It seems to me to be the very opposite of romantic. All those rules about where in a room things have to be, and which direction they must be pointed–it seems to me more pedantic than romantic."

Lee shrugged again, patted his driver on the shoulders to let him know he had a point. "Speaking of romance . . . " he began. Julian leaned back into Lee's arms a few inches, glanced back at him with a winsome smile.

"Yes?" he replied.

"Are you aware of our victim having any, um, paramours?"

Julian leaned forward once more to pay more attention to the road. They were on a quieter street now, so they didn't have to shout at one another quite so much.

"No, I do not," he answered. "I never knew Jocelyn to speak of anyone . . . special . . . in her life. I mean she always had some attractive man on her arm at the galas she'd attend. But I've always assumed they were one of those professional society escorts. You'd see her with one for, oh, a few months or so. Then the next time you ran into her, she was accompanied by someone else. Someone equally handsome and equally wooden."

Lee nodded once. "I see. I only ask because there is this woman, a Canadian who was in the casino on the night Jocelyn died. They apparently met on a cruise not long back and became . . . chummy." He looked at the back of Julian's head to see if the security professional could tell where he was headed with the conversation but got no inkling from his demeanor.

"The woman described their relationship as a big-sister, little-sister sort of thing, but it made me wonder if Jocelyn might be . . ."

Julian whipped his head around with more force than the architect expected. Lee prayed they would not run into the back of a delivery truck or, even worse, the front of some commercial establishment.

"Lesbian? Oh, no, not Jocelyn. I am quite certain about that," Julian replied. He turned his attention back to the street and slowed the scooter some. "She may never have had a long-term relationship with a man, but she always had her eyes set on any man in the room she hoped could provide one."

Lee smiled but said nothing for a few seconds. Eventually, however, he decided to venture, "Were you ever a man she had her eyes set on, Julian?"

Again, his new friend whipped his head around. Only this time he had a look that was more stern than incredulous.

"No, Dalton!" he answered. "Not at all. I can promise you I was never a man she could be interested in."

They were approaching Oil Street, which marked the western edge of the North Point neighborhood. A busker occupied one corner, playing (in random rotation) a guitar, a flute and a harmonica. Lee started some, for the musician looked remarkably like his confidant, the person who had professed an urge to retire from O during their meeting at So Lo Pun village.

Am I being shadowed, Lee wondered. He squinted his eyes and as he did so, the busker–though a keen lookalike–transformed into someone else with a bit less grace and gravitas than his associate.

Julian maneuvered the scooter to a parking space where they could get a better view of the buildings that had been erected there since the architect had left for America some thirty-five years earlier. Lee's gaze trailed up to the top of the many luxury, high-rise residences that made up City Garden.

"Wow," he exclaimed, a small smile breaking across his face. His powers of observation were on full throttle, calculating the angles and torques and cosmetic embellishments he saw on display. He turned his head one direction, dipped it in the other, his smile broadening as he did.

"I must say, Julian, I sort of like how it all flows together, even if . . ."

"The neighborhood's lost some of its old charm?" his friend suggested. Lee nodded but kept smiling, clambered off the scooter and dashed a few steps ahead of his companion to get a different perspective of the towering structures in front of them. "I remember there being some old power station near here, even though it had been decommissioned before I was born," Lee called back.

"It's still here, Dalton, look," Julian replied. The security consultant was pointing to a spot within the housing development where a remnant of the power station could still be seen. "While I was studying at the London School of Economics, I read up on the history of that power station and the World War II battle that took place there. Pretty ferocious and tragic for the locals, as I recall."

"Yes, the Japanese really did them in," Lee responded. The architect felt the developers had done more than a reasonable job of blending the historic building in with the more contemporary towers.

Julian beckoned Lee back to the scooter. "You'll be happy to know that there's still some character left in North Point," he said. "Let's go look."

Julian wheeled the scooter away from the curb, and before Lee knew it, they were on Chun Yeung Street, in the enclave within North Point known as Little Fujian. Here, the small grocery shops continued to vend *tokwa* (Filipino-style tofu), *lumpia* (savory and sweet spring rolls), mung bean cake and other foods enjoyed by the emigrants from China's Fujian province who had settled in North Point decades ago. Lee found that if he closed his eyes, the aromas emanating from the shops could lead him to believe he was in a rural village in the Philippines or Indonesia, not right in the heart of Hong Kong.

But the street and its overflowing market were far more colorful–dare he say garish?–than he remembered them being from his childhood. There were fewer tourists here than at the markets closer to his hotel, but it was bustling and loud, nonetheless. More than once, Julian had to bring the scooter to a complete stop as they tried to navigate the narrow lane and the throngs that occupied it.

As they waited for the crowd to part, they marveled at the massive banners in scarlet, black and gold that screamed both the items for sale and their 'going price.' Then, both men almost became crushed against a vendor stall selling fresh coral trout when a massive tram turned the corner immediately in front of them and drove toward them, taking up two-thirds of the lane.

"Okay, Julian, enough character for me," Lee said, plunging himself into the seat's supple leather.

"I was going to suggest we indulge in some of North Point's legendary egg waffles," Julian countered, "but after that, I think I'm going to need some time before I try to eat anything." He headed them back west, but on King's Road this time. Soon enough, Lee was craning his neck and marveling at a behemoth from the past, a structure that his time away from Hong Kong had almost caused him to forget altogether.

The State Theatre–opened in 1952 as the Empire Theatre–was a stunning but now shabby architectural marvel that had screened hundreds of Asian and Western films during its lifetime. Designed by architects George W. Grey and Liu Sun Fo, the bloated building featured six concrete parabolic arches on its roof, stacked one behind the other like poker chips in a tray. It stopped serving as a cinema in 1997; today, a parade of cheesy retail shops lined its ground floor perimeter and, rising from there, came one gaudy billboard after another, blaring advertisements that almost obliterated from view the intriguing arches above.

"A few years ago, a developer was buying up the retail spaces with the hopes of demolishing the building and replacing it with some new, mixed-use thingamajig," Julian told him as they cruised slowly by the legendary structure. He carefully braked to catch a large sneeze, then asked his passenger, "Have you heard of Docomomo, the global organization devoted to preserving modern architecture?"

"Most definitely," Lee replied. "I'm a huge supporter of it."

Julian nodded emphatically and sneezed once more. "Well, when the locals went ballistic at the prospects of the theatre being torn down. Docomomo stepped up and included it on its 'Heritage in Danger' list. The following year, the government designated it a Grade I Historic Building, given only to buildings of outstanding merit."

"Good," Lee replied. "I hadn't heard that. I mean, sure, it's old. And rundown. But its architecture is sublime, and it was even in a Bruce Lee movie, if memory serves me right."

Julian guffawed at the reference. "Yes. *Game of Death*. 1978. The movie Bruce Lee was filming when he died. It has an awesome fight scene between Bruce and Kareem Abdul-Jabbar, of all people." The architect's jaw dropped a little, and Julian gave his friend a sly wink. "I've watched it five times," he added. "Maybe six."

"You're quite an encyclopedia of knowledge," Lee said with a chuckle. He turned and scanned the landscape for a few seconds. "You know, I don't regret our leaving here for the United States at all," he added finally. "But this place does still tug at my heart."

His companion nodded some. "I understand, Dalton, I do understand. After my lengthy assignments in Tokyo, and especially Bangkok, I have the same feelings for those cities."

After a casual five-minute ride, during which both men seemed to be quietly immersed in nostalgia, the pair approached the intersection at which they had met earlier in the day.

Lee cleared his throat, decided to stay on the back of the scooter rather than disembark it.

"Poor segue, I suppose," he said, "but about this little 'game of death' we're investigating . . ."

"Yes? What's wrong?"

Lee shook his head. "Oh, nothing really. It's just . . . I had a couple of my associates follow up with the sorority sisters you suggested we contact."

"And?"

"First of all, they hadn't heard of Jocelyn's death, so I got to be the bearer of bad tidings along with everything else."

"Oh, I'm so sorry to hear that Dalton. I should have considered that."

"No worries, really. More to the point, they were both in South America on a hiking trip the entire week leading up to and including the day of Jocelyn's death. They sent across some receipts that confirmed their story. Seems we can count both of them out as suspects."

"Ah. Too bad. Maybe I shouldn't have bothered you with the suggestion."

"Not at all, Julian. Your suggestions are always more than welcome."

The security consultant put an index finger to his lips and began to tap them repeatedly. "In that case, there is another thread you may want to follow." He remained quiet for a few seconds and seemed to be silently counting to ten. Suddenly he stopped tapping his lips and barked, "YES!"

"What are you thinking, Julian?"

His friend was now bobbing his head vigorously. "In the back of mind . . . there was something else . . . now I recall what it was," he answered. "Up until about four months ago, Jocelyn had an assistant who oversaw most of her personal details. Her name was Allyson Blackwell or Allyson Blackwood, something like that. Anyway, she wasn't Jocelyn's business secretary, she was more like a personal valet. I met her once. She seemed nice enough. Sort of meek, but Jocelyn always described her as being quite competent."

Lee felt his phone buzzing urgently. He tried to discreetly remove it from his pocket and read the message that had arrived without offending Julian.

"Anyway, the assistant just up and ghosted Jocelyn. Didn't show up for work one day and wasn't heard from again. I had forgotten all about her because she was so . . . forgettable. But the thing is . . ." He turned toward Lee, who had just secreted the phone back into the pocket of his jeans. "The thing is . . . she probably would have had knowledge and access to just about every personal detail of Jocelyn. Her calendar, for instance. Her passwords . . ."

"How she liked her martinis prepared?"

They exchanged a knowing look, before Julian replied, *"Exactly."*

Lee was chewing on something. "Well, my dear friend, thanks for the stellar tour. And you may very well be onto something with this assistant. I've just forwarded those possible names of hers to the team, and I'm certain we'll want to track her down and follow up with her.

"Because I just got a text from Kip Silva saying they found not one but two martini glasses in a dumpster behind the casino. One of the glasses had a trace of rat poison in it but the other did not. The dumpster hadn't been emptied because the sanitation workers on Macau have apparently been on strike the past several days.

"Well, that's fortunate, I guess," Julian said.

"Yes," Lee said climbing off the back of the scooter at last. He doffed his golf cap and extended it toward his tour guide. "But even more fortunate is the fact I've just learned from Kip Silva that the lab was able to collect a scintilla of DNA from the glass that didn't have any rat poison in it.

"Send over whatever information you have about that former assistant, dear Julian, for the one thing they were able to determine from that trace of DNA is that the person drinking that other martini with Jocelyn was absolutely, unmistakably, without a doubt, a woman."

16

Bree fumbled with the enormous umbrella she had brought with her, was exasperated that she even had to manage the monstrosity. But the heavy mist that had developed that afternoon meant she needed more than just some form of headcover for protection. And the bloated, red-white-and-blue bumbershoot she was wrestling with was the only one she could find near the hotel.

She was determined to go back to the market and pick up for Kip Silva that sporty tie she had spotted. He'd look perfect in it, she decided. Its colors would certainly set off his tan.

Surely he'd appreciate the gesture.

Surely it wouldn't seem too forward.

Surely, she thought, *it's the tie that's luring me back there . . .*

The ferry ride across the harbor was uneventful, save for the occasional gust of wind that sprayed mist and sea water upon those who had chosen to stand near the craft's railing. Bree was not one of those–it had taken her far too long to contract the umbrella and snap it shut for her to open it up once more.

As soon as we arrive on the other side of the harbor, I'm ditching this thing for the first small umbrella I can find, she insisted.

The inclement weather provided one key advantage: the marketplace was far less populated than it had been during her first visit. In fact, it seemed almost dreary, with the canvas roofs of some of the stalls dripping rain onto the pavement, and multiple puddles interfering with one's ability to stroll through the neighborhood.

If they had let me design this market, Bree thought, *I'd have equipped it with some awnings that were a lot more colorful and a lot more sturdy.*

It also didn't help that she was still saddled with the garish, gigantic umbrella she'd lugged along. Only one shop had been open near the ferry terminal, and the only umbrella it had in stock was a purple shade with the image of a lime green dinosaur on both sides.

She didn't consider that much of an upgrade, so she stayed with what she had.

"Hey, American lady! I have a lucky amulet just for you! Keeps away all diseases. Wards off evil spirits. Ten dollars. Just for you, lovely American lady."

Bree flashed a brief smile, which faded quickly as she trudged on.

How do they know I'm American? she wondered.

To avoid further come-ons (and the occasional, throaty whistle) she ducked her head behind the umbrella. But after turning slightly to take note of some shiny object inside a stall, and impaling nearby pedestrians in the process, she decided to close up the shade once and for all. Besides, the mist had thankfully let up to the point hardly any protection was really needed.

"Hello, lady! Magic elixir here!"

"Skin balm removes all wrinkles instantly!"

"This amazing bracelet will bring you the love you've been waiting for!"

With her shield now gone, the hawkers called out to her more often and more loudly than ever, urged on by the fact there were hardly any other customers nearby. But she was determined to keep her visit to the market both brief and focused, to fulfill her one objective and then get the heck out of there.

Or was she?

Soon enough, she arrived at the stall where she had seen the tie. But her heart began to pulse rapidly as her eyes darted across the assortment yet failed to land on the tie she had admired on her previous visit. She flipped through a row of ties hanging from a rod, but to no avail.

"Looking for something in particular?" asked an older man wearing a black, conical hat held in place by a thin chin strap. Bree continued to flip through the ties on view, each one crisp inside a cellophane envelope.

"Yes, I am!" she said with more desperation than she meant to reveal. She took a second to compose herself, then continued. "A tie. With red and green stripes? That went this way." Using two of her fingers, she made a quick diagonal motion. The stall owner thought for a moment, then brightened.

"Oh, yes! I know the one! Sorry, I sold it to someone. Yesterday, I think."

Her shoulders slumped, and she turned toward the racks of ties to see if there was another that might be as attractive on Silva as that one would have been.

"Some man bought it. Good looking guy. Very tan. Said he heads up the police force on Macau."

Bree swiveled toward the stall owner, her eyes growing larger by the moment.

"YOU'RE KIDDING ME!" she yelled at him. The proprietor suddenly looked as though she was about to attack him.

"Not kidding," he said meekly. "You know him? He your boyfriend?"

That stopped Bree. "Why, no, not at all. Why on earth would you think that?" She gave the racks one final, fleeting glance but quickly decided her little pursuit now seemed pointless.

"Maybe I have another one like it in the back," he told her. "Want me to look?"

She shook her head and sent him a sympathetic smile. "No, thank you anyway," she answered, patting him gently on one shoulder. "Really, thank you. Maybe next time. I'm sorry if I startled you."

His sour expression told her he knew there almost certainly wasn't going to be any 'next time.'

She turned her wrist to study her watch. If she scooted, she could make the next ferry back to Hong Kong Island. But something told her to slow down instead. Occasionally, a glint of sunshine would pierce the clouds, but it would retreat as quickly as it had arrived. She wasn't sure why, but she felt the need to saunter, to dawdle, to explore.

Or maybe she was sure why she was inclined to stay, far more than she was willing to admit.

The crowd grew some, but not so much as to make the market crowded. Bree paraded past stalls overflowing with scarves and headbands, bracelets and cameos. One particular stall offered rock-mineral necklaces that would blink like turn signals with the push of a button; another focused on 'exotic leather belts,' the authenticity of which Bree questioned.

She found it all alluring and off-putting at the same time. The closest thing she had seen to this growing up was the phalanx of shops in Old Town Scottsdale. Only there, most of the items had a Southwestern or American Indian bent to them. Here, the lineage of the items seemed to veer from rural China to Leicester Square, from the Via Veneto to the Jersey Shore.

She considered grabbing a quick bowl of noodles but changed her mind and began to make her way toward the ferry terminal.

But when Bree rounded the corner, there she was–the beggar, as dirty as before but huddled inside a different vestibule. The rendezvous felt to Bree both serendipitous and fated. The girl was looking in the opposite direction, as if transfixed by something on the horizon. She seemed more composed and dignified than before, but her hair was still a heap of straw, her clothing still ripped and threadbare.

Again, like a marionette guided by strings from above, the girl woodenly turned her head and stared blankly at Bree.

This time, however, it was Bree who thought, *You know me. And you know that you know me.*

The urchin was not uttering the plaintive cry Bree had heard before, nor was she extending her arms toward the crowd. But Bree felt compelled to approach her. To interact with her. Carefully, she sidled across the narrow lane, trying to make her approach as indirect and discreet as possible. The girl was looking off to one side again. Or was she intentionally avoiding the tall American woman who came toward her?

Soon enough, Bree was standing just a few feet away, to one side. The girl pivoted her head in Bree's direction and waited, with an expression that said, *Finally. It's about time.*

The architect flashed a frail smile. "Do you speak English?" she asked hesitantly. Suddenly, she regretted not having taken Dalton up on the free Mandarin or Cantonese lessons he'd offered to everyone on the team before they had left the States.

The girl nodded slowly. "A little," she replied. Bree smiled again, more broadly in an effort to win the beggar's trust. Still, she felt confused.

What now? she wondered. Followed by, *Why am I doing this?*

She swiveled her upper body and cast a brief look at the other pedestrians nearby, none of whom seemed to notice or care about the exchange underway.

"Do you . . . live . . . here?" she finally uttered, swirling a finger in the air to convey the idea of neighborhood. Now that a conversation was taking place, she relaxed her body some, leaned against the handle of the oversized umbrella, the tip of which she now had pointed toward the sidewalk. The girl neither nodded nor shook her head, but merely extended one arm to her right, pointing as she did.

So, at least she has a place to go at night, she told herself.

But then the girl did shake her head and uttered, "Park."

Bree took a breath in. She guessed the girl to be no more than seventeen, although given her appearance, it was hard to know for sure. The architect stood there perplexed for a moment, not sure what to do. Or say. She wasn't even sure whether she needed to say or do anything. Meanwhile, the waif had stopped looking at her and had again locked on some point in the distance, just to the right of Bree's umbrella.

It began to mist again, and the mist quickly turned into a light drizzle. Bree turned to leave, but the girl suddenly thrust her face up toward the tall American, emitted a guttural grunt and extended one hand.

"I don't know what to do here," Bree said to her. "I don't have any money with me. I'm sorry. Look." At that, she reached into one pocket of her jeans, plucked out the slim wallet she'd brought with her and opened it to reveal a collection of credit cards, but no bills or coins. In truth, in another pocket, she had a small wad of bills that she had planned to purchase the tie with. But giving her money away to a beggar she did not know had not been on her plan today and not an idea she particularly relished.

The beggar peered intently at the architect but said nothing.

Bree chose to dart away, but as she did, the precipitation intensified again. After a few steps, Bree stopped and turned around to take one last look at the waif. The girl was scooting under the overhang to avoid the rain that now cascaded from above.

Bree sighed, trudged back to the waif and handed her the large umbrella she'd brought along for protection.

The girl gave her a perplexed look, but one that seemed softer than her previous expressions. "Thank you, Bree," the girl whispered.

It was only as the architect was stepping onto the ferry that would take her back to her hotel that it dawned on her she'd never told the young girl her name . . .

17

The collaborators intended for their virtual meeting to be a well-run strategy session. But it quickly descended into a frantic free-for-all.

"Look, we need to move the assets before somebody discovers them," the American insisted between swigs of beer. "And I am talking about *tonight!*"

"That's preposterous!" the Brit responded. "We can't possibly move it all so quickly. We're not talking about a couple of laptops and printers here. There are logistics that need to be considered."

"I get that," the American said, his swigs from the long-necked bottle coming more frequently now. "But they're getting closer, could move in on us any hour now. This window of opportunity we have is gonna slam shut on us unless we act *ASAP!*"

"I vehemently disagree," the Brit announced. "In my estimation, it will take us a minimum of two days, and perhaps as much as a week, to move everything to a new location. And, old chap, the transfer is probably going to require several trips, which only increases the possibility of our being discovered."

"We don't have the time for all that! Two trips at most. In one night. We can do it if we just hustle a little bit, and you stop coming up with all these excuses for why we can't make it happen!"

Throughout the back and forth, Yang Li had remained silent, quietly working on her granddaughter's shawl. But as the volume of the debate began to rise, she set her project to one side and gave the others a stern look.

"Quiet, both of you!" she began. "No more squawking! You sound like the chickens that run around in my maa-maa's barnyard!"

Both of the men on the call pulled up, assumed looks of sheepish abasement.

"Listen to me. I arrange everything. I know movers. Experts. It will get done but yes, we must plan carefully. They move everything sometime later this week."

"LATER THIS WEEK? We don't have a week, Yang Li! Two days, max. I beg you!" The American took another quick sip of beer. "Chop, chop, and all that!"

Yang Li arched her eyebrows at the poor Chinese slang her American colleague had just used. She leaned toward the camera and gave her associates a menacing look.

"I tell you, we do it when I ready," she began, "I am in charge here because I do good timing." She finished the sentence with an emphatic nod, then picked up her craft project and resumed her work on it.

"It's *have* good timing," the American groused.

"What?" she shot back.

"You don't *do* good timing, Yang Li, you *have* good timing. I thought you spoke better English than that."

The woman scowled at her American colleague, pointed one of her needles directly toward the camera. "WHATEVER!" she bellowed. The three fell silent again, not sure how to proceed.

Unsatisfied, the American decided to push one more detail.

"And you are absolutely certain, Yang Li, that no one will be able to trace the location of the assets after they've been moved, is that right? We just cannot fuck up this plan at this point. It's almost go-time."

Yang Li slowly shut her eyes at the comment. The Brit bulged his, prepared himself for whatever explosion he knew was about to occur.

Instead, Yang Li took on a smile that the Brit could still detect was forced and dripping with acid. Her reply came in a measured tone and was surprisingly articulate.

"I am quite confident no one will be able to trace the whereabouts of the assets," she intoned. "And, after that ridiculous air show you organized hoping to scare Mr. Lee and his team, I am also quite confident that if anyone is going to fuck up this plan, it's probably going to be you, not me."

The others went silent, quickly began to look anywhere else but at one another.

With that, Yang Li leaned toward the camera once more, gave the American a steely look and intoned, "How you like my English now, Yankee?"

18

BAM!

Dalton Lee's boxing glove shoved the punching bag forward far more than he had intended. Enough so that it caused Warren to take a couple of steps back and grip the other side of the bag more firmly.

"Whoa, chill out there, boss," the senior architect said with a laugh. "No need to knock the stuffing out of it."

Lee chuckled privately, more out of ego than out of a response to what Warren had just said to him. It had been ages since the architect had sparred with a punching bag, and it felt good to expend the energy he wasn't sure he still had to expend. The velocity of his arm jabs surprised him, even if his feet felt leaden below him.

He had found it curious when Warren texted him out of the blue, asking Lee to join him at a boxing gym he'd stumbled upon just a few blocks from their hotel. Lee started to decline, fully aware of how out of shape he was. But Warren added, 'There's something we need to talk about,' so he felt obliged to tag along.

He hadn't expected his employee to put him through such a strenuous workout.

BAM! KAPOW!

Warren's eyes bulged some, and he again rolled back onto his heels from the power of Lee's punch.

"Dalton!" he barked. "What are you so angry about?"

That stopped the world's most prominent architect, and most reluctant detective, in his tracks. It dawned on him that he may have been tapping into a reservoir of ferocity that had been gurgling just below his consciousness. A small, but active volcano that had been simmering for many months now and was just this side of erupting.

He decided to be more mindful going forward.

"Okay, you box," he said to his colleague. "I'll hold."

Bad decision. Lee was on his back within seconds, the room spinning in several different directions before he could regain any sense of equilibrium. Warren was bending over him, uttering a mash-up of apologies and profanities.

"Shit! I'm so sorry, Dalton. Dammit, I thought you were holding onto the bag more tightly than you were. Can you hear me? Oh, shit, shit, shit, what have I done? Do you need an ambulance, Dalton? Should I call Lara?"

Lee blinked several times. He meant it as a signal to Warren that he had not lapsed into a coma and could, indeed, hear him. And move. At least one part of his body, anyway.

Warren, of course, interpreted it as a sign that Lee was in some form of distress and needed help immediately. The senior architect leaped to his feet and began to jog away from his superior, yelling "Somebody! Help!"

Somehow, Lee summoned enough oxygen into his lungs to shout, "Warren! No! Stop! I'm fine. I think."

Everyone in the gym pivoted toward the middle-aged Asian American sprawled awkwardly on the mat in one corner. He was sitting up now, but his torso was bobbing and weaving like one of those clown-faced bop bags that's just been kicked by a tyrannical five-year-old.

Warren trotted back to his boss, followed by a gym manager who offered some form of inhalant that smelled to Lee like ammonia mixed with turpentine. He waved off the aromatic spirits, shook his head a few times, then slowly rose from the mat with Warren's help.

"And you were doing so well, Dalton," the senior architect joked.

Lee flashed a weak grin which quickly faded into a queasy smirk.

"As usual," he sputtered, "I underestimated your talents, Warren."

The pair limped over to a bench beneath a phalanx of large windows on one side of the gym. They plopped onto it, side-by-side and Warren began to study his boss's vision. "Are you sure you're all right, Dalton?" he queried. "Your eyes seem to be rolling in different directions."

Lee was getting his breath slowly. "Oh, first time you've noticed they do that, is it?" he answered with a laugh. Warren had the palm of one hand on Lee's upper back. He began to rub it in a circular motion.

"Just don't fire me, Dalton" he finally said with a chuckle that was as hearty as Lee's had been. "I mean, I'm not sure how I'd survive without all of this drama." The remark had both of them now bent over at the waist, laughing toward the floor.

The other boxers looked askance at the mirthful pair, discreetly edged their way to the other end of the gym.

When he had finally regained his composure, and sat back up straight, Lee noticed across the way a series of colorful posters on the opposite wall. The name of the gym floated large above a host of other inspirational messages like 'Power Through,' 'Strength Wins' and 'Box Then In,' all of which were accompanied by a variety of black-and-white photos of boxers from the past, dukes up, fierceness in their eyes.

Most of the boxers were men, but one dark-complexioned woman with a ponytail stood out.

That reminded Lee there was something he had wanted to ask Warren.

"Anisa," he said, still locked on the poster across from them. "What are your thoughts about her . . . distance . . . from the rest of us these days?"

Warren dropped his head, turned away from his superior and began to count the kettle bells lined up against the far wall.

"Well," he finally acknowledged, "that's what I wanted to talk to you about, boss." He paused and looked up at the posters that Lee had been focused on. To one side, a pair of younger boxers were mimicking those in the posters, dancing back and forth and jabbing playfully at one another.

"You want to know what my thoughts are," Warren continued, "and my thoughts are . . . that it may spell trouble for us."

Lee jerked his head in Warren's direction. "What do you mean?"

The senior architect turned back toward Lee but dropped his head again and lowered his voice to a barely audible whisper.

"It means I think it's possible she may be one of them," he intoned. "I think she may be working against us." Carefully, he related the events that had taken place the night he'd followed Anisa across the street and eavesdropped onto her call. Methodically, he replayed word for word what he'd heard her say to the person on the other end of the phone.

Concluded with her final comment, "So you're going to have to be patient and I'm just going to have to stay under the radar a little while longer before we move forward with our plan."

When the prosecutor had finished presenting his evidence, Lee remained silent for several moments. Of course, he didn't want to believe it. Wasn't completely convinced that the clandestine conversation Warren had just described meant what it sounded like.

And yet, the architect had a sinking feeling inside that it most certainly meant what it sounded like. Anisa had been enticing toward him when they first met, then suddenly retreated. Begged to become part of the group, then proceeded to separate from them. Too much about her behavior didn't add up for Warren's explanation not to. Lee had worried for some time that O might try to infiltrate The Lee Group. If Anisa was, in fact, a mole, it could explain how they seemed to know his every move.

Even, sometimes, before he did.

"Well, she told me a few days ago that she was going to try to be more agreeable with everybody."

Warren's eyes became slits as he considered that comment.

"I'd have to say, Dalton, that hasn't been the case," he replied.

Lee nodded his head forward a couple of times before taking a deep breath.

"Okay, well, thanks for the heads up, Warren. I trust your insights, so I'll keep an even closer watch on her. You're welcome to, as well, but I don't want you to feel that you need to take that on as your responsibility. You have lots of other things to focus on right now." Slowly they stood, but before they moved away from the bench, Lee reached out and clapped a hand on Warren's shoulder.

"Oh, and don't worry," he said. "I'm not going to fire you." They both chuckled at that. But Lee then shifted his expression to one of dead seriousness. "I may dock you several month's salary, Warren, but I'm not going to fire you," he added. He glared at his employee for a moment, but quickly flashed a wide grin to confirm to him that the comment had been in jest.

Lee took a couple of steps toward the exit to the gym, moving directly into the path of the two young boxers who had been sparring with one another. The collision catapulted Lee onto his back again; once more, his eyes resembled dice tumbling wildly across a craps table.

Warren shut his eyes, leaned his head back and softly moaned, "Oh, jeezus!" Then the senior architect sprang into action once again, dropping beside the splayed torso of his superior and patting him on the cheeks.

"Dalton! Are you all right? Can you hear me, Dalton? DALTON!"

19

The world's most prominent architect sat slumped in his hotel room's luxurious armchair, his feet propped up on the ottoman before him, one hand cradling an ice pack against his right temple. He'd considered adding a hot water bottle to the recuperation regimen but decided that just might be overkill.

Beside his feet lay the acrostic. He had just deduced the solution to one of the final clues.

S. Like most fried foods and some spouses

His lettering in the answer field was clean and precise.

B-A-T-T-E-R-E-D

He tossed the acrostic to one side and decided to skim the headlines in that morning's newspaper:

'Strawbuck Captures Preakness, Is Poised to Take Triple Crown'
'Scientists Connect Havana Syndrome to Microwave Transmissions'
'Dubai Reports Record Revenues from Oil, Petrochemical Sales'

Well good, he thought. *Maybe now Dubai won't balk at paying my fee for designing that concert hall they want.*

The stars that had been swirling in and out of his line of vision ever since his collision in the boxing gym had finally retreated, but he was left with a dull headache and a sharp pang in his right side.

So, of course, that's when his phone decided to blow up. First came a text from Julian: 'Found Allyson Blackwell, Jocelyn's former assistant. She's working at the Kellett School now. See contact info below.'

Lee forwarded the text to Lara and Kip Silva. The moment he was notified that the forward was sent, a call came in from Kip Silva.

"Dalton, are you all right? I hear you had a run-in with . . . um . . . a couple of pugilists?" Lee tried to ignore the faint snicker he was sure he heard coming from the other end of the call.

"Something like that," Lee responded, wincing as he shifted his body in the chair. "What's up?"

Silva cleared his throat and assumed a more sober tone. "Thought I'd update you on some developments here. First of all, it seems Alex Wentworth did not fly back to Canada when she was scheduled to."

Lee shifted in his chair again, winced again. "That's odd. She seemed anxious to get back home."

"Yes, she did. But then again, if she belongs to O and they have any additional assignments they need her to undertake . . ."

Lee nodded, and as he did, the ice pack slipped from hand and landed on the seat cushion beside him. Cradling his phone to his ear, he lifted the pack with the fingers of his right hand and tossed it over the back of the chair and onto the carpet.

"I was thinking the very same thing," he replied. "So, where is she now?"

Lee's question was met with a telling silence. Finally, Silva responded, "We're not sure. I mean, we don't know. It seems she's vanished off our radar."

Lee rolled his eyes and turned to gaze out the window on his right.

"Well, that's not very encouraging." He paused to reposition his body in the seat cushion once more. "Do you have any good news to share?" he added. "Did the martini glasses yield any more valuable identification. I could use some good news right now, Kip."

The line went quiet again. "No to the martini glasses. The DNA sample we found was quite small, and it seems even that got contaminated some during the trip to our lab. Other than the gender of whoever was drinking from that glass, we're not able to determine much else with any degree of certainty."

Lee sighed heavily. It was more of a 'life sigh' than a comment on the compromised DNA, but Silva took it as the latter.

"But . . . well . . . I can't necessarily call it *good* news, but I do have something under the category of helpful news. It appears the mysterious phenomenon of the roulette ball landing in the wrong pocket has been solved."

"And?"

"There may have been some sort of hanky-panky going on in the casino's back office. However, in this case, whoever was in charge of the wheel just mis-programmed the pocket that the pill was supposed to drop into. Human error, in other words."

Lee considered this for a few seconds and frowned. "In other words, Alexandra Wentworth's windfall was . . ."

"Entirely coincidental," Silva concluded.

"Hmm," Lee replied, still frowning. He turned toward the window again. Only now did he notice a small billboard across the street that was broadcasting a public service announcement intended to protect residents against online scams. In large block letters, it warned:

DON'T BE FOOLED!

"Do you need us to send you to a doctor, Dalton?" Silva suddenly asked. "You sound uncomfortable. And you really should be mindful of a blow to the head. They can lead to some serious complications afterward if you're not careful."

Lee smiled weakly. "No, I'm fine, Kip. There may not be any squash matches in my immediate future but I'm only nursing some bruises, a little soreness of the ribs and a mild headache. Fortunately, I have some very good pain meds."

"All right, then." A pause, followed by, "Oh, I almost forgot. You and your team are cleared to visit Jocelyn Cheng's office and residence whenever you feel up to it. I may want to join you. No rush, but I know you're probably interested to scope those out as part of your fact-finding.

"Well, that's a positive development," Lee replied. "Thanks, and yes, it may be another day or so before I'm ready to do that. I'll ping you when I'm ambulatory again."

"Good. Be sure to let me know if you need anything." Silva clicked off, but Lee stayed on the line.

What with suspects emerging but then quickly vanishing, and the matter with Anisa weighing heavily on his soul, he felt like he most definitely was in need of something.

But exactly what that was, he did not know.

20

Bree stood outside Lara's hotel room, hesitant and uncertain. More than once, she had raised her right hand and balled in into a fist to gently rap on the executive assistant's door. But she'd brought the fist back down to her side when caution got the best of her.

She really needed Lara's help, though. So, she raised a fist once more and allowed it this time to tap lightly against the door.

"Lara, it's me, Bree. Can I have a minute? I need your advice."

She could hear footsteps coming across carpet and then the door opened. Bree expected there to be a stern look on Lara's face. Instead, the woman's expression was one of concern.

"Are you all right, dear?" she asked. Widening the gap between the door and the door jamb, she added, "Come on in."

The younger architect shuffled into the room, head lowered. Despite her view being mostly that of the carpet, Bree couldn't help but notice how the tidiness of Lara's room was diametrically opposed to that of Liam's room down the hall.

"I hope I'm not hitting you at a bad time," she stammered. "If it is, I can come back later."

"No, it's fine, Bree," Lara replied. "I was just about to go online and see if I could rummage up a few more details about Jocelyn Cheng's financial affairs." She paused, gazed more intently at her younger associate. "But Liam's on that task as well, so . . ." She placed a hand on Bree's shoulder. "Is something wrong?"

Bree shook her head and smiled weakly. "I'm all right, really" she replied. "It's just . . . my online sleuthing skills seem to have escaped me. Or I'm having problems with the wi-fi here, I'm not sure what the problem is." She paused. "I can't seem to get into any of the portals I would normally use to access her appointment calendars." Bree looked up. "I feel so stupid, Lara. I'm feeling a little useless to the team right now, I'm afraid."

Lara allowed an uncharacteristic smile to cross her lips and lifted her chin an inch or so. "I think I know what the problem is. Follow me. And, you're not at all stupid, Bree. I find the skills you bring to the team immensely valuable."

"You do?" Bree said as they padded toward Lara's desk.

"Why yes, dear. Who else on the team would have the audacity to tackle someone in a drugstore and snatch their cell phone away from them the way you did in Manhattan? Or use your strength to boost one of our former employees up onto a carport so he could do reconnaissance on a suspect, the way you did in Miami?" Lara narrowed her gaze at her coworker, then added, "I certainly hope you realize I would certainly never do such things."

Although Bree knew that statement could be interpreted more than one way, she grinned and reddened some at the woman's backhanded compliment.

"Now," Lara began as she logged onto her laptop, "the problem you've been having is likely due to the fact we're having to enter an odd string of characters after our password before our system will let us in." The elder architect swiveled toward her colleague and arched a brow. "Part of its latest update, I'm afraid. Just before we left the States, I explained the change in a much-too-long email which, I suspect, no one fully read. Liam and Anisa had the same problem when we first got here. My apologies."

Bree ducked her head but said nothing, allowed the executive assistant to type away on her keyboard.

After a couple of moments, Lara sat back in her desk chair. "And *voila!*" she announced, as a scramble of images and text arrived on her screen.

"Thank you, Lara!" Bree replied, placing her palms together and clapping quietly. "I'll go back and read that email you sent. I promise."

Her superior smiled but seemed determined not to let the unusual camaraderie end so quickly. "Well, since you're already here, why don't we just explore Ms. Cheng's appointment calendar together, shall we?"

Bree nodded and then offered Lara a helping hand when the elder stateswoman of The Lee Group ventured off into some far-flung corner of the web by accident. Soon enough, however, they were back on track and had found a version of the casino executive's calendar of appointments that Bree had saved to the cloud.

As Lara navigated to the weeks just before the woman's murder, Bree blurted out, "Have you ever known anyone who was homeless, Lara?" The senior architect stopped typing and cocked her head.

"No, no, I can't say that I have. In Finland, we have several government programs in place to prevent it from occurring. We do have unhoused people in Finland, but far fewer than there are in America." She reared back a few inches and scrutinized her colleague. "Why do you ask?"

The younger architect scrunched her nose and shrugged her shoulders. "Oh, I don't know. I've just become more aware of it lately, I guess." She started to tell Lara about the young woman she had come upon in the markct in Kowloon but changed her mind.

"I feel terrible admitting this," she continued, "but I think I've always viewed homeless people as more of an eyesore than anything else, but . . ." She looked down at her lap for a few seconds, then returned Lara' gaze.

"But what?" Lara asked.

"But . . . maybe . . . not so much anymore."

Lara continued to study the face of her colleague, wondered what had prompted her to offer such a revelation and confide it to her right now.

"Your friend, Carole," she began as she resumed typing on her keyboard. "What do you think her perspective on those people would be?"

That made Bree start. She'd never heard Carole talk about the homeless per se, but she knew Carole was always a champion for the disadvantaged. Especially those who were female . . .

She started to ask Lara what made her think of Carole, but they had a task in front of them, and she chose instead to redirect her energies toward that. "Oh, I'm sure she would be nothing but sympathetic," was all she said.

Lara studied her a bit, then returned her focus to the computer. "Well, I'm sure you'll sort it all out in time, Bree. No one really sets out to be unhoused, of course. And as discomforting as homelessness may be, those without a home are human beings just like the rest of us." She shifted in her chair a bit and straightened her posture. "Now, let's see, where are we within this calendar."

Bree craned her neck toward the computer display as Lara carefully scrolled through the entries in the file.

"I think I'm going to zero in on the week right before her murder," Lara said as she sped up her scrolling through the document. "I'm not even sure what we're looking for, and what we're looking for could be anywhere in the weeks–or maybe even the months–before her demise. Still, if it's true she did ingest the poison within a couple of days before she collapsed in the casino, that might be the most sensible timeframe for us to explore, wouldn't it?

Bree nodded and scooted closer toward the desk. Lara used the cursor to move the content on the screen to exactly one week before the casino executive's death, a day which contained no entries.

"A little strange she had no social engagements on that day, don't you think?" Bree asked.

"Well, it's always possible," Lara responded with a slow drawl, "that she had some sort of social engagement that day that she didn't want anyone to know about." She winked quickly at her colleague, then scrolled down through the file.

The following day included one entry in the morning–"Meeting at Macau Chamber of Commerce," and another in the afternoon–"Nails Magnifique–Irma."

Lara frowned. I doubt her nail technician is the one we're looking for," she said. "Although, in a way, that would be the perfect guise for one of their murderers to assume, isn't it?"

"Is it likely they would have served her a martini while she's getting a mani-pedi?" Bree wondered aloud. They looked at one another and let a couple of beats go by before shaking their heads 'no' in unison.

"Even if they did," Lara pointed out, "that salon is a good twenty minutes from the casino, as best I can tell. Doesn't really explain the second martini glass being in the dumpster behind the casino, does it?"

Bree chewed on the inside of one cheek and admitted she had to agree with Lara on that point.

The next day on the calendar also bore no appointments, but the day after that showed her attending a gala at the Macau Cultural Centre intended to raise funds for a local "Visit the Elderly" initiative. "She would have had an excellent opportunity to have her fill of martinis there," Bree suggested.

"That's true," Lara intoned slowly. "But that was still a good four to five days before she died." Now it was Lara who was chewing on the inside of one of her cheeks. "Let's keep looking shall we?"

Three days out, the calendar revealed two appointments in the morning, one with the casino's attorney and another with a television reporter who wanted to do a story about the new gaming mechanisms the casino was installing. "Seems benign enough," Lara said.

They both started, however, when they spotted the entry for lunch that day:

1:15 p.m.–Lunch with my sis, J. at Chez Toulouse

"That would be Jacquelyn," Bree blurted out. "Maybe Anisa has been right all along!"

"Maybe," Lara echoed. "Except . . ."

Bree turned toward her superior. "What is it?"

"Well, again, the restaurant. It seems it's here on Hong Kong Island. Doesn't explain the other glass being in the dumpster over on Macau."

Bree's shoulders dropped. "This is starting to feel as useless as I felt when I first got here," she groused.

Lara scrolled to the next day in the calendar, suddenly sat up straight.

"Well, look at this would you? What do you know. And only two days before she collapsed on the casino floor, too."

Bree leaned forward to see what Lara had found on the calendar. At first she read the entry silently, but as she got midway through the words, she began to recite them out loud.

3:00 p.m.—Drinks with Allyson Blackwell. My place.
FIND OUT WHY SHE GHOSTED ME.

21

Everyone was quiet in the limo car that was transporting them to Macau. The mist and showers of the days before had ended, but there was still no sun to be found. The sky was the color of flint and the water that stretched out on either side of the harbor bridge looked like a perfectly ironed bedspread.

Bree was poring through a book on the nuances of feng shui. Liam was checking Australian football scores on his phone and Anisa looked to be napping, her head resting against the window beside her. Warren appeared to be making copious notes on a legal pad; in fact, his writing was gibberish, a pretense he was using while he kept watch on Anisa.

About halfway across the bridge, Lara leaned over and nudged her boss's shoulder.

"I have to say, Dalton, I'm more than a little disappointed in you," she said softly.

He turned toward his executive assistant. The wrenching act caused him to wince some.

"*Of course* you are," he replied. "But what is it precisely that has caused your disdain for me this time?"

Lara twisted her mouth a bit, both as a response to his rebuke and an effort to keep from laughing at his comment. She glanced at the top of his head.

"Your hat," she answered. "It's the same baseball cap you wore on our flight over." She paused and shot him a look as sardonic as the reply he'd just given her. "I've sort of taken a fancy to guessing what form of headgear we're going to see you in on any given day. I was hoping you might show up in a sombrero, or maybe one of those horned helmets the Vikings used to wear." She paused again, looked away from him. "I fear your creativity may be slipping."

Lee let out a short guffaw, returned his attention to the acrostic in his lap:

U. Permanent-record entry?

He counted how many letters the answer contained and frowned. Fifteen. When the answers were that long it took him much longer to ferret out the solution. The architect chewed on the pencil's eraser for a moment, then nodded and guffawed again. Lara swiveled in her seat to see what he was up to, but he met her gaze and overtly bent back the cover of the puzzle book to shield what he was about to write.

Pressing the pencil lead into the page, he entered in bold, block letters:

I-N-S-U-B-O-R-D-I-N-A-T-I-O-N

When he emphatically completed the last serif in the final letter 'N,' the pencil lead shattered to pieces.

***

Kip Silva appeared more tan, more fit and more dashing than ever. Lee wondered if the police officer drank a pitcher of testosterone each night, just before whitening his teeth with some sort of bleaching agent. Normally, Lee would be put off by such an emphasis on appearance, but Silva was so likeable, the architect found it easy to overlook his colleague's apparent obsession with appearance.

Noticing that Bree was scurrying to take the last remaining seat next to Silva, Lee limped forward quickly, cut her off at the pass, dropped into the chair and launched the meeting with a startling comment.

"I think I know who killed Jocelyn Cheng and why," he announced.

The bustle that had accompanied everyone taking their seats

and situating their accessories on the table in front of them stopped immediately, and the room remained quiet until Liam, after several seconds, softly replied, "Dude!"

The architect put one palm up and assumed an apologetic expression.

"I didn't mean I know *the identity* of the individual who caused her death," he said. "What I meant was, I think Jocelyn, being such an astute businesswoman, was probably helping O from a financial standpoint. Maybe she was helping raise funds somehow for their little scheme. Maybe she was managing whatever investments they have. Whatever it was, I'm led to believe that the person who took her life was probably the person within O she likely interacted with the most–their treasurer, if you will, or if they're especially well-organized–their CFO.

"Maybe O killed her," Bree interrupted, "because they discovered she was embezzling money from them. Makes sense to me."

Lee turned to his assistant. "Lara, you and Liam have been looking into her financial affairs. What do you think?"

Lara glanced at Liam, who indicated he was fine with her taking the lead. "Well, I think what Bree proposed is certainly a possibility . . ." She glanced again at Liam before continuing. "But I can't say we've found anything to support that idea." Liam nodded his head in agreement. "There were the unusual transactions we found around the time of her murder, but nothing we've seen indicates she was skimming money from anyone."

Liam raised one palm. "That said, I've only . . ." He smiled and dipped his head in Lara's direction before continuing. "I mean, *we've only* been able to sift through the accounts that are in her name. I did find one account she opened that was under a corporate name of some sort, but it only had about twenty thousand dollars in it. And that's the only account under that particular corporate name–or any name similar to it–that I've been able to suss out.

"None of those accounts showed anything that would suggest she was shredding money from anybody, much less from our terrorist friends."

Lee nodded, studied the table for a moment. "Well, it is just a hypothesis. But if it's got any teeth to it, that would probably mean we might want to look within the victim's inner circle for someone who has some financial chops. He pivoted toward Kip Silva. "Anything about either the Canadian woman who was at the casino, or Jocelyn's younger sister, that would suggest they hold an MBA in international finance?"

Silva studied the ceiling for a moment, then shook his head.

"Not that I can think of," he answered. He shuffled the file folders in front of him some, then flashed a high-wattage grin at Lee. "But then, we all know who we're dealing with here," he added. "Masters of disguise, masters of multiple identities. One of them could be the world's top mathlete, or a former top executive of the World Bank, but we'd never know it. They'd make us think they were a simple tradesman, a simple shop owner . . ."

"Or a simple roulette croupier, perhaps?" Bree was glaring at the police officer with a mischievous smile. For a few seconds, he was taken aback by her comment, but he quickly recovered and met her expression with one just as shrewd.

"Perhaps," he said softly.

Lee inched forward in his chair. "I also think it's essential we follow up as soon as we can with this Allyson Blackwell that a contact of mine passed along to me as a person of interest," he said. "It appears she might have the very financial background I was talking about. And Lara and Bree also just discovered she might have had the perfect opportunity to inflict some harm on our victim."

Silva expressed how impressed he was with this new information; at the other end of the table, Bree beamed with delight.

"Excellent," Silva said. "Let's see if we can persuade her to come in during the next day or so." He glanced around the room, slapped his right palm on the tabletop and then rose quickly from his seat. "Okay then, let's go visit Jocelyn Cheng's office and apartment and see what we can learn there, shall we?"

**

When they entered her penthouse suite atop the Lucky Fortune Casino building, Dalton Lee felt an odd shift inside. But he couldn't discern what had caused it.

The accommodations were stylish but not overtly opulent. A long leather sofa backed up to the wall facing the apartment's front entrance; in front of it was a chrome and glass table accented with a mix of travel and lifestyle magazines. A large abstract painting (a print, Lee was fairly certain) hung above the sofa. Its geometric shapes made no political or social statement, but they did complement well the colors and forms on the pillows that adorned the sofa. A thriving, indoor bamboo palm stood tall in one corner, and along the wall to the left of the door was a credenza or cabinet of some sort that looked like it might be an entertainment center. However, a discreet lift of its top panel by Warren revealed it to be a bar equipped with a few crystal decanters that were assembled in a tidy row and brimming with vodka and gin.

"This place looks too perfect," Anisa suddenly announced, a slight scowl on her face. "It feels like it's been hermetically sealed."

Yes, maybe THAT'S what had me feeling so queasy, Lee thought.

Warren was still standing beside the bar, a quizzical look on his face.

"What is it, Warren?" Lee asked.

His employee cocked his head both ways, then took in a breath. "They found two martini glasses in the dumpster out back, correct?

"Yes, that's right," Silva answered.

Warren nodded for a few seconds. "Well, if that's the case, they weren't from here. This credenza is fully stocked with barware. There's not a single martini glass missing from the set."

At that, the team remained silent, but not for long.

"Unless someone restocked the bar with new martini glasses," Anisa surmised, "after they plied her with the one laced with rat poison."

For a few more minutes, the team continued to inspect the living area, which Liam started to refer to as 'the showroom.' Kip Silva noted that the carpet had been recently vacuumed, and Lara mentioned she could not find a speck of dust anywhere, not even along the baseboards.

To the right of the sofa was a French door leading into an anteroom that served as the casino executive's business office. When he stepped through the entryway, Lee felt a return of the unease he had experienced when he first entered the suite's front door. Only now, the sensation had magnified into something profoundly unsettling. Still, the source of his discomfort, and even its form, was difficult to pin down. It felt like one part nausea, another part hypertension, yet another part chills.

All he knew for certain was, *something was off.*

The room was more sumptuous than the one upfront, with mahogany 'rail and stile' paneling gracing all four walls. Each floating panel was rectangular and sported at its center a hand-carved 'button' with a design that looked rococo from afar but proved, upon closer inspection, to bear distinctively Chinese symbols.

Cheng's desk was situated in the back right corner of the room, facing diagonally toward the front corner, on their far left. To the left of that was another bamboo palm, and behind it, and against the back wall, was a small, empty wastebasket. While working at the desk, Cheng sat in an unusually high-backed leather chair, which would have afforded its occupant a commanding, almost regal, presence. Lee envisioned Jocelyn Cheng sitting erect in the chair and Nefertiti on her throne suddenly came to mind.

In the back left corner of the room was a conversation pit formed by two love seats and a square, metal coffee table with a glass top that appeared to have the same magazines on it as its counterpart in the front room. Forming an 'L' in the front left corner were two mahogany bookcases, one running along each intersecting wall. Lee strolled over to examine what was on the shelves and was disheartened to see only a dictionary, a thesaurus, a photography book devoted to the flora of Macau, a copy of *The Teachings of Lao-Tzu* and a complete set of *The Harvard Classics.*

Not a single book about architecture to be found, Lee muttered silently.

Anisa suddenly appeared behind his right shoulder.

"Don't you find it rather curious, Dalton," she began, the lilt of a flirtation in her voice, "that there's not a single business management book on those shelves?"

Lee turned only to discover her face was much closer to his than he had been prepared for. Instantly, he didn't feel quite so uncomfortable.

Even his pains from the boxing encounter seemed to melt away.

"Or any books about casinos or real estate," he added. As quickly as possible, he turned back to the shelves so he would not succumb to the overwhelming urge he had to grab her by the shoulders and kiss her on the lips.

Kip Silva opened the drawers of the executive's desk and gave out a low whistle.

"What is it?" Bree asked, sidling over toward him. He shook his head.

"Nothing unusual, which I actually find unusual," he replied. He lifted a small stack of paper. "Letterhead, in the center of the drawer, looking as if it's never been touched. A letter opener, positioned vertically, about six inches to its right. And about six inches to the left of the letterhead, a stack of envelopes that match the stationery. A full stack, as if none of them have been used." He closed the drawer and moved gingerly to his right to exit from behind the desk. "Good thing she was such a small woman," he said, panting from the effort. "I don't know how anyone much bigger than her could squeeze back here to sit down."

"Well, you do have an athletic body, Kip," Bree offered. "Maybe it's all those muscles you've built playing so many sports that's making things so . . . tight?"

The police officer glanced at her and beamed his iconic smile at her. "You know, you're probably right, Bree, you're probably right. I guess I should focus on doing some more aerobic activity to slim down a bit."

Bree's perky expression clouded. "Oh, I didn't mean to imply there's anything wrong with your physique, Kip. Not at all. I just meant that . . ."

"No offense taken," he replied. "Your comment does remind me though that I've been meaning to hit the treadmill for some time, and that I really should follow up on that."

On the other side of the room, Lara frowned at the pair overtly.

"Meanwhile, OVER HERE," she announced at a volume just slightly beneath that of a bellow. Once she had the pair's attention, she dialed down the volume and softened her tone. "Over here is something I find rather curious."

The two sauntered over to the conversation pit she was next to, as did Lee and Anisa. Crossing her arms, Bree examined the area, then issued her own frown.

"What is it, Lara? What do you see? I don't see anything."

Lara gave her colleague a slight smirk. "Look down," she replied. "At the carpet."

Bree did as she had been instructed, but her expression didn't change. "I still don't get it," she said, shaking her head.

Lara leaned over and lifted one leg of the table that rested in front of the seating arrangement. "This table is quite heavy. But its legs haven't left much of an indentation in the carpet the way a heavy table should after being in place for a while."

Lee stepped forward. "Which implies this furniture has probably only been here for a short time," Lee added. He shot a glance at Kip Silva. "I assume this suite has been closely monitored since the murder?"

Silva nodded. "It has. We've had a series of . . . rotating guards from a security company we contract with . . . stationed . . . at the . . . front . . . door." He ran out of steam as the import of what he was saying became clear.

"A security company that *O* may very well have infiltrated," Lee intoned.

"But if all this furniture was recently installed," Anisa countered, "surely there would be surveillance footage showing that?"

"And what I don't get," Liam interjected, "is why they'd even feel the need to shuffle the cards in here at all. What's up with that?"

The police officer looked pained. "I have no answer to your question, Liam," he said. "And to your question, Anisa, all I can say is, 'It's complicated.' The casinos, of course, do have security cameras running twenty-four, seven." He paused to give a half-hearted laugh. "But being the private person that she was, Jocelyn didn't like the idea of her personal suite being on camera all the time. And . . ." He tilted his head one way, then the other and shoved both hands into his pockets. "On top of that, the casino has been undergoing some renovations over the past couple of weeks. They've been bringing in some new gaming tables, some new furniture for the dining areas. So, even if there were footage of furniture being unloaded here, it'd be tough to know which delivery was the one meant for this particular unit.

He exhaled heavily, "As I said, it's complicated."

"What all this is," Warren suggested, "is *weird*."

Lee felt his phone shimmy. He discreetly removed it from a pocket and saw it was from the confident he had met with in So Lo Pun: 'Any progress on my retirement?'

He tapped out a quick: 'Working on it,' then caught Lara's eye to say he was ready for the group to return to their hotel. Silva promised to have the building's security footage reviewed and share it with Warren. "Although I can't say I'm optimistic we'll discover anything useful."

On their way out of the suite's front door, Bree sidled up close to her boss.

"Dalton, there's something very odd about the office portion of that suite," she whispered.

He nodded. "Yes. I agree. I felt it as well."

Bree gave Lee a serious, almost stern, look.

"No, it wasn't something that I felt," she replied, keeping her voice as quiet as possible. "It's something that I saw. Something a person who was truly into feng shui would never, ever allow."

22

That evening, Liam was pumping hard the pedals of the stationary bike he had commandeered in one far corner of the hotel's gym.

And yet, he was still bored.

Usually, he could spend an entire night–even an entire overnight–studying the blips and pulses on the app he had shown to Warren a few days earlier. He found it fascinating both from an informational and visual standpoint. It could pinpoint people missing at sea and those buried beneath an avalanche. Motorists who had fallen asleep at the wheel and driven into a mossy ravine and embezzlers who were hiding in some remote, Alpine cabin.

What it had not yet done was pinpoint the whereabouts of his wonderful sister, or the other friends and relatives associated with The Lee Group whom O was holding captive.

Which made him question, of course, whether they were still alive.

He ratcheted up the resistance on the bike and repositioned the tablet computer sitting on the shelf in front of him, so it would be less likely to bounce as he pushed the 'pedals to the metal.'

Tonight, he had detected an unusually large sonar blip emanating from somewhere within the jungles of Brazil. But the profile of the blip didn't match the details of any of the devices he kept on file–the devices known to have been carried by Dalton's parents, Bree's friend, Warren's wife, Anisa's cousin and the others when they were abducted. He knew, of course, they would no longer have possession of those devices. The hope was that maybe one of their phones or tablet computers had been tossed into a drawer nearby or was being scrutinized or was in the process of having its contents swiped, by one of their captors.

Still, he knew that even if that were the case, the time that would have elapsed since the owner had been taken hostage could now in some cases be measured in years, not months. The odds of the app delivering a perfect match with a device still owned by one of their loved ones might at this point be approaching those of winning a national lottery.

His breath was becoming belabored now, and his t-shirt was beginning to carry the unmistakable odor of underarm perspiration. He started to launch a different browser to check out some soccer scores, but a wave of guilt washed over him. *Dalton pays you very well,* he scolded himself. *And you get to work in a singlet or board shorts whenever you feel like it. So, man up and keep on going.*

That prompted him to resume a little task he'd been distracted from the night before when room service had brought his order of fish and chips. He chuckled and shook his head when he recalled the smile and flirtatious look of anticipation the young mate who brought the food gave him as he was about to exit Liam's room.

"Aw, nah, thanks, mate but I'm not really into that sort of thing," he'd told the server gently but firmly, something he'd grown accustomed to doing most everywhere he went. But the more he reflected on the incident, the more he wondered whether he had entirely misinterpreted the dude's intent.

Huh, maybe he was just hoping for an extra tip on top of the standard service charge, he thought. *Didn't consider that.*

He opened the Tor browser on his desktop and was into the dark web in seconds. He'd been playing around with email addresses Jocelyn Cheng might have been using surreptitiously to see if he could ferret out some details about any financial connection she might have had with 'O,' or some other insight into the reason for her murder.

He knew the likelihood of his finding something revealing was about as likely as his successfully stuffing a kangaroo into an overhead luggage compartment. Still, he was damn good at this sort of thing if he did say so himself.

He slowed his pedaling, let go of the bike's handlebars, took the tablet computer off the shelf, grasped it at both sides and allowed his thumbs to hover over its virtual keyboard for a few seconds as he tried to conjure up an off-the-radar email address the murder victim might have used.

Eventually he typed, Jocelyn.cheng@luckyfortune.com.

Nothing came up in the results list. He kept going.

Jocelyn.cheng@luckyfortunecasino.com.

Again nothing.

jcheng@luckyfortune.com.

jcheng@luckyfortunecasino.com.

Cheng.jocelyn@luckyfortune.com.

Jocelyn_cheng@luckyfortune.com.

Nothing clicked. He exhaled heavily, aware that she might very well have used some random address to shield her identity, something like martinilover@luckyfortune.com, or even macaumadam@ luckyfortune.com.

Out of frustration, he slowed his pedaling even more and started punching the keyboard with both thumbs, entering whatever string immediately came to mind.

It was with the sixth or seventh entry that he landed upon what appeared to be a mother lode of emails written and received by the victim in the time leading up to her murder.

Whoa, how did I miss this before? he wondered. He scrolled back up to look at the address that had yielded such a bounty of communication. That's when he realized he'd stumbled upon the account by making a typo.

jchong@luckyfortunecasino.com.

He studied the address for several seconds before he realized it wasn't really a 'typo' after all.

Ah, I get it, he exulted to himself. *She changed the 'E' in her last name to an . . . 'O.' Sneaky.* He let out a depressing sigh.

What kind of stranglehold does that organization have on the people it recruits? he wondered.

The account he had hacked into appeared to have been operating for only two years or so. Still, it yielded a treasure trove of emails, probably a couple of thousand in total, he estimated.

Rather than scroll through all the subject headers in search of something compelling, he decided to search the emails for a few 'incriminating' words and phrases. Searching for *O* wasn't going to be feasible, so he tried 'organization' instead. It popped up about twenty times, but usually in the context of, 'Our organization is well-positioned to deliver innovative and entertaining gaming supplies to today's destination casinos.'

He veered in a different direction. He tried 'freedom' (knowing what an obsession that was to the members of *O*). Again, it came up several times, but in more generic references.

'Revolution.' That generated a few hits, all of which had to do with roulette wheels.

'Overthrow.' Nothing.

'Transformation' More nothing.

Frustrated by his lack of success, he considered a short break, thought about going into the hotel's restaurant to grab a ham sandwich (as health conscious as he was, he'd already had enough poke bowls here to last a lifetime). He had finished his workout and now was just sitting on the bicycle seat, listlessly nudging the pedals forward with his toes.

That's when an instant message came in from Anisa. 'Any chance I can stop by for a minute? Have an idea I'd like your take on.'

His expression went from a frown to a scowl. It wasn't that he didn't like Anisa. He just didn't trust her. Only a couple of nights earlier, Warren had confided his suspicions of Anisa to Liam, which didn't help her cause. But he was intrigued to find out what idea she had that made her seek out his opinion.

And, he had to admit, *she is kind of hot . . .*

'Not right now,' he replied. 'Will hit you back later.'

He shifted in the seat and turned back to his sleuthing. Scratched his head, folded his arms in front of him, then leaned forward intently. Decided to drop the search approach and go back to the victim's inbox to study the emails and their subject headers. He scrolled down a ways to begin his review at the emails that the casino executive had received about a year ago.

But most of the subject headers seemed mundane and transactional.

'Register for this year's convention in Manila.'

'Replace three windows, get one free.'

'Your astrological reading for the week of January 23.'

The more he reviewed the account, the more he was beginning to think it may have been one she had created to manage spam messages.

He flipped over to the repository of emails she had sent, stopped when he came upon one in particular with a subject header written entirely in Hanzi characters. It intrigued him, mostly because it was the only email he had come across with a subject header written in that style. He opened it, and found that it contained one short sentence, also in Hanji.

Quickly he swept the text, copied it, opened a sophisticated translation app he'd downloaded a few months ago and dropped the message into the app's blank field. Hit 'Translate' and waited. The app churned for only a couple of seconds before delivering its final take on the wording.

The screen read: 'Help me. I've made a mistake and they are coming after me! I just know it!'

Liam glanced over to see who it was that Jocelyn Cheng had sent the email to.

That's when he fell off the bike and landed on the floor in an awkward heap.

23

Kip Silva shuffled a few papers in front of him, stared directly at the middle-aged woman sitting across the table from him and The Lee Group.

"I want to thank you, Ms. Blackwell, for coming in to talk with us this morning. I'm sure Ms. Cheng's death was a shock to you given your previous employment with her."

The woman he spoke to, attired in a tight brown suit with a light-blue blouse underneath, gave him a vacant look and said nothing in reply.

The police officer ducked his head slightly in anticipation, then glanced at Dalton Lee and arched both eyebrows.

"Okay then, well we understand you worked for Ms. Cheng for a little over a year or so?"

The woman uttered something, but her volume was so soft, and her words so rushed, no one at the table could decipher what she said.

"I'm sorry, Ms. Blackwell, could you please speak up a little bit?" Silva asked.

The personal assistant flinched slightly, coughed once, then said, "I'm terribly sorry. What I had said was that my tenure of employment with Ms. Cheng actually lasted two years and three months."

"Thank you for that, Ms. Blackwell," Silva replied. With his left hand, the police executive reached into a bowl near his right elbow and plucked from it an orange Chupa Chup, which he quickly unwrapped and plopped into his mouth.

At the other end of the table, Bree wore a beatific smile on her face.

"Would you be willing to share with us, Ms. Blackwell, why you left your job? And you're not required to answer that question if you don't want to."

The woman shifted uncomfortably in her chair and frowned.

"I'll just say I was not . . . um . . . let's just say I discovered that Ms. Cheng was involved in some . . . activities I did not care to be associated with."

At that, Kip Silva ducked his head again, and Lara abruptly stopped taking notes.

"Are you willing to share some details about that?"

Her gaze listed off to the left and toward the floor before she replied with, "Not particularly."

"Did you report these activities to us or to any other law enforcement organization in the area?" She looked at her skirt and then at the floor again.

"No," was all she said.

Dalton Lee was studying Allyson Blackwell as she spoke. He detected the slightest whiff of perfume coming from her, but the scent was neither remarkable nor memorable. He also noticed how she kept massaging the buttons on her suit jacket and shifting in her chair at least two or three times every minute or so.

She's afraid of something, he surmised.

That reminded him of the victim's cry for help via email that Liam had told him about, and that he needed to revisit the casino executive's suite as soon as possible to follow up on Bree's observation. Given what he wanted to check on, he figured he'd probably need Liam and Warren to accompany him.

He also noticed that Silva seemed more rumpled than usual and that his mood was anything but chipper. The normally charming superintendent-general was swirling the Chupa Chup in his mouth now as if taking a throat swab and was glaring like a coyote at their reluctant guest.

Finally, he removed the lollipop and resumed the interview.

"So, Ms. Blackwell, I believe you had drinks with Ms. Cheng just a couple of days before she passed? She asked you to her suite, I believe. Can you describe for us what sort of mood you found her in that day? Did she seem agitated. Or wary, perhaps?"

The woman looked befuddled for a few seconds, but then the clouds suddenly seemed to part.

"Oh, that? No," she said. "That didn't happen."

Kip Silva thrust his upper torso over the tabletop.

"I'm sorry?"

Allyson Blackwell didn't shift in her chair now but instead sat tall in it.

"Ms. Cheng did invite me to come to her suite. But then she cancelled a couple of hours before our appointment. She just said she wasn't feeling well and that she wanted to reschedule. But then before she did that, she . . . well, you know, she . . ."

It was as if a vacuum cleaner had sucked all the energy out of the room. Dalton Lee closed his eyes and dropped his head to his breast.

"How did she communicate that cancellation to you?" Silva probed.

The personal assistant tilted to one side and procured her cell phone from a large purse that was sitting on the floor next to her.

"By text," she answered. She held the phone in the air, activated a couple of buttons, did some scrolling and then handed the device to Kip Silva. "There. You can see for yourself."

He scanned the screen for a few seconds, winced, then handed the phone to Lee, who inspected it briefly before handing it down the line to his colleagues. The investigators all looked at each other as if trying to decide who was going to be the first to bolt from the room.

"All right, Ms. Blackwell. Well, I'm a bit embarrassed and terribly sorry to have inconvenienced you," Silva said. This time, Lee could tell the magnanimous smile that Silva gave to the woman was entirely artificial.

When the assistant had left the room, Lee clapped Silva once on the back.

"My bad, Kip," he said. "I should have investigated that line of reasoning more thoroughly before you went to the trouble of bringing her in."

"We're terribly sorry, Kip," Bree chimed in. "if there's anything we can possibly do to . . ."

Lara cut her off. "I'll send over all the information that Liam and I have found regarding those large payments and withdrawals to and from Ms. Cheng's account in the days leading up to her murder, and the offshore accounts she had open. And Anisa has been looking into her legal affairs and may have found a couple of interesting things of note. We think we've culled through it all pretty carefully, but maybe your team will notice something we've missed."

Silva smiled weakly, nodded once and rose from his chair, followed by Dalton Lee and the rest of The Lee Group.

As they all headed toward the door of the meeting room, Bree cleared her throat to make sure Lara noticed she was sending her a double helping of serious side eye.

24

"Boss, should we be worried that there might be a surveillance camera watching our every move right now? Just because it's well after sundown doesn't mean 'O,' or the Macau Police Force, is fast asleep."

Warren was standing to one side of the front door leading to Jocelyn Cheng's suite; Dalton Lee stood on the opposite side. Liam was hunched in between the two, using his skill as an expert safecracker to jimmy the lock without a key.

"I guess we'll find out, won't we?" Lee replied dryly. The architect was mostly back to his normal health and had decided to forgo asking Kip Silva for a key to the suite. "I want to explore this theory without the police looking over my shoulder," was his explanation to Warren and Liam as they all headed toward the casino.

They had finessed their way past the security guard in the casino lobby by claiming they were there to ensure the suite was cordoned off properly. The guard examined Dalton Lee's official-looking but very generic business card, fell for the story and quickly went back to the video game on his phone. Now, Lee insisted, he only needed a few minutes to examine the suite and satisfy his curiosity.

Once Liam was able to get the front door open, Lee surprised him by darting toward the French doors that led to the victim's office. They found it untouched from their visit the day before.

"What's this theory of yours, Dalton?" Liam asked.

The architect didn't respond for a few seconds, choosing instead to wander over toward the corner where the desk was situated. He stood in front of it, arms folded, brow scrunched in contemplation. Then he slowly nodded a couple of times and very softly said, "Yes, I do believe Bree may be right about this."

He swiveled toward his colleagues and unfolded his arms.

"Actually, Bree spotted it, but it reinforces something that was swimming around in the back of my head," he replied. He turned back toward the desk, extended one arm toward it. "Feng shui says an office desk should always face the door that people use to enter the room. To be welcoming to new business opportunities, and all that." He paused and swirled one finger around in the air to indicate the entire room. Then stopped and pointed it toward the opposite side of the room. "But this desk sits at a diagonal, facing that corner over there. That's . . ."

"Bad feng shui," Warren filled in, beginning to nod along with Lee's narration.

"Not something Jocelyn Cheng would have done?" Liam added.

Lee nodded but did not directly answer his employee. He sauntered around the corner of the desk that was closest to the mahogany paneling and the bamboo palm that took up so much of the space between the desk, the chair and the wall.

"This is all . . . much too crammed together. It's not . . ."

"Natural," Warren chimed in. "Like the rest of the suite. It's not . . ."

"The way it was when she was actually working in here." Liam enjoyed becoming part of the deduction game, was eager to offer his observation.

"Precisely, Liam," Lee said. "I can't help but wonder whether this corner is so cramped because O pushed everything back here to discourage people from lingering around this corner. For some reason."

The architect turned his attention to the wall behind, and to the side of, the desk. He pushed against one of the floating panels, but the wood felt solid. He then ran his fingers first along the grooves that formed the floating panels, and then across the carved buttons at the center of each panel.

All seemed to be as it should. He turned back toward the desk and the empty wastebasket situated behind the desk and against the back wall caught his eye. He scrunched his face again, began to stroke his chin.

"Odd place for a wastebasket," he told them. "You'd really have to contort your body to toss something into it from the desk chair, wouldn't you?" He strolled around to the other side of the desk, both to better gauge its relationship to the chair and to inspect it more closely.

Everything seemed normal. But when he picked up the wastebasket, he noticed it was situated directly in front of one of the decorative buttons in the paneling. Lee again traced his fingers across the carved flourishes that comprised the ornamentation. Then, on a whim, pressed the center of the protruding button with his index finger.

A panel on the opposite side of the desk quietly began to retract from right to left into the wall, revealing a dark portal to some additional room beyond.

"What. The. Fuck!" Warren said.

"Shazizzle!" Liam exclaimed as he dashed toward the opening.

"Liam, wait!" Lee barked. The world's most prominent architect thrust a palm into the air as he made his way from the far side of the desk to the entrance to whatever netherworld he had just unveiled. Together, they crept beyond the threshold and, when their eyes had adjusted to the darkness, allowed their jaws to go slack at the almost supernatural vision in front of them.

Which was, a long, narrow room filled to capacity with illuminated computer screens and bulky servers. And–at the farthest end of the hallway–a phalanx of tower-like structures that Liam quickly recognized to be base stations capable of generating intense, electromagnetic pulses.

Microwave transmissions, to be precise.

25

The *cha chaa teng* café in the Kennedy Town neighborhood of Hong Kong was empty save for the three individuals in a corner booth whose heads were well down into their overflowing rice bowls. For several moments, no one said anything. Their chopsticks darted toward– then away from–the center of the table as they procured a variety of meats, fish and vegetables. The trio was almost graceful in the way they manipulated their utensils to obtain their food without knocking into one another.

But once they had filled their bowls, they slurped and gulped their meals, happy to disregard what most would consider basic table manners.

Eventually, the American set his chopsticks on the rest sitting beside his bowl and wiped his mouth with the paper napkin the server had provided him.

"So, Yang Li, where do we stand with the microwave stuff?"

The woman chewed on a sliver of Hainanese chicken for several seconds before answering.

"Happening later tonight, overnight. Everything set. We move it all to another location. Much better location. My people say it take two or three trips but can do it all tonight."

"Remarkable!" the Brit said between gulps of pork.

"Thank God!" the American retorted. He took a sip from his bottle of beer, then took a bigger gulp in celebration of the news.

The threesome went back to their ballet with the chopsticks. Eventually, the Brit turned to his co-conspirator.

"So, Yang Li, exactly where are we moving those precious assets? And please tell me they won't get damaged during the transfer. We spent at least two million euros as I recall just to procure and install that equipment."

The woman's expression curved into an almost coquettish smile as she chewed on a slice of chicken.

"Microwave stuff going to private place no one know about. Very hidden," she said softly. She swallowed once before continuing. "And no damage. But we test it to make sure after the move it do what we want it to. We start our plan very soon."

They all nodded, resumed their meal. But as was the case on the veranda a few days before, a quiet feeling of unity–and success–pervaded their table. They looked at one another with knowing smirks on their faces, raised their chopsticks first above their bowls and then toward the center of the table.

There, they clicked the utensils against the others five times in rapid succession.

Any committed member of O would recognize the cadence as their covert way of reciting the mantra that bound them all.

Power to the cause.

26

Lee's middle-of-the-night text to Kip Silva about the secret room behind Jocelyn Cheng's office and the dangerous equipment that it contained set off a flurry of communication and concern.

Silva replied: 'Meet you there with my investigators around 7 a.m.'

Lee arrived fifteen minutes earlier than that but had to wait for Silva and his team before he could gain access to the executive floor and Jocelyn Cheng's suite. The architect was outwardly calm as he waited beside the security desk. Inside, he was frantic for the Macau police to show up, seize the equipment and cordon off the area.

But when they all descended upon Jocelyn's Cheng's suite, they found the door unlocked and slightly ajar.

"Oh, no," Lee exclaimed as they entered the suite. The door to the victim's office also stood wide open and slightly off of one of its hinges. More concerning, though, was the condition of the door that led to the room containing the equipment they had come to inspect. It leaned precariously to the left, almost entirely off of its track, as if tossed to one side by some rampaging monster.

Racing past the entryway, they expected to perhaps find some of the systems repositioned from their original positions. What they encountered instead was nothing, save a chaotic jumble of cables and cords that dangled from the ceiling, sprouted from the walls and snaked across the vast concrete floor.

Spiny, sinister tendrils that seemed to be taunting Kip Silva and his police force, but even more so Dalton Lee, sneering directly at the world's most prominent architect, "Just like before, you arrogantly thought you had us in your grasp and could thwart the revolution we're destined to deliver.

"Only, this time Dalton, you have completely, spectacularly failed to stop us."

27

The male contingent of The Lee Group was away, preoccupied with the cache of microwave equipment in Jocelyn Cheng's suite. So, Bree viewed it to be the perfect time to delve more into the casino executive's social life.

She had to admit, she was feeling more confident about her value to the team. Her noticing how oddly the victim's office furniture was arranged had led to the discovery of that equipment in the adjacent room. There was no doubt about that.

Although Lara had paid her a nice compliment the day they were reviewing the victim's appointment calendar, she couldn't help but acknowledge that the contributions Lara had brought up were all in the category of accidental. Almost comical.

Now she wanted what she brought to the team to be more serious. More mindful.

More *intentional*.

She typed in the new login credentials Lara had shared with her and was soon on the internet. They had thoroughly perused her appointment calendar, she believed, so she decided to dig more into the victim's public activities from whatever news coverage of them she could find. She did, however, choose to use a search engine that claimed not to retain a history of what one entered.

"We can never be too discreet in our investigations," she remembered Lee once telling her.

She shifted in her desk chair, swept a strand of hair back over her right ear and leaned closer to the screen to examine the search results for articles about Jocelyn Cheng that had been published over the previous year. *Hmm,* she thought. *Dalton told us she was publicity shy, but there sure are a lot of results here to wade through.*

The aroma presented by the cranberry-orange muffin she'd picked up in the hotel lobby before settling down to her work distracted her. As her eyes flitted over the search results, she absent-mindedly plucked off a morsel of the muffin and plopped it into her mouth. Followed by a second and then a third. The bread treat proved so delicious, however, that she eventually gave up on her piecemeal approach to consuming it and picked up what remained and devoured it in two large gulps.

I may need another of those before I'm done with this research, she told herself.

She tried to click on a link to an article that piqued her interest, but the oily residue from the muffin caused her finger to glide across the surface of her mouse.

Oh, great, she told herself, *now I'm going to have to clean all this up, or I'll never be able to type.*

After a few spritzes of cleaner on both the mouse and her keyboard, she was finally ready to concentrate on her assignment. It didn't take long for Lee's comment about Jocelyn Cheng's public shyness to begin to make sense to her: most of the articles she had unearthed were less about the casino executive than they were about her prolific and impressive philanthropy. Several of her gifts had gone to smaller projects, like dance companies and theater groups, or libraries and public fountains. But many had also gone to substantial endeavors, including the region's new performing arts center and the construction of an expansive park on Macau's Cotai peninsula.

The more Bree read about Jocelyn Cheng's generosity, the more her admiration for the woman grew. There were only a couple of photographs of the casino executive attending a fund-raising gala, and Bree noted that in those, the philanthropist's attire was anything but flamboyant. She tended toward tailored suits in black or white and jewelry that was subdued, not showy. The executive seemed to almost disappear in the photos; more prominent, in most cases, was whichever tall, handsome, silver-haired man was standing by her side.

However, from what we know, she was one of the most powerful women in the region, she thought. *Isn't that fascinating?*

Another thought crossed her mind.

Carole would have adored Jocelyn Cheng, she said to herself. *They share the same vision.* Then she had to correct herself. *SHARED the same vision, that is.*

She skimmed across a few more headlines on the search results page, headlines that enumerated several other ways Jocelyn Cheng had contributed to the community:

'Cheng Foundation Announces Gift To Regional Culinary School'

'Local University Announces Cheng To Fund Hospitality Program'

'Lucky Fortune Casino Hosts Regional Tech Expo'

She was about to call room service and ask them to deliver two more muffins when she stumbled upon the article that shocked her sensibilities and locked in her reverence for Jocelyn Cheng. Its headline read:

'Casino Exec Donates $5 Million To Pediatric Cancer Center'

The fact that Jocelyn Cheng had agreed to fund the cancer center for children didn't really surprise her. What took her aback was the paragraph that read:

"Despite the hospital board's insistence that the new center be named after her, Jocelyn Cheng, the CEO of the Lucky Fortune Casino Group has graciously declined that offer. She has asked instead that the new cancer center be named in honor of two children in Macau who have recently passed away from different forms of cancer. Both were children of employees of the consortium. Daisy Lim was a three-year-old with leukemia and five-year-old Timothy Ma was battling bone sarcomas.

"In addition to having the cancer center named after the pair, Jocelyn Cheng has said she will personally cover any medical bills not paid for by the families' insurance plans."

Bree pushed herself back in her chair, found herself on the verge of tears. First, because of Jocelyn's Cheng's magnanimous gesture. And second, because O had coldly murdered such a generous, selfless soul.

What a legacy to leave, Bree thought. *What a resume of admirable achievements she has.*

She couldn't help but wonder what sort of legacy she, Bree Westerman, would leave. She didn't really consider her life thus far to have been pointless–as a member of The Lee Group, she had helped stave off at least three terrorist plots that would have had devastating consequences and possibly led to democracies crumbling on several continents. But all of that effort was clandestine. Behind the scenes. Not the sort of thing you waved in front of people in your obituary.

The fingers of her right hand played with the computer mouse, began to twiddle the desktop as she considered exactly what kind of impression she was going to leave behind.

Then the headline of yet another news article about Jocelyn Cheng caught her eye.

'Casino Exec, Philanthropist Jocelyn Cheng Dies Unexpectedly'

A subhead added:

'An autopsy is underway into the CEO's cause of death'

She already knew all the details covered in the article . . . knew far more details, given all that had transpired since the article had been published. However, one paragraph at the very end of the story made her pull up:

"A spokesperson for the Lucky Casino Corporation says Ms. Cheng's generous offer to fund both a new bird sanctuary on Macau, and a center for Macau's unhoused population, will move forward in spite of her death."

Bree procured from the desktop a couple of stray muffin crumbs and placed them one by one on her tongue. Savored the sweet combination of orange and cranberry.

Read the paragraph one more time, nodding very slowly as she did.

28

Dalton Lee was reading up on microwave transmissions. In their most benign form, they relay information from one point to the next and beyond. They help satellites talk to one another and often facilitate deep-space radio communications. They can even support radars, sensor systems and radio navigation systems.

They also, he learned, are being connected to 'Havana Syndrome' illnesses, mysterious maladies that have afflicted government officials and military personnel with severe headaches, a ringing in the ears, cognitive fog and–in the more extreme cases–death.

Transmissions that could have been generated by the very equipment they had stumbled across in the room behind Jocelyn Cheng's office.

Had that equipment still been there.

Had it not all been whisked away overnight to a different location somewhere in the region.

"They're always one step ahead of us," Dalton Lee lamented to Warren. "How does *O* always seem to know what it is we're about to do and when it is we're about to do it?"

Warren had a strong inclination as to who might be sharing that inside intelligence. But he chose not to raise the issue with his superior just then.

"So exactly what do you think *O* is planning to do with all that equipment?" he asked Lee instead. "And how do you think Jocelyn Cheng was involved?"

Lee was gazing out the window of his hotel room, his back to Warren. He spotted, near the waterfront, a billboard encouraging people to get tested for STDs. It proclaimed:

WHAT YOU DON'T KNOW
CAN HURT YOU!

"I don't know, Warren," he replied without turning around. "But if I had to venture a guess, I'd say they intend to use it to attack some influential people. Business leaders and political leaders, perhaps. Whether just in this area or beyond, I can't say. But when they've accomplished that, when they've diminished whoever they've targeted, they'll . . . take over somehow. Take control." He studied the skyline for several seconds, then allowed his gaze to float back to the billboard.

"And as for Jocelyn Cheng's connection to it all, I don't know that either. But given what her former assistant said to us, I assume she was involved in the plot somehow, maybe chose to back out of it at the last minute for some reason, and that's when they decided to . . ."

There was a knock at his door. Warren went to open it and found Lara on the other side.

"Sorry," she said. "I would have texted you, but I was on my way to the gift shop, so I thought I'd pop in and tell you in person. Kip Silva's team just sent over the surveillance tapes from the casino and the residential wing of the building. Perfect timing for you and Warren to look over them, I presume?"

"Thank you Lara," Lee replied.

"And another interesting development."

Lee arched an eyebrow in anticipation.

"They just found Alexandra Wentworth. In Uruguay."

Lee's eyebrow arched even more. "*Uruguay?* What in the hell is she doing *there*? And how did she end up in South America when most every law enforcement agency in the world was supposed to be keeping an eye out for her?"

Lara sent him an exasperated look. "Apparently she's a master of disguise. And a collector of forged passports. Somehow, she made it past security at Hong Kong International and hopped a flight to Rio, then took a bus from there to Montevideo. The Uruguayan police caught up with her in–are you ready for this–one of the state-run casinos. She has two bodyguards bringing her back here as I speak." She glanced at her watch. "In fact, they've probably already landed."

Lee mulled over the new data. It certainly made the Canadian woman look suspect. On the other hand, it wasn't O's style to let their assassin jet off to some other continent before they had uncoiled whatever plot they had in mind.

"All right. I assume we'll learn more from her once she's back in custody here." Lara nodded and began to shut the door when Lee added, "And, by the way, while you're in the gift shop . . ."

Now it was Lara's turn to raise an eyebrow.

"Would you mind picking up for me some extra-strength pain reliever? The largest package of it you can possibly find, please."

***

It took a couple of hours for them to access the surveillance tapes recorded in the casino. The hotel's wi-fi seemed to be acting up and the bandwidth on Dalton's laptop wasn't equipped to provide a quick download. They thought about asking Liam if they could use his more powerful computer instead, but just as Warren was about to text him, the laptop signaled the download had completed.

"Do we even need to be looking at these files, boss?" Warren asked. "We know now it wasn't the martini she got served at the roulette table that did her in. So . . ."

Lee had launched the files which, to his relief, were remarkably clear. "That's true, Warren," he said. "But I'm interested in seeing Alexandra Wentworth's behavior while she was there if she shows up on the tape. That might reveal something to us. Maybe."

Warren nodded and leaned forward as the tape begin to play. The first images seemed to come from a camera mounted just above and behind the roulette table where Jocelyn had been sitting. Neither she nor Alex Wentworth were in view and the tape projected only mundane movements by the croupier, those arriving at and departing the table and the drink servers, including Regina Bauer.

"It's like watching a tape of the travelers coming and going from one of the lounges at Heathrow or LaGuardia," Warren said after a few minutes. "Lots of movement, little action."

Lee agreed, but kept his eye on the tape, nonetheless. He glanced at the clock in the lower right of the screen and estimated what they were viewing had probably taken place about forty-five minutes before Jocelyn Cheng had collapsed on the floor.

"I'd fast forward it," Lee said, "but I'm afraid we might miss something."

A few seconds after Lee expressed that thought, Warren reached over and grasped the architect's forearm. "Hold up, boss," he said. "Back it up a few seconds." Lee did as Warren instructed and hit 'Play.' The tape moved forward, but he didn't see what had prompted his colleagues sound of alarm.

"There! Stop!" Warren barked. Lee hit 'Stop' and looked at his employee, who had one arm outstretched. "There!" Warren repeated. "In the black dress. Isn't that . . .?"

Lee moved closer to his laptop and squinted. Finally, he detected what had set Warren off.

"Jacquelyn Cheng, Jocelyn's younger sister," he intoned, a wisp of intrigue in his voice.

"Talking to that server we interviewed," Warren added. "The one from Nebraska." They watched the pair converse for several moments. At times, the sister's hands became animated, as if she were tossing a ball back and forth between them. Regina Bauer remained stolid, however, with an expression that perpetually seemed to say, "Can I go now?"

"I thought the sister said she was working in Shenzhen the day Jocelyn died," Warren said. "I thought it wasn't until a few days after Jocelyn's death that she came to Macau to talk with us and Kip Silva."

"So did I," Lee replied.

The discussion between the two women went on for another

minute or so, until the server glanced at the roulette table, then back at Jacquelyn Cheng. Quickly, she turned toward the back of the house and gave a brief nod to the other woman to follow her. They disappeared from view and stayed out of sight for about five minutes. Eventually, Regina Bauer came out from the back, sauntered over to the bar and collected a couple of mixed drinks that had been waiting for her at the nearest well. Jacquelyn Cheng didn't reemerge.

"What do you think that was about?" Warren asked.

Lee chewed the inside of one cheek and slowly shook his head. "What I think is that we probably ought to ask *them*," he answered firmly.

As it turned out, the tape ended just before Alex Wentworth arrived at the roulette table. And Lee was getting eye strain. So, he and Warren agreed to exchange places before they watched the other surveillance footage. Lee had to remind his employee that due to Jocelyn Cheng's penchant for privacy, the footage would not show the outside or interior of her suite. Instead, it would broadcast images from where people accessed the elevators on the ground level that took passengers to the floors above.

The tapes proved to be even more tedious than those taken in the casino. An elevator door would open, and a handful of people would scurry out, followed by a couple of people taking their place in the car. Another would arrive, but this time no one would exit it, causing those who had been waiting for it to charge into the car as quickly as possible. And sometimes those leaving a car would collide into a small group of people who had impatiently gathered too close to the doors and failed to step back to allow the passengers to exit.

The scene repeated itself several times, to the point that Warren began to yawn.

"Want me to call downstairs and order us a couple of grilled cheese sandwiches?" he asked his superior. "With extra pickles on the side?"

Lee had been studying the tapes as intently as possible, but Warren's suggestion made him pull up. A grilled cheese sandwich on that shokupan bread would be a welcome break from the tedium. But he decided they needed to stay true to their task.

The sandwich, and the pickles, would have to wait.

The tape continued to play with little that was meaningful taking place, save for the moment when a bottle of red wine pushed through the bottom of a paper sack someone was holding and smashed to pieces on the terrazzo tile below. The two young Chinese women on camera looked at each other, startled, until the doors of a car arrived right in front of them. Choosing to be irresponsible in the moment, they dashed into the car and punched repeatedly the button that would cause its doors to close, vanishing forever from the camera's view and the pinot noir stain that billowed across the floor.

"I hope there was a surcharge on their bill when they went to check out," Warren said, shaking his head.

The tape continued, much as before, until Lee spotted two other women disembarking from one of the elevator cars.

"Whoa!" he barked. "Zoom in on them, can you?" Warren sized up the icons on the app he was using and found where he could enlarge the image, but only by about 25 percent. "Those two," Lee said, pointing at the women at the center of the screen. They were smiling at one another and waving goodbye as they headed in opposite directions from the elevator bank. As one of the women turned away from the other, a tattoo on the back of her hand came into view.

"Isn't that . . .? " Lee began. Warren leaned forward and let out a long, low whistle.

"It is," he replied, shaking his head and looking back at his boss. "Once again, Jacquelyn Cheng and Regina Bauer."

29

Anisa had finally persuaded Liam to meet her at the amphitheater in Tamar Park in Hong Kong's Admiralty District. She was well aware that both Victoria Park and Hong Kong Park would have been closer. But she also knew those would be teeming with children clambering all over the playground, or seniors working to perfect their tai chi.

She wanted a place with fewer distractions. Fewer people. Fewer intrusions. So, knowing they would likely be deserted, she chose to sit at the far end of the concrete amphitheater steps that looked out over the skyscrapers on Hong Kong Island. And waited.

"G'day, Anisa."

She was impressed. He was only a minute or two late. *Not bad for a surfer boy from the land of the long weekend,* she told herself.

"Right on the dot," she said perkily. He took a seat beside her and rolled his eyes.

"Let me guess, I'm an Aussie–and I like to surf and wear shorts most of the time–so that means you think I'm nothing but a wheelbarrow."

She scrunched her face a bit. "Wheelbarrow? I don't get it." Liam snickered and glanced off at the towering glass structures in front of them.

"A wheelbarrow. Somebody who only works when they're pushed."

She tossed her head back and let out a laugh, then quickly pulled it in. "Sorry. I've never heard that one," she said. "A wheelbarrow." A sly smile remained on her face as she lifted some strands of hair off her forehead and tucked them behind one ear.

Liam leaned forward, rested his elbows on his knees. "Well, I don't know any Jordanian slang, so I guess we're even, huh?"

She let out a short laugh, looked off in the distance.

"Well, maybe if you're nice to me I'll teach you some." He returned her smile, but she continued to be focused on some dot far beyond the edge of the park.

"So, you wanted to see me? Get my opinion on something?"

She shifted her weight on the step and finally looked back at him.

"Yeah, but first, how's your work coming with that special software of yours? And your investigation into Jocelyn Cheng's finances. Finding anything interesting?"

He glanced at her, went back to studying the skyscrapers beyond.

What's she up to, he wondered. *Why's she being so nicey-nicey all of a sudden?*'

"Um sort of, not really." He halted, wary of what he should share, given Warren's recent assessment of her motives.

As if she could read his mind, Anisa's posture became more formal, and she took on a more professional expression. "That's all right. You don't have to tell me anything. It's not like we're, you know, *teammates,* or anything."

Liam closed his eyes for a half-second, felt like the cad he'd been called more than once over the years.

"Sorry, it's just . . ." He let out an exasperated sigh, hung his head. "The fact is, I'm not really finding much of anything. And suddenly, Lara is, like, the queen of internet research, locating all these details, like the mysterious deposits, and who made them." He was studying the buildings again, assumed a hangdog look. "I mean, she's being great about it and all, acting as if I'm partly responsible for finding some of the information we've dug up."

He tugged on the bottom hem of his shirt, put his hands behind his head and stretched his legs out in front of him. "But the fact is, I feel more like a blister than anything else."

166

Anisa turned to him. "Okay, and a blister is . . .?"

Liam returned her look with an impish smile. "You know, a blister. Someone who only shows up after all the hard work's been done." She shook her head and chuckled into her palms, which she had cupped in front of her face. He nudged her gently with one shoulder.

"What about you? Anything on the victim's legal front you care to share? Share with, you know, your . . . *teammate?*" Just then, a sea eagle swooped low in front of them and let out a long set of screeches that sounded like a squeaky toy being repeatedly stepped upon. To Liam, the bird's call resembled a warning, and he had an odd feeling it might just be.

"Right, well, I haven't found anything out there, on the interwebs," she replied, winking as she emphasized the last word in the sentence. "But . . . I was able to hack into some of the files on her personal computer, and . . ."

Liam leaned toward her. "And . . .?"

"And . . . it appears she was planning at some point to file a lawsuit against her predecessor. For sexual harassment."

Liam pulled his head up at that. "So, *that* would likely be 'the cloud' he left under."

Anisa cocked her head. "Except, all I saw was a preliminary draft of a suit. With lots of typos. But it was fairly explicit."

Liam nodded. "If the dude was really harassing her, he probably decided to skip out rather than let the lawsuit go public. It may even have been part of some deal they struck privately. Especially if he was nearing retirement."

"He was sixty-three."

"Well, there you go."

They fell silent for several moments. Then she nudged his shoulder with hers. "Anyway, I was also thinking he may have paid her to drop the lawsuit. It never got filed, I do know that." She stopped to let that sink in before continuing. "So, as you're researching her finances, you might look for a nice fat deposit into her account that would confirm such an arrangement. It probably wouldn't have been in the millions, but you might look for a six or seven-figure amount dropped into one of her main accounts. Probably deposited a couple of months before, or after, he left the company last summer."

She shot him a smirk. "Maybe you can show Lara you're not such a hand truck after all."

He chuckled. "It's wheelbarrow."

"Whatever," she shot back.

He tried to study her without her noticing, would look away each time she turned her face toward him. "Thanks for the tip," he finally replied. They both contemplated the exchange for a while. Then Liam broke the reverie with, "So, do you still think *O* had nothing to do with Jocelyn Cheng's murder?"

He hoped she'd provide some definitive evidence that she'd been joking when she'd announced that. But all she said was, "Let's just say I'm going to go along with the prevailing wisdom for the time being." A long pause, then, "But don't be surprised if this whole little escapade turns out to be something far different than what it appears to be."

Liam found the comment irritating. "Why do you say that? Do you have some sort of evidence you're not sharing with us? What gives?"

She was looking away from him. "Do facts and evidence even matter these days?" she said with a hint of defiance in her voice. After a while, however, she turned back to him, sent a sympathetic look his way.

"I'm sorry, Liam. I was just raised to be suspicious. Of everything. And everyone. Don't forget, I have some skin in this game as well." She waited, then softened some more. "It's just that you're putting a lot of energy into this project, and I'd hate to see you be disappointed if it all goes south in some way. If it turns out *O* didn't murder her. If it turns out to be some sort of charade meant to distract us from some other catastrophe they have planned somewhere else." She waited for a few beats, then added, "Or, if it turns out they did commit the murder, but we're still not able to stop them from wreaking whatever havoc they've got planned."

He remained quiet for a few moments, studied the sun which was beginning a slow descent in the western sky. When his composure had finally returned, he said, "Hey, I thought you called this meeting because you wanted my input on something. Seems to me it's been the other way around."

She shifted some. Now she was looking off into the distance again.

"I did. I mean, I do. There's this thing I'm working on. And I thought maybe . . . I could convince you to be a part of it too. In a way. Maybe."

A slight chill ran through Liam. It sounded like the classic lead-in to a con of some sort. Still, he was interested to hear what she had to say.

"Would it pay?" he suddenly said, point blank. "I could really use some extra avocados these days." He turned away but pivoted back quickly. "That means hundred-dollar bills, by the way."

She snickered. "That's one bit of Aussie slang I know," she said with a wink. Then, her demeanor turned serious again, and she added, "It could pay."

She began to tell her tale to him. Used words and phrases like, 'freedom,' and 'government overreach,' and 'liberation.' He flinched when she mentioned 'hostages' but found himself being reeled in by her passion and her commitment to her cause. She spoke softly, non-stop, for almost five full minutes.

When she finally reached the end of her elevator pitch, she looked at him warily. "So, what do you think? You in?"

Liam sighed deeply and audibly. "Anisa . . . we both owe Dalton so much." He looked into her eyes and let that float out there above and between them for some time. Then finally added, "I could maybe be supportive."

She didn't smile at his response. She only nodded. Then she jumped up from the concrete and wiped off some gravel that clung to her jeans. "Great. We'll be in touch," she told him.

He rose to join her. When he was fully standing, she said. "Oh, there's one more thing." She stepped forward, threw her arms around his neck and pressed her lips firmly against his. He was immediately intoxicated by the mixture of jasmine, rose and orange blossom she was wearing and, as if being manipulated by a puppeteer, found his arms encircling her waist without expecting them to.

Gently, she pushed herself away from him, flashed her biggest smile of the day and started scampering off toward the amphitheater's exit.

"What . . . was *that?*" he called out as she retreated into the distance.

"From the day I first laid eyes on you," she called back as she rounded a corner and vanished from sight.

30

The Alex Wentworth they confronted in the interview room within the Macau Police Headquarters complex was a far cry from the Alexandra Wentworth they had confronted on previous occasions. Her complexion was sallow, her expression was forlorn, and it seemed she had developed jowls where there had been no jowls.

Her shoulders were slumped, and she hung her head, looking up at Kip Silva through heavy lids. One could easily interpret the posture as one of remorse or shame, but Dalton Lee deemed it more likely it was one of nervous wariness. On her right sat her attorney, a frail, middle-aged Macanese man who kept wiping his nose with a small handkerchief.

I bet HE couldn't knock me over in a boxing gym, Lee thought.

"You understand why you're in here, Ms. Wentworth?" the superintendent-general intoned. She rolled her eyes, then uttered a quiet, "Yep."

Silva shuffled through some papers, then looked up and met her gaze.

"What were you doing in Uruguay?"

She took a quick breath as her mouth contorted into an obvious smirk. "Gambling," was all she said.

She began to survey the rest of the people in the room, eventually raising an index finger and swaying it back and forth in front of Lee and his entourage. "Do all these Mouseketeers really need to be here for this?"

Lee flinched, but Lara clipped his lower shin with the heel of her right shoe before he could respond. Silva decided to ignore the comment and press forward.

"You boarded a flight for Rio using a forged German passport that identified you as an 'Ingrid Geissner,'" he stated. "You then checked into a hotel using a passport allegedly issued to a Cheryl Ann Dowd of Dubuque, Iowa." He paused but stared even more directly at the blonde across from him.

"We checked, and there is no Cheryl Ann Dowd living in Dubuque, or anywhere else in Iowa for that matter," he announced dramatically. "So, Ms. Wentworth. What gives?"

She turned casually toward her attorney, who sniffed a couple of times and then leaned over to whisper something in her ear. After he returned to his original position and daubed his nose with the handkerchief yet again, she tilted her head in her attorney's direction and said, "Rudy Giuliani here says I don't have to answer that question."

Silva sighed and cast a brief glance toward Lee.

"You don't have to answer the question, Ms. Wentworth, but you could make your life, and ours, *so* much simpler if you did." She looked over at her attorney who rapidly shook his head.

"Sorry, I plead the Fifth, or whatever it is one pleads these days," she replied. She then effected an artificial smile and added, "And I liked it so much more when you called me Alex."

The superintendent-general sighed again, more heavily this time, and raked the fingers of one hand through his hair.

"Well, Ms. Wentworth, this isn't the United States of America, it's Macau, and besides, you're Canadian not American. It doesn't work like that here."

She gave a 'so what' shrug of her shoulders; her attorney blew loudly into his handkerchief. Silva studied the woman for a few more seconds, then collected the papers in front of him and put them into a neat and tidy stack.

"You haven't really broken any Macanese laws, so we're not prepared to charge you with anything . . . yet," he said.

"Good," she replied.

"*However,* we are in discussions with the Canadian government about having you extradited back to your home country. So, we'll be holding you until we've reached some sort of consensus with Ottawa about that, which could take as little as a few days, or as long as a couple of weeks."

"Jeezus," the blonde responded. She looked at her attorney, who indicated with a nod to the door behind them that it was time for them to go. An assistant with the police force stepped forward to escort her to her quarters. But after they had risen from their seats, she extended her right palm and said, "Can I say something?"

Silva looked up at her and nodded. "Sure," he replied. As discreetly as she could, Lara opened the leather portfolio she had in her lap and prepared to scribble a few notes.

"I know you think I killed Jocelyn," Alex Wentworth began, "but I didn't. Everything I told you earlier was true. I came to admire her during our cruise together and I really appreciated the interest she took in me, even it was sort of . . . short-term." Lee worried the woman was about to have another emotional meltdown, but suddenly she seemed to pull herself together.

"I have my issues. I have a gambling problem and I may have a few little things I'm running away from that might . . . show up on a background check." She paused to steel herself. "I admit I've made a few mistakes in my life, but murdering Jocelyn is definitely not one of them." She put both palms on the top of the table and leaned forward both to brace herself and assume a stance of power. "If I were you, I'd look into that hag who brought Jocelyn the martini I sent her," she continued. "I'm not sure what was going on that night, but she was acting very odd, pointing at Jocelyn and having these covert conversations with others on the side."

"What others?" Silva countered. "What do you mean?" A smirk returned to Alex Wentworth's face, and she pushed herself back from the table.

"You're the detectives," she replied. "You figure it out." With that, she swiveled around and headed for the door, followed by the police escort and her attorney.

When the clamor had subsided, Silva turned to the world's most prominent architect. "What do you think?" he asked. Lee scratched the back of his head for a few moments.

"I think she knows exactly how to make a grand exit," he responded.

Silva nodded then whispered to Lee, "Any chance we could talk privately?" Lee arched an eyebrow but quickly nodded.

"Team, I'll meet you out front in a few minutes," he said to his associates. As they were departing, Bree glanced over her shoulder, a definitive scowl on her face.

When the door closed, Silva reached into a jacket pocket. Lee expected the police officer to pull out a Chupa Chup, but he instead removed a gold-colored pen and started scribbling on the back of one of the pieces of paper he had put into the neat and tidy stack. When he was finished, he tore off the corner of the paper and handed it to Lee.

"I have a meeting in ten minutes, so I can't talk now. Meet me at this address tomorrow morning about nine. We can talk more privately then, under the guise of being tourists visiting Macau's premier landmarks." Lee nodded, tucked the address into a shirt pocket and collected his things.

"Did I hear that you all decided to take the helicopter over here this time?" Silva asked.

"We did!" Lee responded enthusiastically.

"And that you got more than a little bit nauseous during the trip?"

Lee's smile dropped. "No! Not really, well, maybe a little." He looked embarrassed, then began to chuckle. "Let's just say I'm glad I put on an extra layer of antiperspirant this morning."

Silva patted his colleague on the shoulder. "Don't feel badly, Dalton. It's happened to me as well. Next time, bite into some ginger or peppermint before you board the copter. Helps enormously."

Lee found the recommendations odd but nodded his approval, nonetheless.

"And was it just me, or was Bree in a particularly sour mood this morning? Any idea what that might be about?"

Lee shook his head and shrugged his shoulders. "I'm doing my best just to focus on the dramatic events unfolding before us," he said. "I can barely keep up with all the additional drama my team sometimes brings to the table, much less sort it all out."

Silva flashed him a sympathetic smile, then rose from his chair. "Come on, I'll walk you out."

As Dalton stood he turned toward Silva. "By the way, that's a great tie you have on. Remember where you got it?"

Silva glanced down at the red-and-green-striped rep tie he was wearing. "Yeah, isn't it great?" he replied. "Found it over on Kowloon, near the Ladies' Market, of all places. You should go over there if you haven't been yet. They have lots of stuff for guys, and probably for less than a third of what you'd pay in the States."

Silva opened the door for Lee and followed him out of the interview room and down the hall toward the building's front lobby.

"And Dalton, I really like your . . . uh . . ." Silva raised one finger and swirled it just above his head.

"Pith helmet?" Lee responded. "Yeah, thanks. I thought it rather jaunty and particularly appropriate given it's derived from the salakot headgear worn in the Philippines."

With that, Lee strode to the front door, bade Silva farewell and joined the rest of The Lee Group outside.

31

"Is everything finally in place?"

Yang Li nodded rapidly but said nothing. She was zeroed in on her handicraft project, her fingers fidgeting even faster than her head had moved.

"That's good!" the Brit replied in between swallows of his roast beef sandwich. They had resorted back to meeting online, for they felt trying to be all in the same place at the same time was risky at this point.

Their screens flickered, and then the American appeared in the upper right. He was unshaven, and his hair wasn't combed. Yang Li looked up from the project in her lap and let out a short burst of a laugh.

"You just get out of the shower, just get out of bed?" she said, a smirk anchored on her lips.

"Pretty much," the American replied. "So, all the equipment has been tested?"

Yang Li's fingers continued to manipulate the needles as if she were on speed. "Yes, sir!" she answered. "Everything test A-OK."

The American became absorbed by Yang Li's artistry. "You told us you were making a shawl but that's gotten much bigger than any shawl

I've ever seen. What are you really making, some sort of bedspread? She laughed once more and shook her head.

"None of your business," she said, chuckling. "Any more questions?"

The Brit leaned toward his camera. "What would you estimate to be our 'go time,' Yang Li?"

Her hand movements slowed, she looked down and to the left, seemed to be calculating silently. Then she nodded once emphatically. "Before the end of the week," she said. "Three, four days maybe. No more."

That seemed to satisfy everyone, even the American who just seemed eager to return to his slumber.

"And we have everyone in place to assume the leadership positions once we've disposed of . . . you know, the status quo?" he asked.

For the first time, she looked directly at her camera. Her lips pulled taut, and her gaze became intense.

"You know we do," she replied. "We moving people into place for more than two years now. Number two in every jurisdiction. Ready to move forward once their superiors have been . . . disposed of. Ready to dismantle all government regulations in their countries."

She tilted forward, and her grimace turned into a grin.

"All loyal to the cause. All committed to the cause. All prepared to do anything . . . to anyone . . . for the cause."

She nodded emphatically once more and returned to her handicraft, a sinister smile spreading across her face.

32

"It's really none of my business, Bree, but do you mind telling me why you want an advance on your salary? Are you in some sort of financial distress?"

His senior architect was standing beside the desk in Lee's hotel room, appearing demure and reluctant, which most people knew was not her usual self. Her fingers were interlocked in front of her, and her expression was one of shy embarrassment.

"Yes, things are fine," she replied softly. "And well, it *is* your business, actually. So, I'll understand if you prefer not to do it."

The architect looked his younger associate up and down, took note she hadn't answered his question about why she wanted the funds.

"How much would you say you need?" he asked as he launched the banking app on his phone.

She sighed heavily, looked off toward the back of his suite. "Oh, I don't know, Dalton, not a lot. Maybe two thousand, or three?"

Lee started. "Three thousand isn't a lot? I think that's a lot!" he said, one finger poised expectantly over his phone. Bree winced, but he waved off her reaction.

"It's fine, Bree, really. Don't fret about it. You were extremely helpful in pointing out to me how Jocelyn Cheng's office furniture was so oddly arranged. Very astute of you to notice that. So don't think twice about your request. In fact, it's done! *Finis.* Transferred into your account."

For some reason, Bree felt the urge to honor Lee's act with a curtsy.

Lee set his phone on the desk. "Now, I'd really love to discuss the case with you, but Kip Silva has asked me to meet him in Macau so he can update me on what his team has been able to unearth. We're going to be taking a little walking tour of the historic sights, which I am sure would bore you beyond all measure, otherwise I'd ask you to join us."

Bree opened her mouth to say something but, sensing she was about to disagree with his assumption, he rose from his chair and cut her off before she had a chance to utter a word.

"So, I'll catch up with you later, and I hope the advance serves your needs, whatever they are." He took her by one forearm and gently directed her toward the door.

She nodded, scrunched her shoulders a bit, smiled weakly in defeat and trudged through the doorway. But before the door closed behind her, Lee called out to her.

"Yes?" she said expectantly, poking her head back into the room.

"Everything truly is okay, isn't it?" he asked.

Her face relaxed, and she beamed back at him through the portal. "Yes, Dalton, everything's fine," she assured him. "In fact, in an odd way, I haven't felt this good in a very long time."

***

"Well, I have to say, Dalton, you look quite dapper in that *portuguesa.*"

Dalton glanced up and smiled at the headgear he had chosen to wear that day–a black felt hat like those traditionally worn by Portuguese riders during Lusitano dressage competitions.

"Yes, well, you know what they say, Kip. 'When in a former Portuguese territory, do as the . . .'"

The police officer (casual as could be in a maroon, long-sleeve t-shirt and simple gray slacks) flicked the portuguesa's brim with the index finger of his right hand.

"Probably a smart idea to wear it, given the amount of sun we're supposed to get today," he said. "Although, you might get a little steamy under all that felt. And people might wonder where you left your horse."

They both let out a light chortle at that. The day was warm but not stifling; occasionally, a wisp of a breeze kept them comfortable and brought to them the aroma of roasted almonds from the street vendors nearby. It was the sort of day Lee could take great joy in, were it not for the fact that a murder–and an imminent terrorist plot–dominated their thoughts.

As if he had been reading the architect's mind, Kip Silva suddenly allowed his smile to drop. His pace slowed, eventually he fell a few paces behind Lee, and his face took on an expression of concern–or maybe fear?–that Lee never imagined the police officer could display.

"What is it, Kip? What's wrong?" Lee asked, turning to rejoin his colleague.

Silva shook his head once, then slowly resumed his gait. When he had caught up with the architect, he whispered, "It's just . . . we know what they're up to now. But I'm beginning to worry, Dalton, that we may not stop them in time. My team is doing everything they can to determine where they might have moved their arsenal but, so far, no luck. If we can just identify who murdered Jocelyn, we can probably coerce them into revealing where the equipment is." He turned his head and squinted at Lee. "But are we really any closer to knowing who killed her than we were a week ago?"

He quietly studied the sidewalk for a moment before continuing. "I guess the uncertainty of everything is starting to weigh on me, Dalton, that's all."

Lee did his best to comfort the police officer. But the fact was, he shared his friend's concern. "I'm sure we'll have a breakthrough soon, Kip," he replied, sounding nowhere near as confident as he had hoped he would. He let Silva catch his breath some more, then suggested, "Come on. Let's keep walking."

They resumed their stroll and soon arrived at the ruins of St. Paul's Cathedral (or, as Kip so eloquently pronounced it, Ruinas de São Paulo). The crowd of tourists was much larger than what Lee had anticipated, but he was pleased to see them showing respect for the iconic structure. Their brightly colored t-shirts and shorts, bobbing up or down the steps that led to the towering façade of the cathedral, looked especially vibrant against its stolid, gray stone.

Lee himself considered the ruins quite sad, felt they resembled a lonely, defiant dowager who refused to submit to the shifts of time. Or, for that matter, much of Venice. Which was not entirely a coincidence, he noted, since most historians believed the church had been designed in the seventeenth century by an Italian Jesuit (a fact that helped explain its former nickname, 'The Vatican of the Far East').

They chose not to ascend the steep steps to the façade, which was all that remained of the structure after a fire swept through the cathedral in 1835. Besides, Lee had delivered several lectures on both the façade and its ornate carvings, which depicted everything from a Portuguese ship, to Jesuit saints, to flowers native to China and Japan, as well as numerous creatures described in mythology.

"It really is the perfect symbol of the multicultural heritage of Macau, isn't it?" Lee said to Silva. The police officer nodded in agreement.

"Yeah, back then, people of different cultures came together in our churches." He paused, then offered a brief chuckle. "Today, they come together at our casinos."

"A different form of worship," Lee retorted, smiling.

As they headed toward their next stop, Lee turned to Silva and began, "Um, speaking of casinos . . . Alexandra Wentworth. What do we make of her?"

The police officer blew air out of his lungs and shook his head. "She's a puzzler, that's for sure. I don't think I've ever dealt with anyone like her. I wouldn't be at all surprised if she's an operative of O," he replied softly. "So much about her seems . . . sketchy." Silva was studying the pavement again as they sauntered their way toward their next tourist site, but he looked up at Lee to make a point.

"But then again, almost all of her story checks out. We've run a background check on her and there's nothing unusual there. She grew up in what seems to have been a normal family in Western Ontario, got an undergraduate business administration degree from George Brown College and an MBA from McMaster University in Hamilton. She's bopped from one trading company to another but has generally stayed with each one for at least three or four years, and her responsibilities have grown with each job change.

"Before this recent erratic behavior of hers, there's no criminal background to speak of."

Silva peered at Lee, took on a sober expression.

"I need to be careful here, Dalton," he added, glancing over his shoulder to ensure no one was eavesdropping, "but as much as I'd love to lock her up for a couple of months, we still have nothing to charge her with. She wasn't under any form of house arrest, and she hasn't violated any of our laws, really. The issue of forged passports is something for Canada to address." He stopped and lowered his volume. "The best I can do is drag out the extradition process for as long as I can, come up with some excuses for delaying it." He kicked to one side a small tree branch that had landed squarely in their path. "But I can only do that for so long. And that isn't very long."

They chose to stroll east toward the Guia Fortress, with its signature lighthouse and chapel. The sun had become more intense, making Lee glad that he had chosen a piece of headgear sporting such a wide brim. But when they arrived at the fortress, he had to remove the hat so he could take in all of the three-hundred-foot-tall lighthouse. Completed in 1865, it was the first western-style lighthouse in East Asia with a beam that could be seen more than thirty kilometers away on a clear night.

"It's still in use, isn't it?" Lee asked.

"Yep," Silva answered. "And they're now using its coordinates to represent the official geographic location of all of Macau."

Of greater architectural interest to Lee was the adjacent chapel, founded two centuries earlier by an order of missionary Clarist nuns who lived on the site. Lee knew the chapel's stunning Asian- and European-themed frescoes from the seventeenth century had been hidden and forgotten about until 1998, when routine construction led to workers rediscovering them.

And yet, to his dismay, the government of Macau continued to approve new construction projects much nearer to, and taller than, what was allowed in the chapel's vicinity. As a result, he had strongly supported a local conservation group when it submitted a report to UNESCO stating the government had failed to protect Macau's cultural heritage against the threats.

That reminded Lee of a topic he needed to bring up with Silva, a topic he found awkward to broach. But broach it he must.

"So, Kip," he began hesitantly. Silva glanced at the architect and was taken aback some by the unusual tilt to his eyes. "So, one of my associates, Liam, says he's come across an email Jocelyn Cheng sent you a few weeks before her murder saying she was feeling threatened and asking for help."

Silva's expression morphed from curiosity to chagrin. Several moments went by before he finally nodded and said, "Yes, Dalton. She sent me that." He looked up sheepishly at the architect, then continued. "And ever since her murder, I've been struggling to deal with the fact that . . ."

"That you didn't do anything about it?" Lee caught his breath. He hadn't meant to come across so accusatory. "I'm sorry, Kip. I didn't mean to . . ."

The police officer shook his head. "No, you're right. To some degree, anyway." He let out another sigh. "Her email arrived right before I was heading to Bali for a five-day holiday. I told one of my lieutenants to check into it, but then outright forgot about it. To be fair, Jocelyn had a bit of a reputation for being melodramatic about her safety. She'd claim people were stalking her, watching her on the street, but it was never anything we could actually verify. And when I got back from Bali, I ran into her at a couple of public functions, asked her how she was doing, even if there was anything she wanted to discuss with me, and she looked at me as though she had no idea what I was talking about.

"I assumed it was somebody's prank, or maybe some sort of spam, especially since it came from a different address than the one she had used with me before." He stopped again, sighed yet again. "But I can't tell you how much I've regretted not following up with her in a more private setting, found some safe place where she could have felt more comfortable confiding in me.

"And then, of course, it wasn't long after that when . . ."

Lee decided to drop the topic for the time being. He hadn't been very responsible with his own emails of late and understood how time and tension can make it easier for things to fall through the floorboards.

But still, Lee thought, *he's the head of the public security police force in Macau. And she was one of Macau's most prominent executives and philanthropists. One would think . . .*

Just then, a young girl on a scooter approached on Lee's right. The wheels of her toy ran over his right foot, causing him to wince. The girl looked back over her shoulder and sent the architect a big smile.

"Sorry about that, Dalton," Silva said. "Macau is seeing more and more tourists these days. How's your foot?"

Lee waved off the incident. But rather than walk to their next venue, the pair chose to take a cab to the A-Ma Temple, built in 1488 to honor Mazu, the goddess of the sea and guardian of sailors and fishermen. Lee was well-versed in the legend that claims when Portuguese sailors landed near the temple in the 1600s and asked villagers what the name of the place was, the villagers misunderstood them to be asking for the name of the temple. The villagers responded 'A-Maa-Gok (which means 'Pavilion of the Mother'). But from that point on, European documents referred to the entire area as 'Macau.'

Lee had always loved this traditional, Ming-Dynasty temple compound, which comprised six distinct structures. He adored the dignified symmetry of its Gate Pavilion, flanked by two stone lions. He swooned over its Hall of Benevolence, the oldest structure and the one with a psychedelic mix of purple and aqua blue and Chinese red. And he completely plotzed over its Buddhist Pavilion, featuring a vibrant array of cone-shaped incense coils descending from the ceiling.

Lee was eager to discuss with Silva what his team had recently discovered, but he also wanted to show respect to the throngs of tourists and villagers who were there to pay tribute to their deceased ancestors. Out of habit, he bowed his head while the teenagers, middle-aged housewives and elderly men around him either offered up silent prayers, or lit long, tapered incense sticks that emitted the unmistakable scent of sandalwood. Lee considered lighting some sticks in honor of his captive parents but decided not to equate them with the dearly departed. Instead, he offered a brief but fervent prayer for their quick release.

After a moment, he felt a gentle nudge to his ribs. "You're tapping your foot incessantly, Dalton, so I'm guessing that means you want to discuss the case some more," Silva whispered. The police officer tilted his head to one side. "Follow me out to the grounds," he added. "We can talk out there."

They strolled over to one of the more secluded sections of the compound's gardens. They pretended to be admiring the flora and trees until they were certain no one was within earshot. Another slight breeze kicked up, enough to tousle Silva's otherwise perfect hair.

"Chupa Chup?" the policeman asked as he pulled two out of his pants pocket. "They're both watermelon. They're the ones Bree gave me."

Lee shook his head. "No thanks," he replied. The architect carefully let go of the branch he'd pulled down with his left hand as part of their pretense of inspecting the foliage. A chorus of children's voices began to float toward them. The laughter and chatter seemed to draw near, then suddenly veered in a different direction. After a moment, the garden became tranquil again, almost eerily so.

"Kip, there's something else I haven't shared with you yet," Lee said in a hush. He went on to tell Silva what he and Warren had found on the surveillance tapes.

"Wait, they were together in the casino *and* by the elevators leading up to Jocelyn's suite?" Lee confirmed to Silva that he had understood correctly. "Well, that is a little bizarre, isn't it? I'd never guess those two even knew each other, much less were so . . . chummy." The police officer stroked his chin, then glanced at Lee. "I'd say we probably need to have a little conversation with them, wouldn't you?"

"Together or separate?" Lee wondered aloud.

Silva stroked his chin again. "Good point. We might be able to turn one against the other if we interview them separately. Or at least see if their stories jibe." He considered the options, then looked at his phone. "Let me think about it, Dalton. I have to get back to headquarters for a meeting. I'll shoot you a text once we have something lined up with them. We'll be quick about it, I promise."

Silva's countenance brightened just as the sun disappeared behind a bank of clouds. "Who knows?" he began. "Maybe we're about to make some progress after all."

Lee nodded and smiled but was disappointed the tour was coming to an end. He had hoped they might go on to visit The Moorish Barracks – with their peculiar mix of Arabian and Gothic columns and latticework. Built in the 1870s to house a regiment from a Portuguese province of India, it now served as the headquarters for the territory's Marine and Water Bureau. And he was especially disappointed they wouldn't be taking in the charming Taipa Houses and Museum, five pastel-green villas built in 1921 that are the epitome of Portuguese architecture during the colonial era. A few years back, Lee had been commissioned to deliver a series of lectures at the museum focused on architecture across the region, an appearance that fell through when a cyclone brought flooding to the area.

They summoned a car that would drop Silva off at his office and Lee at a dock where a ferry would take him back to Hong Kong.

As the ferry churned beside Lantau Island, Lee ran through everything that had occurred over the past few days. His portuguesa was now balanced on his lap, and he gently stroked its brim and crown as he watched a flock of sea birds dip and swoop above the placid water. He felt more sanguine after the tour of Macau, and he allowed himself the luxury of savoring the fresh, brisk air and the relative serenity the journey across the bay now afforded him.

But the birds soaring alongside the ferry suddenly began to veer away from, then toward, one another, at times bumping in midair. Those that had been gliding gracefully above the bay just a few moments earlier were now jerking in one direction, then the opposite. Accompanying their volatile movements was a shrill, almost frantic call that rose, then fell, then surged once again, louder than before.

At the same time, Lee felt a click, followed by a low buzzing at the back of his head. He gripped the brim of his hat, waited for the pulsating to come to an end. It did, returned for another minute or two, before finally stopping altogether.

Meanwhile, the birds resumed their tranquil flight, seemed oblivious to their erratic display.

Squinting at the vista beyond the boat's windows, Lee chewed the inside of his right cheek. Slowly placed the portuguesa on top of his head.

The weather was still brilliant, the water was still calm. However, the world's most prominent architect now found himself on edge.

Something told him the yet-to-be-explained alliance between the casino waitress and Jacqueline Cheng was likely more pernicious than the tapes revealed.

Something told him they had very little time left to stop O from launching whatever catastrophe they had in store.

And some subtle, ill-defined something told him the person who had murdered Jocelyn Cheng was on the verge of eluding their grasp.

33

Lee's dreams that night were feral and fantastical. They began with him sitting at a table before several tall stacks of headgear. Frantically, he'd try one on, then another, struggling to find the hat that would perfectly suit both his mood and the shape of his head. None satisfied him. Not the bowler, which he replaced with a visor, followed by a fedora, then a beret, then a stocking cap (and so on, and so on and so on). As his dissatisfaction with the hats that he put on grew in intensity, his discarding of them grew in velocity, propelling him, eventually, into a state of panic.

That was followed by yet another nightmare in which he was piloting one of the skywriting jets he had seen the day he'd first met Julian. Except, the plane was out of control and none of the instruments on the panel in front of him made any sense. Frantic, he looked out the window only to see a billboard floating in the airspace beside him bearing the warning,

YOU'RE HEADED IN THE WRONG DIRECTION, DALTON!

That then morphed into another psychedelic episode in which he was sitting alone in a vast movie theater. The enormous screen began to unreel, in rapid-fire motion, images of the many people he had met throughout their time in the region. Kip Silva's secretary became the cartoon character who had spoken to him from the bus, who then transformed into the busker on the street corner, who became the driver who'd taken him to So Lo Pun. With each transformation, the next face took on increasingly maniacal characteristics–horns, fangs, pulsating lesions, a ruthless sneer.

The reel ended, and Lee bolted up in the bed. "That's it!" he exclaimed. "That's it!" He shook his head once, revisited quickly all the visuals he had just seen, then nodded emphatically that what had just dawned on him was absolutely, totally right.

"Yes, that's definitely it," he said more quietly before. "*That's* how I can engineer my confidant's escape!"

***

"Where are you, RIGHT NOW, Dalton?"

Julian's exhortation was so loud, the architect had to pull the phone back several inches to avoid injuring his eardrum. At the same time, a tiny smile creased his lips.

"Where I usually am at eight in the morning, Julian. In my hotel room. What's up?"

Lee could not discern from the jarring introduction whether Julian was thrilled beyond measure or substantially dismayed. He quickly discovered it was the former. "I know this is sort of 'out there,' but I wanted to invite you to a night of entertainment. Someone I met during my stint in Thailand is in town and I want you to see her perform. And should you be worried about taking time away from the case, I think I have some valuable information about it that will help you considerably."

Given Julian's track record, Lee was skeptical about any new lead he might have. But he hated to dampen his friend's enthusiasm.

Someday, I'll probably want someone to give a damn about the advice I have to share, he surmised.

"All right, Julian. What time and where? And what sort of entertainment are we talking about?"

"The club Octavia. I'll send you the address. Meet me at the front door around nine. Dress casual."

"And the entertainment?"

There was a long pause on the other end of the line before Julian responded, "You're not afraid of snakes, are you?

***

Lara entered Dalton's room with brio–the paragon of officiousness and efficiency. She'd let him know by text that she had a few things she needed to discuss with him. Since he was still waiting for Kip Silva to let them know when Regina Bauer and Jacquelyn Cheng would be coming in for interviews, he suggested she come whenever she was ready.

She was ready.

"To begin, I have excellent news," she said, smiling as much as Lara might ever smile. "We've been selected to design the concert hall in Dubai."

"So quickly?"

Lara allowed her wisp of a smile to widen into a hint of one.

"I rushed over to them a comprehensive portfolio of our work and our responses to all of their final questions," she replied. Her smile faded, however, and was replaced with a look of sheepishness.

"What?" Lee asked.

"Well, I also lied a little. I said we'd be able to start work on the project in . . . about a month or so."

Lee grimaced but quickly recovered from his reaction.

"That might be rushing things just a tad, but given the speed at which O likes to operate, our services here may no longer be needed by then." He hesitated for dramatic effect before adding, "Whatever the outcome."

"They need you to sign the pages in this contract I've tagged with a yellow note," she said. "Once you've done that, I'll send It off to them and invoice them for the deposit they've agreed to."

Lee thumbed through the sheaf of papers and noted the abundance of yellow notes it contained. "This may take me a while," he intoned.

That prompted Lara to frown and return to her more dour, businesslike self. "Now, about the case in front of us. I . . ."

"Excuse me, I just have to ask . . ." Dalton wore an impish grin, which to Lara softened the fact he had rudely interrupted her. "I just have to ask . . . did you ever lie to your parents? I can't imagine you lying to them, but . . ."

"I certainly never lied to my mother. No reason to. Right up until the time she vanished at sea, she was my very best friend." Lara shifted in her chair, tugged at the lower hem of the skirt she was wearing. "It will probably come as a surprise to you, given everything I've said to you about him, but I've only lied once to my father."

"About what?" Lee countered. She shifted again, then gave him a steely expression.

"Just before I went off to university, he demanded I never pursue architecture as a profession," she replied. "I told him I'd stay as far away from it as possible."

Lee scoffed and sent her a look that told her he found that to be a pretty bold thing to do.

Lara cleared her throat and returned to the notes she had called up on her phone. "So, as I was saying, I believe Liam and Anisa have confirmed an interesting detail they were speculating on. They've found what appears to be several five-figure deposits into one of Jocelyn Cheng's primary checking accounts over the course of about eighteen months. She noted the deposits in her banking software as 'Consulting Income,' but the kids guessed they were payments from her previous boss, intended to persuade her not to move forward with a sexual harassment suit she was threatening him with. That's why he left the company. Liam and Anisa told me this morning they've now confirmed that those deposits indeed came out of the ex-boss's accounts."

"Wait, did you say Anisa? Why are she and Liam hooked up together on this? I thought she was focusing on Jocelyn legal affairs?"

Lara cocked her head to one side before answering. "Well, Dalton, I think it's because in this case the legal and financial issues are so intertwined. Anisa came upon the draft of the lawsuit the victim was planning to file and Liam volunteered to help her determine whether

Cheng's predecessor agreed to pay her off if she dropped the suit."

Lee looked as if he had just learned that a close classmate had died from a massive heart attack, or that someone had hacked into his investment portfolio and drained it to zero.

"Turns out, he had," Lara added, hoping that would snap Lee back into the room with her.

Lee's body appeared to relax, but he still bore a troubled expression. "Anisa should have brought that lawsuit to *my* attention, not Liam's," he muttered. Lara looked down at her lap, tugged the hem of her skirt once more.

"Maybe I should move on to something else," she offered, returning to the list on her phone. She did some scrolling, then stopped and exclaimed, "Ah, yes, Chez Toulouse."

"What's that?" Lee said. "The place where Anisa and Liam were collaborating on their project?"

Lara shook her head slowly. "It's a restaurant here on Hong Kong Island where Jocelyn Cheng was scheduled to have lunch with her younger sister a couple of days before she died. We thought it might represent an interesting opportunity for the sister to have spiked our victim's drink with rat poison. But as it turns out . . ."

Lee had completely relaxed into the armchair again and was whisking croissant crumbs off of his shirt. He pulled up, however, upon hearing Lara's disclaimer.

"As it turns out, what?

"Well, Jocelyn's calendar indicated the appointment, and that she was looking forward to it. But when Bree called the restaurant to confirm they had dined there, they said they didn't show any reservation on that day in either of their names."

Lee scrunched his face. "Maybe Jocelyn or Jacqueline had an assistant make the reservation for them and that person put it in their name instead?"

Lara first nodded then quickly shook her head.

"Yes, but we looked into that. Jacquelyn doesn't appear to have an assistant, and Jocelyn's former assistant had already departed, and they didn't show any reservation in the name of the replacement, either." She hesitated, then added, "And if I were making a lunch reservation for you, Dalton, I'd almost certainly make it in your name, not mine."

Lee nodded, stared into a distant corner of the room.

"I suppose you're right," he said at a level just above a whisper. He continued to study the far corner for another minute or so, then added, "So, yet another dead end, I guess."

Lara's head bobbed back and forth. "Maybe not, but probably. I mean there's still the question as to why her calendar said she was looking forward to a lunch with her sister at a restaurant that doesn't show them having any reservation. Maybe they planned to just drop in and then changed their mind at the very last minute and dined elsewhere. Or maybe the restaurant's system deleted the reservation somehow."

Lara now paused to collect her thoughts. "It doesn't mean Jacquelyn didn't have any chance at all to lace Jocelyn's drink with the poison. But we can probably say that if she did, she definitely didn't do it at that restaurant on that day."

Lee nodded again, seemed now to be churning on the topic as much or more than Lara had. Then he took a deep breath in.

"Lara, can you send me a screen capture of the notation in Jocelyn's appointment book? I'd like to see it."

She nodded and entered his request into her phone.

"Is there anything else?" Lee inquired.

His assistant glanced up and nodded.

"Yes, I think there's just one more thing," she replied. Her sour look went soft, and the edges of her mouth began to contort a bit, as if she were trying to restrain a laugh.

"The newsboy cap you're wearing," she began. "I could be mistaken, but I think it still has the price tag on it."

34

"Driver, pull over here please."

The young woman taking Lee to the Club Octavia slid the town car alongside the curb about fifteen meters from the corner. Dalton was relieved to discover that the busker was not in the middle of a performance but instead was leaning against the side of a building, taking a long drag from a cigarette. A dirty tarp lay on the sidewalk, only a smattering of small bills scattered across it.

The musician did not see Lee until the architect leaned over and placed five, Hong Kong one-thousand-dollar bills under a rock that was holding down one corner of the tarp. At that, the busker pushed away from the building, flicked the cigarette to one side and approached.

"Sir, that is very generous of you, I must say," the musician said. "Thank you." The busker was grizzled, wore a small sage-green cap with patches that seemed to indicate some form of military service, and spoke with an accent that sounded half-Chinese, half-British.

"What, sir, would you like me to play for you? I know just about every song from every continent, except Africa. Name your music and I will gladly perform it. And again, thank you for your remarkable donation."

Lee smiled broadly. "I'm really not here for entertainment," he replied quietly. "Actually, I have an assignment for you."

The performer leaned back a bit, peered at Lee warily. "Assignment? What type of assignment?"

The architect took a step forward and widened his smile even more. "Really, it's a simple assignment but a very, very important one for which I will reward you even more than I already have. Much more, in fact."

The musician seemed to relax but stayed put, waiting for some additional information to emerge.

"By the way, my name is Dalton," the architect said with a quick bow. "What's yours?" The busker responded in kind, half-heartedly, shot a quick glance at the car Lee had arrived in, decided this benefactor out of nowhere must be all right.

"Just call me 'your friend,'" came the response. "What's the assignment?"

Lee studied the pavement between them for a couple seconds, then met the busker at eye-level again and smiled his biggest smile yet.

"Well, 'my friend,' let me ask you this. You've told me you can play just about every song imaginable." He paused, creating a moment of intrigue for the musician.

Then he added, "How good are you when it comes to impersonations?"

✦✦✦

Later, on the way to the club, Dalton spotted atop the roof of a warehouse a billboard encouraging residents to read the local newspaper as they commuted on the area's mass transit system. Its message was:

READ BETWEEN THE LINES!

Yeah, I really need to get better at that, he reminded himself.

The driver flipped on the windshield wipers as a series of light showers passed overhead. The evening had progressed from twilight to darkness quickly, and the shimmering lights of the restaurants and clubs and other commercial enterprises they passed began to reflect and blur in the puddles that were forming in the street. Lee chastised himself some for taking time away from the case to go clubbing with Julian. Still, the security professional had teased him with the prospect of some helpful intelligence.

So, I'm not being a complete slacker, he thought in defense.

Upon exiting the car outside Octavia, Lee instantly saw Julian, whose face brightened when their eyes met. It warmed the architect to see someone so joyous at his arrival, and he broke out in a spontaneous grin in return.

"You made it!" Julian exclaimed as he enveloped Lee in a massive bear hug. Lee pounded the security official rapidly on the back, in part because he was pleased to see him, and in part because he was having difficulty breathing, so smushed into Julian's ample bosom he was. "You're just in time," Julian exhorted. "I can't wait for you to see the show! And I love your headwear. What . . . is it?"

Lee smiled and lifted his right hand to touch the rich cloth on top of his head. "A *corno ducale*," he replied. "It's what the doges of Venice wore back during the Renaissance."

Julian's smile broadened. "You'll fit in perfectly in this club!" he pronounced. "Come. You'll see."

Lee found the interior of the bar to be over the top and then some. Its palette combined excesses of gold and jade and blue and violet and indigo. It was as if a muster of peacocks had taken up residence in the place and had decided to unveil their trains simultaneously. Several young women in contemporary and classical outfits occupied swings that hung from the ceiling; others bedecked with multicolored balloons were dancing on tall podiums scattered throughout the expansive room. One woman in a tiger suit prowled among those seated, occasionally cracking a small whip on the back of a chair. Meanwhile, a bodybuilder in boxer shorts flexed his muscles in a towering birdcage off to one side.

Julian had commandeered a table near a small stage that was theatrically lit, but completely empty. Overall, the room was populated with patrons but not terribly crowded.

"It's early yet," Julian explained. "The crowd will grow once the show begins." A heavily tattooed young woman bedecked in feathers that reached from the back of her waist to above her head glided over to them and asked if they wanted a bottle of champagne.

"I can get a glass of champagne anywhere," Lee said, finding himself suddenly in a jovial mood. "Let's go local, shall we?"

Julian burst out in laughter and embraced his companion with a squeeze similar to what a vise might deliver. "Yet another reason why I like you so much, Dalton!" he proclaimed. "So very, very much!" He let go of his grip (*just in the nick of time,* a breathless Lee thought), turned toward the server and said something to her in Cantonese.

She nodded once, glanced at Lee and began to answer Julian in English.

"Well, our *Chuan energy drink* is very popular," she uttered slowly. "It comes with vodka, vanilla, lychee liqueur, pepper honey and lime. Or there's our Mango Pomelo, with mango, coconut cream and grapefruit pulp."

"The first one," Lee said quickly.

"Make it two," Julian said in English.

Once the server was out of sight, Julian leaned to his left and shoved his shoulder against Lee's. "I think she likes you, Dalton," he whispered into the architect's ear. "I think she wants you."

"What makes you say that?" Lee countered. All the stimuli around him had him feeling more than a little punch-drunk without his having taken a sip of anything.

"Well, her name is Chloe, and I rarely see her look directly into someone's eyes. Abuse issues, I suspect." He bumped Lee's shoulder with his, then leaned away. "She couldn't take her eyes off of you though," he said. "Of course, you are a very handsome man, so I'm not surprised."

Lee felt himself blushing. The flattery was appreciated and oddly comforting.

"Is she the one with the snakes?" he asked.

Julian threw his head back and emitted a loud guffaw. "No. She'll be on soon. You're so funny, my friend." He pulled in a bit, let his smile drop. "And I really need to apologize to you for sending you down so many unproductive rabbit holes over the past few days.

This time, it was Lee giving Julian a squeeze.

"Oh, Julian, It's fine, really. They all seemed to have merit at the time. Please don't worry about it. You of all people should know that leads, that turn into dead ends, are all part of an investigator's work."

Their cocktails soon arrived. Lee was delighted to discover that, contrary to most of the opulent bars he had visited over time, this one was generous with its alcohol. "Wow, that pepper honey packs a punch," he blurted out after his first sip. Julian laughed heartily again, slapped his companion on the back but then sat up as a drumroll came across the speaker system.

"Gentlemen and ladies, welcome to Club Octavia." Lee could see the emcee in a booth at the back of the club, a young woman bedecked in stunning geisha attire. She caressed the microphone in a suggestive way and seemed to stare directly at Lee as she wet her lips for her next pronouncement. "We are very happy to have you here," she continued. "We are also very happy to showcase for your entertainment tonight one of the world's most renowned snake charmers. Please sit back in your seats, relax and savor the amazing artistry of Dara Nalazanji!"

The long drumroll ended with a sharp cymbal crash, followed by a sinewy young female slinking onto the stage, a tall wicker hamper under one arm. She pranced to one side of the stage then the other, lifted the hamper above her head, then undulated her abdomen while a flute trilled a mystical tune in the background.

Lee found the performance oddly enchanting. The woman wore a transparent veil, a bikini top sporting several of the royal colors and an ankle-length skirt in blue and gold that had a slit up one side. He found the dancer's routine more hypnotic that erotic, for she seemed emotionally removed from the room, as if she had been sent into a trance before going on stage.

"She's your friend?" Lee whispered to Julian.

The security consultant nodded and leaned toward the architect. "Yes. I met her in Thailand while I was on assignment there several years ago. She was just starting to learn the craft then. She is much more proficient at it now, I see."

The woman set the wicker basket on the stage and revolved around it, first clockwise than counterclockwise. Lee noted how much of the act involved her hands and that they looked strong enough to crush the basket if she wanted to. When she completed her second revolution around the hamper, she removed its lid and continued to move her torso like a curtain billowing in a light breeze. In the background, the flute became louder and more intense.

Julian elbowed Lee and pointed to the hamper. "Watch this," he said.

A few seconds later, the head of a cobra appeared a few inches above the open hamper. It weaved one way, bobbed the other, then reared back as if inspecting and judging the audience in front of it. It elevated itself further, about another six inches or so, and then a second head appeared just above the hamper's rim, causing those seated near the stage to shift and murmur. As the second snake elongated its neck, the entertainer extended both of her arms in front of her. As if performing a routine that they had executed a thousand times, the two serpents coiled themselves around her limbs in unison at a syncopation that matched that of the flute.

It was when they had both slithered all the way to her shoulders that the third snake in the hamper came out of hiding. It seemed more agitated than the other snakes, darting its head and tongue toward the spectators in an aggressive manner. That led to those nearest the performance scooting their chairs back a few inches and one woman leaving her seat and darting to the back of the room.

Lee was completely captivated by the act. Captivated, that is, until the dancer lifted the hamper above her head, descended a short flight of steps at one end of the stage and then set up shop right next to his seat. The architect stiffened as the snakes ducked and raised their heads that way then this, moving closer to Lee with every thrust forward. He clutched the underside of his chair as the snake on the left darted toward him then retreated, and the snake on the right glided to the floor and began to make its way up one of Lee's pant legs.

The third snake remained erect in front of him, staring him down as if to say, "Just try me."

"My snakes like you," the dancer breathed. "They find you very intoxicating." Lee glanced at Julian who shrugged his shoulders and sent Lee a bemused expression.

"I'm flattered, I guess," Lee replied, a forced smile frozen upon his face.

Suddenly, as if prodded by a fast-forward button, all three snakes coiled themselves around Lee's thighs, arms and torso. Although terrified, the architect silently acknowledged they weren't really causing him any discomfort. Somehow, their heads and tongues pointed away from him at all times, and their hold on him wasn't constrictive at all but instead felt like gentle hugs from three loose straps. His eyes were almost bulging from their sockets, and somewhere in the darkness of the club, a woman shrieked. But Lee remained relatively calm, his pulse close to normal.

Then the flute trilled continuously for several seconds, and all three snakes beat a fast retreat into the hamper they had slithered from. The dancer smiled, slapped the lid tightly onto the basket, scampered back to the stage and took several bows before exiting stage right. Julian stood and applauded both the entertainer and Lee, prompting others throughout the room to do the same.

"You were outstanding, Dalton!" Julian gushed. "I've never seen anyone maintain their composure the way you did!"

Lee was breathing fast and wiping off some slimy residue the snakes had left on his clothing.

"The least you could have done was warn me," he countered, chuckling.

"But that would have spoiled the fun of it," Julian countered.

A magician appeared to be setting up for his set when the dancer (sans snake basket) suddenly dropped into the chair on the far side of Julian.

"Thank you for coming, Julian, you're looking fantastic, love!" Despite her exotic name, Dara Nalazanji sounded as if she hailed right out of London's East End. "Oh, how I have missed you and how I miss Thailand!"

Lee became fascinated once again with the entertainer's hands. He decided they must be as developed as they were because of her need to manage reptiles that moved every which way at a moment's notice. The dancer, sensing what Lee was thinking, glanced at Julian. "Your friend, does he know?"

200

Julian shook his head, pivoted toward his companion and extended an open palm in Lee's direction. Dara, meet my dear friend, Dalton Lee, one of the world's most renowned architects. Dalton Lee, meet my dear friend, Dara Nalazanji, one of the world's most renowned snake charmers." The entertainer extended her right hand to Lee who found the grip much more substantial than he expected.

"Or, as I knew her when I first arrived in Thailand, *Darren* Nalazanji." The dancer arched her eyebrows and gave Lee a knowing smile.

"Aha. I see. Thailand. Of course. Well, it's a pleasure to meet you . . . Dara."

She nodded and beamed at the architect. "Oh, you were a wonderful foil for my act, lovey. I spied you in the audience early and just knew you'd be cool as an ice cube about it all. The snakes are completely harmless but lots of people go bonkers when the snakes approach them. I choose my 'straight men' carefully, don't you know, and I think my choice tonight was spot on!"

The lights lowered again for the magician to begin his performance. Dara leaped up from the chair and gave Julian a peck on one cheek. "Thank you, doll, for bringing your friend to the show. It's just brill to see you. I'm here the rest of the week, so maybe we can have a drink and reminisce about all those fun times we had in Bangkok?"

"Let's do that," Julian replied. "I'll call you later to set something up."

Spotlights shone on one of the magician's assistants wheeling out a long box with a woman's head poking out of one end and her golden slippers poking out of the other. Julian let out a soft sigh, nudged Lee and bowed his head.

"I've seen more than my share of ladies sawed in half," he whispered. "Let's move to a private viewing area where we can . . . discuss a few things."

They rose from the table. Julian took Lee by the wrist and guided him to a staircase behind their table, which led them to a small, glassed-in alcove that overlooked the main floor.

"This is cozy," Lee said settling in. The architect surveyed the luxuriously carpeted floor as if he had lost something valuable. "No snakes here, it seems," he announced.

Julian responded with a faint smile. Suddenly, his demeanor seemed more sober. Another server, wearing a red bunny suit, hopped to the table to take their order. When she had returned to the bar, the security professional leaned toward the architect and placed a palm over his nearest forearm.

"Dalton, I think I may have stumbled upon who was behind Jocelyn's murder," he said as quietly as possible. Lee pulled back, allowed his jaw to drop some. Julian released the architect's forearm but moved in even closer. "Have you interacted at all with one of the waitresses at the Lucky Fortune casino? A Rebecca Baumann, or something like that?"

"It's Regina Bauer, and yes we have," Lee replied. "She's an odd duck, but I have a hard time envisioning her masterminding a murder. Why do you ask?"

Their drinks arrived. Julian handed a credit card to the server. When Lee began to protest, Julian shoved a firm palm in front of him to quell the architect's objection. The server chose to process the charge at the table, which irked Julian. But he didn't show it, extending instead a false smile that served as a reasonably effective façade for his impatience. When the rabbit finally turned away, he relaxed his body again and placed both elbows on the table.

"I think she and Jocelyn's sister, Jacquelyn, conducted the murder together. I think one of them, or both, belong to The Organization. Um . . . 'O,' I mean."

A slight trill went through Lee. The fact Julian had determined some unholy alliance between the two women seemed only to reinforce what he and Warren had spotted on the surveillance videos. "What makes you say that Julian?" he probed. What do you know?"

The security consultant reached into the inside pocket of the sports jacket he was wearing and extracted a piece of typing paper that he unfolded gingerly. "I'm sorry, Dalton, I'm not very tech-savvy. I think you can read this. But if not, let me know."

The type was grainy but legible. It resembled one of those old telegrams, written all in caps, with words strung together without punctuation:

**SO THE OPERATION WAS A SUCCESS,
THEY FINISHED IT THEY FINISHED, JOCELYN,
JACQUELYN AND REGINA DID
YES AND NO ONE KNOWS THE BETTER
NOW WE CAN MOVE FORWARD
WITH WHAT WE NEED TO DO
AND TAKE OVER THE WORLD
WHEN WE'RE READY, RIGHT**

Lee turned the paper over, but it was blank on the other side. "What is this?" he asked, puzzled.

Julian sniffed, put both hands in the air. "Dalton, you won't believe it, it was the most amazing coincidence! I was having dinner at The Governor over in Central a couple of nights ago and these two men are at a table on the mezzanine right above me. They are talking and one says to the other one, 'So the operation was a success?' and I'm barely listening because I assume they're talking gall bladder or maybe a hip replacement. But then they mentioned Jocelyn's name. And then her sister's. So, I started paying closer attention and that's how the conversation evolved." Julian leaned back in his chair and studied Lee's face. "I mean, I doubt it's incriminating enough to stand up in a court of law, but it sounds damning to me."

He stopped, turned remorseful. "They left immediately after that. If they hadn't, I would have tried to detain them somehow and contact you or Ray Silva."

Lee re-read the message, shook his head. "But what is *this*?" he said, holding the paper aloft and waving it back and forth.

Julian looked sheepish. "When they started talking, I flipped on the voice-to-text app on my phone," he explained. "That's a print-out of what it recorded. It's grainy because I can't figure out how to change the ink cartridge in my printer."

Lee chuckled, squeezed his friend's upper arm. "You know, you could have just let me read it off the app," he said as he refolded the paper and handed it back to his companion. Julian returned it to his jacket pocket, turned a slight shade of red.

"I didn't think of that. I told you I'm not very tech savvy." He sighed heavily, looked off into the distance. "That's why it's time for me to retire, I guess."

They both turned forward to watch the magician below, who was now doing a card trick with someone he had pulled from the audience. As the trick unfolded, Lee filled Julian in on the images he and Warren had seen on the surveillance tape as well as the discovery of the microwave equipment in Jocelyn's office and its subsequent disappearance.

Julian began to rub Lee's upper back with one palm.

"My friend," he began, "I am worried. If I know anything about The Organization, it's that they are relentless and will move faster than a cheetah to consolidate their power and then abuse it, all under the guise of 'liberty' and 'freedom.'

"I pray that equipment you just described to me gets found immediately and, if I had to guess where they may have secured it, I'd say probably in the Zhuhai Park just outside Macau. Lots of large, industrial warehouses there, and it's very close to the Zhuhai-Macau bridge for easy transport.

He stopped to take a long sip of his beverage, leaned into his friend, gave him a severe look.

"But, wherever it is, Dalton, I'm betting they will begin to use it, if not tomorrow, then maybe just a day or two later. You're closing in on them and I don't want to be alarmist, but nothing terrifies me more than the idea of O sensing it's been backed into a corner."

35

Bree found the weather almost insufferable.

The sidewalks were damp with sweat, the air was dense and drippy, even though no rain was falling. Her lungs felt heavy and especially so in the tighter quarters of the *Star Ferry* she was taking across Victoria Harbor to Tsim Sha Tsui.

This time, she had decided to forgo an umbrella, and she was beginning to regret the decision. Nonetheless, she was committed to doing what she had come here to do. It was something she felt *compelled* to do, something she felt *fated* to do.

Her worry, of course, was that she'd be unable to find the girl. That the beggar would be in some completely different location in the market, would have decided not to come out on such a horrid night or maybe even had relocated to Hong Kong Island, Macau or perhaps even Shenzhen.

But Bree came upon the waif within ten minutes of arriving at the ferry dock, sitting in a lotus position just inside a vestibule only a few hundred feet from where Bree had left her a few days earlier. The architect stood apart from the waif for several moments, tucked beneath a stall's overhang, just watching her and waiting. The beggar's cry for attention from the few passers-by seemed more muted than before, as if she were already resigned to the fact she wouldn't be attracting much in the way of donations this evening.

Bree noticed the girl's face looked unusually dirty. And her clothing seemed more tattered, as hard as that was to believe. But the revulsion Bree had felt before did not materialize. She continued to peer at the girl from several meters away and offered a silent prayer of thanks that her fate was not that of the beggar's.

As if by magic, the shoppers in the area first dwindled, then vanished altogether. Bree decided it was time to make her move. As she approached, she expected the urchin to send her way one of her knowing looks, or perhaps even a smile of recognition. But the girl seemed to look right through her, acted as if she did not know her at all.

The architect patted her chest and said, "Bree. I'm Bree. Remember?" The girl nodded dully, but her expression remained blank. Her Eurasian features gave her a feline quality, with a face that served as a mask that made her emotions inscrutable.

The waif remained stoic. Bree hadn't planned for that, didn't know what to say or do next. But when a pedestrian skittered around a corner, then slowed as if considering whether to toss a few coins the girl's way, the urchin turned and stared at Bree. As if she were waiting. For something.

The pedestrian reconsidered, briskly moved on.

Bree glanced over one shoulder, noticed once again there was almost no one on the street, even though the market had at least another hour left before it was scheduled to shutter for the evening. She returned her gaze to the girl who resembled a statue, unmoving and unmoved.

Maybe I shouldn't do this, she worried. *Maybe she'll be embarrassed or insulted.*

Then the scent from sandalwood candles in a stall nearby wafted her way. She committed to moving forward.

Deftly, the architect reached into the inside pocket of the raincoat she had thought to bring along and removed a white envelope that was slightly larger than those found in a typical business office. She allowed the faintest of smiles to cross her lips, bent slightly and tossed the envelope onto the girl's lap. Then she pivoted and darted away, not looking back to see whether the beggar was registering some response or rummaging through the envelope.

"That was for you, Carole," she whispered to the stars above her.

Had Bree expected some response from Carole, or the universe in general, she would have been disappointed. Lightning did not pierce the sky; thunder did not roll. The air remained supremely sultry, her hair had grown lank from the moisture.

She did, however, feel a trill of warm satisfaction pulsing throughout her system. For she knew, if her calculations were correct, that the funds she had just placed on the young girl's lap, enabled by the advance that Lee had given her, would handle the urchin's living expenses for more than a year.

Possibly even two.

36

A tale of two interviews:

Jacquelyn Cheng strode confidently into the meeting room, shook the hands of Kip Silva, Dalton Lee and Warren Jackson, smoothed her skirt and took a seat across from all three. Lee had given permission to Bree, Lara, Liam and Anisa to remain at the hotel to pursue their investigations.

"Thank you for coming in again, Ms. Cheng," Silva began.

"I'm happy to," she responded. "I know all of this must be exhausting for you. How can I be of help?"

Silva looked over at Lee. The architect nodded his head, indicating the superintendent-general should move forward as they had discussed.

"Ms. Cheng, could you tell us about your relationship with Regina Bauer, a server at the Lucky Fortune casino?"

The woman's chipper expression dimmed; one side of her mouth turned downward.

"Relationship?" she countered. "I'm . . . not sure what you mean by that."

Silva paused, looked once again at Lee.

"You do know Ms. Bauer, correct?"

The sister of Jocelyn Cheng shifted in her seat. "Yes. Of course.

Regina has been working for Jocelyn's company for a while now, a few months, I believe."

Silva nodded, flashed one of his klieg-light smiles.

"Excellent. So then, would you explain this to us?" He swiveled in her direction the laptop that was open in front of him, reached around one side of it and, with his left index finger, pressed a button on the keyboard. The video of Jacquelyn and Regina Bauer chatting near the casino's elevator bank began to play, followed by them sharing a brief hug and then waving goodbye.

The designer's faced drooped entirely for a moment. Then she rallied a broad smile. "Right. Yes. That would be Regina and me, probably right after one of our sessions."

"Your sessions?"

The young woman glanced to one side for a moment. Lee couldn't tell if she was recalling the details of the meeting or concocting them on the spot.

"Yes. Our sessions. Regina–as you probably know if you've spoken to her–is not one of the casino's most polished employees. Not her fault really, given her background. She grew up in some town called Broken Bow and only took a course or two at the local community college before dropping out. And Jocelyn told me she actually does her job reasonably well, apparently. But Jocelyn felt Regina didn't really embody the corporation's . . . brand . . . the way she wanted her to. Or, I should say, as Jocelyn *needed* her to.

She straightened her spine and lifted her chin.

"Jocelyn thought, maybe, given my skill set, I could pass along to Regina some of the nuances of serving the casino's more upscale customers. Show here, for example, that one does not drop a cocktail in front of someone as if it were a scalding potato but instead presents it to them with some sense of flourish. That you then ask the patron, 'May I bring you anything else?' not 'What else do you want?' Nuances like that."

Silva nodded. "I see. And how many times a week, and for how long, have these 'sessions' as you call them been taking place?"

"Not every week," she quickly replied. "Maybe once or twice a month. And I'd guess I've been helping her for . . . a couple of months, maybe?"

"And how long does a typical session last?"

She tilted her head up and squinted some before responding, "About an hour or so. Never more than an hour and a half."

Silva tapped his pen on the tabletop in front of him, stopped when he had decided how to move forward. "So, from the video, do we assume correctly you conducted these sessions in one of the private residences within the casino's tower wing?"

The young woman nodded. "In Jocelyn's suite, actually. She'd give me access to it whenever she was out of town or was going to be gone from the suite for most of a day. If the suite wasn't available, I'd sometimes meet Regina at the casino, and we'd use a small training room there. But most of the sessions took place in Jocelyn's quarters because it's more private, of course." Now it was Jacquelyn Cheng flashing a broad, emboldened smile at the interrogator.

Silva sat back in his chair, turned toward Lee and sent him a look that said, '*Sounds plausible to me.*'

But Jacquelyn Cheng wasn't finished.

"It turns out, Regina is a fast learner," she continued. "I think she's made amazing progress in the time I've been working with her, and I must say, I take great pride in seeing that she's embraced, and executed, just about everything I've told her to do."

***

Regina Bauer was leaning forward in her seat–the very same seat Jacquelyn Cheng had been sitting in two hours earlier–one finger extended toward the computer in front of her and a scowl on her face.

"That ain't me."

Dalton Lee let a brief chuckle emerge; quickly cupped a palm over his mouth.

"I'm sorry?" said Silva.

"I said, 'That ain't me.' That's somebody else. Not me." The server started punching her chest with one finger. "This . . . this is me," she droned. She extended the finger back toward the computer and jabbed in the direction of the scene that was playing out before her. "That," she said. "That ain't me. Got it?" Bauer fell back into her chair, crossed her arms in front of her. The expression on her face morphed from one of dissatisfaction to one of defiance.

Silva sighed heavily and Lee chuckled softly once more.

"What's so funny?" the server asked, glaring at the architect. But her tone now was more one of awkwardness than aggressiveness. She could tell Lee was chuckling at her expense.

Silva ran the palm of his right hand along the back of his neck.

"Nothing, Ms. Bauer, nothing," he replied. "So, Jacquelyn Cheng. Jocelyn Cheng's sister. The other woman in the videos. You know her, is that correct?"

This time, Bauer's look shifted from defiance to wariness.

"Sort of," she replied. "I know she's the big boss's sister. *Was* her sister, I mean." She looked down at her lap and suddenly wouldn't look Silva directly in the eye, a shift that Lee found interesting.

"But I've only talked to her maybe once or twice. You know, 'Hello, Ms. Cheng, how are you today?' 'Do you want another vesper martini, Ms. Cheng?' That kind of thing. But that's about it." She halted for a moment, seemed to search for her next words. "I mean, I'm civil to her, and all. But if we passed each other on the street, I probably wouldn't recognize her. And vicey versa, I'm sure."

"Oh, wow," Warren mumbled.

Lee found the whole episode both fascinating and unbelievable. It felt like they were sitting inside a surrealist painting that someone was spinning first clockwise, then counterclockwise. He leaned toward the server, decided to make absolutely certain the crazy-clock situation unfolding before them was precisely what they perceived it to be.

"So, you're saying you've never spent any private time with Jacquelyn Cheng?' he asserted, more as a statement than a question. "You've never been involved in any sort of . . . sessions . . . with her? At the casino?" He nodded toward the computer in front of her. "Or, in her sister's suite?"

The casino employee glanced up at him, took on the look of a peeved bulldog. "What do you mean 'sessions?' Are you saying you think I need therapy or something?"

She pulled in some, but soon enough, the kettle began to rattle and whistle again.

"Look, I told you once and I'm not going to tell you again. That ain't me!" The server breathed in through her nostrils and pushed herself toward the men in front of her. "And one more thing I'm gonna say and you're probably not gonna like hearing it."

Silva raised one hand to interrupt her.

"Ms. Bauer, I'm actually going to say something to *you* and you're probably going to *love* hearing it."

"What's that?" she asked.

The policeman smiled from ear to ear then whispered, "You can go now."

***

Lee and Silva were standing in front of the receptionist's desk, chatting over what they had just experienced. Every now and then, the assistant adjusted her glasses with the cat eye frames but otherwise she seemed fixated on some document that was up on her computer screen.

"So, what do we know, Kip?" Lee asked his colleague.

Silva thought for a moment, his fists thrust into the pockets of his khaki slacks. "What I know," he said, "is that I liked this job a whole lot more when I felt sure I knew whom I could trust." Lee sent the policeman an understanding look but said nothing.

After a minute, Silva added, "And what do *you* think?"

Lee started rocking back on his heels and shook his head.

"Well, what I *think,* is that somebody–or some bodies–just lied to us."

At that, the receptionist cleared her throat, removed her glasses from her face and slapped her palms onto the desktop.

"If I learned anything from my criminology professor at the University of Macau," she announced, "it's that the ones you think you can trust the most are the ones who are most likely lying to you."

The two men looked at each other, then at the receptionist, then back at each other, stunned at the young woman's sudden declaration.

Her point made, the receptionist casually replaced her glasses onto the bridge of her nose, positioned her hands back over the keyboard and redirected her attention to the document in front of her.

37

"I need to move forward quickly, Liam. Are you still with me on this?"

They were in Anisa's room. She had made it clear that the aroma and anarchy that pervaded his room squelched any romantic spirit in her.

He wound his arms around her waist, pulled her close. "Of course, I am," he replied, kissing her on the bridge of her nose. "Are you still with me on *this?*"

She squinted at him; pecked him on the end of his nose in return. "Yes . . ." she said, drawing the word out into two long syllables. "For certain. Why . . ."

He unwound his arms from her and thrust both hands into the pockets of his jeans. "I just want to be sure you don't plan to jet off to South Africa and into the arms of your ex when I'm not looking."

She stepped forward, swatted at his chest, then stepped back.

"No worries there," she answered soberly. "I don't have the inclination at all, and even if I did . . . with what's in front of us, I don't have the time."

He nodded, took on a serious expression. "So, what's your timeframe? *Our* timeframe, I mean. Right now, I'm just sitting in front of my laptop screen, trying to get a bead on whether any of those blips could belong to . . . you know . . ."

She studied the carpet for a few moments before responding. "In a day or two. I can just tell things are on the verge of boiling over. I want to make my move before everything starts to unfold."

Liam nodded at her comment, moved forward to take her back into his arms.

"Okay then," he said softly, nuzzling his nose against hers. "Make your move. Know I'll be right there beside you when you do."

38

There was a clinking of some type of service item against a glass. Shortly after that, someone bellowed "ATTENTION! ATTENTION, EVERYONE!"

Servers scurried from one person to the next, collecting napkins and plates from those who had finished.

The American stood in front of a small stage at one end of the room and raised his left arm.

"Ladies and gentlemen, *mesdames et messieurs, nǚshìmen xiānshengmen.* I am happy to announce that the Great Transformation is about to get underway."

All the attendees in their ball gowns and tuxedos turned toward the speaker, murmured their excitement and politely applauded. The spectacular view from the top of the Oceana Insurance Building, in Macau's Praia Grande Central District, only added to the air of festivity.

"Very soon, our initiative will begin to roll out not just in this region but in major capitals throughout Asia," the American continued. Rather than a tuxedo, he was clad in a dark gray suit with pants legs tailored a little too short, a white button-down shirt and a blue tie that dangled down to just below his belt buckle. "Very soon," he continued, "those leaders in the region who don't deserve that title and have been suppressing the liberties of freedom-loving people everywhere will begin to feel our impending wrath.

"Literally."

A chorus of guffaws pulsed through the crowd. One Macanese woman in a long pink dress bent over to slap her thigh and in so doing, spilled her cocktail all over the floor.

"Very soon, my friends," the American was now shouting, "we shall assume the positions of power we have sought for so long and vanquish those who naively believe that restrictions and regulations and collaboration are more worthy that unfettered, unbridled, individual impulse!"

A moderate whoop erupted from those assembled. Servers bobbed and weaved between those who occupied the floor, refilling their glasses and offering hors d'oeuvres.

"How will we know when the plan is in process?" a sonorous male voice called out.

"Yes! How will we know? How will we know?" others chimed in.

The American ducked his head and conferred with his colleagues who nodded at him to answer the question. He smiled brightly and assumed a stance that would allow him to boom even more loudly.

"You will know, trust me, my comrade," he replied. "First, you will hear a smattering of reports of people in the region suffering from dizziness and nausea. That will either be preceded, or followed by, a ringing in their ears or a headache that will become quite severe. Bank presidents, police officials . . . yes even heads of state will be the victims of this onslaught." He paused, took on a more serious tone. "However, we cannot guarantee that civilians will not get caught in the . . . microwave crossfire . . . we intend to unleash."

The buzz of the crowd was subsiding as they became more focused on what the American was describing.

"Are you talking about Havana Syndrome?" some woman exclaimed. "Don't people go on to suffer brain injuries from that?"

The American continued to beam from the front of the room.

"Let me just say that given the assault we're about to unleash, I feel certain the effects will almost certainly be referred to as Macau Syndrome going forward." He stopped, caught the eye of the woman who had posed the question. "And yes ma'am, debilitating brain injuries are a very possible outcome."

The crowd elicited a low rumble, like an engine about to be revved.

"The brain injuries, they're often permanent, aren't they?" The speaker was an older woman with a strong Scottish accent.

"Most definitely," the American replied quickly. "That is our hope. The quicker we complete our rightful ascendancy, and restructure the governments throughout the region, the faster the masses can savor true freedom."

The rumble accelerated. Someone offered a quiet, "Hip, hip, hooray."

"May I ask . . . ?" It was an Australian male in his seventies who was leaning on a cane. "Will our money be safe while this is happening?" Again, the American glanced at his counterparts and again they nodded their assent for him to answer.

"My friend, when we take over, there will be no need for money. Commerce will proceed from human good will. The gold standard, credit ratings, bank-based lending, they're all artificial constructs that limit wealth to those already wealthy. When we replace the establishment with our own leaders, things like deeds, property liens, asset accounts and the like will all vanish and be ridiculed as vestiges of the old economy. The pre-Transformation economy."

The rumble grew into a low roar. It was as if the crowd's cocktails had all been spiked with adrenaline.

"Very soon you will be able to say whatever you want, do whatever you want, go wherever you want to go and be with whomever you want to be with and not worry about how it might affect someone else or how it might offend them." Here the American scrutinized the audience like a periscope probing the ocean's surface. He was confident they had reached the level of joyous frenzy he had hoped to achieve.

"Within reason, of course," he quickly added as an almost inaudible whisper.

More liquor flowed, more laughter poured forth, from somewhere the sound of violins appeared.

"Just a minute, everyone, just a minute." The American extended one arm in front of him, palm down, as he tried to quiet the assembly.

"Before we devolve into complete debauchery, Yang Li has something to share with us. She's been claiming it was a shawl for a niece or granddaughter of hers, but it turns out it's something altogether different."

At that, the back curtains of the stage located behind the American slowly opened, and a small spotlight illuminated a spot just above the American's head. If there wasn't an actual drum roll, everyone heard one in their head as a swath of fabric in the shape of a square slowly descended from above. It had more heft than a scarf but less than a full quilt. It seemed to be a tapestry of sorts, populated with images of herons and cranes, apples and pears, gingkoes, dove trees, ponds and lakes.

But when the fabric stopped descending, and the spotlight concentrated on its very center, it became apparent why the woman had taken so much care in its crafting. For there in the center, in an ornate script font, was a capital letter 'O.'

Upon its reveal, the terrorists fell silent in reverence and raised their glasses toward the tapestry. With little to no prompting they uttered adoringly their anarchic mantra, "Power to the cause."

39

Lee needed to get out. Walk the streets. Ponder the case. Plan a little switcheroo.

It was the acrostic that had motivated him to get away from the hotel suite. He only had a couple of clues left to solve and one had stymied him for days.

W. Type of room that can be frustrating

The answer had six letters in it, but neither 'dining,' nor 'living,' seemed to match the tenor of the clue. That morning, the solution had finally dawned on him:

E-S-C-A-P-E

And so, he did.

He'd chosen the perfect day to do so. The temperature was warm but not hot, the air was dry and calm. The afternoon sun, muted by thin horizontal clouds, softly illuminated the skyscrapers around him, creating a rosy, relaxed vibe to his stroll.

Which didn't last very long.

"You're slipping, Dalton," a voice called out to him. "You've been here for almost two weeks, and you still don't have an idea as to who murdered Jocelyn Cheng or where all that equipment is sitting. I'd say something like 'tick-tock,' 'tick-tock,' but I'm afraid at this point, you may have missed the boat altogether."

The architect slowed, pivoted his head to the left, then to the right. No one. Or, perhaps more likely, no *thing*. He was walking alongside a building that was under renovation. But the workers appeared to be on break, the plywood facing the street bore no placards or posters sporting people or cartoon characters that might have unleashed the monologue he'd just heard.

"Down here, Dalton. I know *you're* used to being the one to put out fires, but for now, you're going to have to surrender that responsibility to me."

He focused on the sidewalk, where one of Hong Kong's iconic fire hydrants held sway. (Fortunately) it did not have a physical mouth that moved, but from a certain angle, the fireplug resembled a large red bug with two bulging eyes and a mouth formed by the ridges that encircled its base. He also noticed the base sported the number 283 in yellow.

He had been born in February of 1983.

Rather than deliver his usual sarcasm toward whatever voice he heard, he decided instead to engage his critic.

"So, what do you suggest we do about all that?" he inquired. He hoped if he made it about the team, rather than him individually, the voice might ease up on him.

The ploy seemed to work.

"You might want to think about the comments you've heard over the past few days," it replied in a tone less harsh than the one it had used before. "One comment in particular might provide some helpful wisdom. But you really need to pick up your pace, Dalton."

That jolted Lee. Only because he had already sensed, somewhere at the back of his subconscious, that something someone had recently said mattered far more than it seemed to at the time.

"I mean, it's not like your parents' lives are at stake, or anything," the hydrant continued. "It's also the lives of those who matter most to your team. Oh, and don't forget all the muckety-mucks in the region who could suffer greatly if you don't solve things lickety-split. Wouldn't *that* be an awful amount of carnage to have paper-clipped to your resume?"

Lee was irked now. "Anything else?" he spat. But the hydrant went cold on him. He turned away and noticed that a teenage boy strolling down the sidewalk in the opposite direction was eyeing him with concern.

The architect resumed his stroll, but suddenly stopped, thrust out his right leg and gave the hydrant a swift kick in the side before moving on. He was disappointed the fireplug didn't respond somehow to the attack. Then he realized if his hoping for a response from an inanimate fireplug wasn't the perfect definition of crazy, nothing was.

Lee reached up and stroked the front of the light cotton beanie he was wearing. Although its ribbed texture was comforting, he suddenly was filled with overwhelming sadness. He veered across the sidewalk to the building under renovation and rested his head against the façade. Fought the tears, as he always did, by rapidly taking several shallow breaths.

This secret, he thought. *I'm not sure how much longer I can bear it.*

Sunlight burst through the clouds just then and spotlighted Lee like a performer on a stage. The rays comforted him, healed him, energized him. He turned away from the building and resumed his walk. He wasn't happier, particularly, but he was lighter in spirit.

Except for one small thing:

"You might want to think about the comments you've heard over the past few days. One comment in particular might provide some helpful wisdom."

At some cellular level, he knew it was true. But for the life of him, he couldn't determine which comment it was he should focus on. There had been so many of late.

On his right, toward the harbor, the International Finance Centre complex now loomed above him. Lee had always admired the sleek grace of its two office structures, even though he couldn't help but think that One ifc resembled an electric shaver, and that the much taller Two ifc looked remarkably like . . . well . . . a pleasure toy.

He knew the first building, opened in the 1990s, rose thirty-nine stories and contained four trading floors as well as the offices of many prestigious firms. Its younger and bigger sibling, however, loomed eighty-eight floors and housed twenty-two trading floors, making it the second tallest skyscraper in all of Hong Kong.

Both were designed by his good friend, Cesar Pelli, and he

loved that, together, they offered everything from an exhibition area devoted to Hong Kong's monetary history, to several global financial institutions, to a host of double-deck elevators, to a concierge serving all its tenants. He also loved that the developers chose not to allow the buildings to carry the name of any of their marquee occupants or have any floors ending in the number 'four,' since in Cantonese and Chinese, the word for that digit sounds remarkably like the word for 'death.'

Which brought the architect back to the murder of Jocelyn Cheng. By pinpointing who killed her, he knew they could easily (if not comfortably) 'encourage' that person to tell them where the microwave systems were now located and stave off the personal suffering and political tumult that *O* was preparing to inflict.

As if he had been reading Lee's mind from afar, Kip Silva that very moment sent the architect a telling message: 'We've thoroughly searched Zhuhai Park. No microwave equipment. However, just got word Alex Wentworth says she's now ready to confess to something. Will let you know when we have a meeting with her scheduled.'

Well, that's interesting, Lee told himself. *However, Kip said she was prepared to confess to 'something,' not, 'a murder.'*

His finger flew across his phone's keyboard: 'What's the plan regarding Jocelyn Cheng and Regina Bauer? Do we confront them about their contradictory stories?'

Lee had to wait a couple of minutes for a reply. Finally, it came: 'Still figuring that out.'

He was about to put the phone back in his pocket when it started to buzz.

"Where are you RIGHT NOW, DALTON?" Lee smiled, glanced toward the nearest street sign.

"Um, somewhere on Finance Street. Where are *you*, Julian?" In the background, Lee heard a loud whoosh, followed by several clicks and clacks.

"I'm getting my car washed," Julian shouted. "Hey, my snake charmer friend told me to tell you she thinks you are incredibly handsome. I told her that was too bad because I have already claimed you."

Lee chuckled and felt himself flushing. "Well, thank you, Julian but I don't think I'm really available to anyone right now. (*Except maybe Anisa,* he thought, *and we know how unlikely it is that will be going anywhere, anytime soon.*)"

He heard Julian sigh above the sounds of the car wash. "That's too bad," the security executive replied. "Hey, I was calling to see if Zhuhai Park yielded anything?"

"Unfortunately, no. But thank you for the suggestion, Julian. It made perfect sense at the time."

"Well. I'm trying my best." He sighed once more, a sigh more noticeable as the noises made by water blasts and high-intensity vacuums seemed to be subsiding. "Are you available for a drink soon? You sound like you could use a little getaway from all the clamor of the case and all? Tomorrow sometime? My treat?"

Lee didn't really feel like he had the time to relax right now, but he had a hard time resisting Julian's warm invitation. "Sure," he said. "Text me where and when and I'll meet you. But, Julian, only one drink. I need to stay alert as I can for whatever is about to unfold."

"Understood," Julian answered. "I'll send some details soon. *Ciao, mio caro.*"

Lee muted his phone and shoved it into a front pocket. His stroll became more of an amble. The clouds had expanded to engulf the sun altogether, casting a gray and quiet calm across the harbor and Hong Kong's spectacular skyline.

Still, the world's most prominent architect felt oddly emboldened. Something Julian mentioned during their conversation reminded Lee of a little research he needed to conduct. Research into a topic that had been gnawing on him for a few days now.

A little research he believed could very well break open the case and identify exactly who it was that had killed Jocelyn Cheng.

40

The world's most prominent architect decided he wanted to take in a quick sauna at the hotel before heading off to dinner. He needed to sort through all the information and misinformation that had landed in his lap over the past several days. So, when he arrived at the sauna, he was secretly delighted to find it unoccupied.

Which reminded him that it had seemed to him over the past week or so that the entire hotel had grown much quieter for some reason.

Once the door closed behind him, he picked up a long-handled ladle sitting in a bucket of water just inside the door. Scooped some water onto it, then poured the liquid over a pile of black lava stones that rested in a horizontal trough a couple of feet away. He then repeated the steps, just to be sure he generated the amount of steam that he desired.

Enough steam to shroud him entirely as he sat in contemplation on the sauna's top row.

After taking his seat, he pulled tighter around him the large towel he was wearing, reclined his upper torso against the wall behind him, tilted his head back and took in the billowing vapor, which filled his lungs with the soothing scent of eucalyptus.

His body was relaxing, but his mind was racing. With the cryptic comments from the fire extinguisher that he had conversed with on his walk. With the contradictory statements from women who, in fact, seemed to be conspiring with one another.

With that wisp of a theory he was developing as to who might have done in Jocelyn Cheng.

Like the steam, those thoughts and several others swirled around him to the point that he found himself on the verge of drifting off.

And then the door swung open, and the towering figure of Liam came charging into the cubicle.

"Oh, sorry boss, I didn't realize you were in here," he proclaimed as the sauna door slammed behind him. "You want to be alone? I can come back if you want."

Lee smiled weakly and shook his head.

"No, Liam, it's fine," he replied. "However . . ."

Liam waited expectantly. "Yes, Dalton?"

"I think it's customary in better hotels to wear a towel in the sauna. Or swim trunks. *Anything.*"

Liam glanced down at himself, ducked his head sheepishly.

"Crikey, it is? My bad. We're more cazh about that sort of thing back home." He swerved around, bolted out the door, then returned a couple moments later, swaddled from just below his chest to just below his knees.

"Better?" he asked. Lee nodded and, with an outstretched arm, invited his young associate to take a seat on the tier below him.

They sat in silence for some time, the steam enveloping them the way a dense fog might overtake a small, secluded valley. After a while, Lee shifted and cleared his throat.

"So, Liam, what plans do you and Anisa have?"

The lava rocks on the other side of the cubicle gave off a long soft hiss.

"Plans?"

Lee issued a discreet smile, knowing Liam could not see it.

"I know you probably haven't noticed, but *I've* noticed you and Anisa becoming somewhat of an . . . item?" he said. "You've started sitting beside one another at our meetings and I've seen how she looks at you, and you look at her, when the other is speaking."

"Oh, you mean *those* types of plans."

The architect found that a curious response but decided to press on with the point he wanted to make. He shifted his weight and once again breathed in the menthol air.

"Anyway, I just wanted the two of you to know that whatever your plans are, you have my blessing. Not that you need it, of course. I just thought you'd appreciate knowing that any feelings I had for Anisa are now . . . muted. So long as your relationship doesn't interfere with our work, it's fine. I'd even go so far as to say I'm very happy for the two of you.

"Really, I am."

The sauna remained quiet for a couple of moments. Eventually, Liam replied, "Okay, thanks."

"I just want the two of you to feel comfortable being open about your . . . situation."

Liam just nodded at Lee, squinting some as he did. "Okay, thanks," he repeated.

No one said anything for a few minutes more. Lee silently wished his young employee would vacate the sauna so the architect could think about the case . . . and the rest of his life. But he wasn't about to come right out and ask him to.

After a time, the steam began to evaporate to where they could more easily make out one another's forms. Liam shifted and looked up at his superior. "Now, can I ask *you* a question, Dalton?"

"Of course, Liam. Shoot."

The Aussie glanced down at the wooden slats that comprised the floor of the sauna, then looked back up at Lee. "That swim cap, or whatever it is you're wearing."

Discreetly, Lee allowed his left hand to trail upward and touch the latex cap pulled tightly over his head.

"Yes, what about it?"

"Well, I mean, we're in a hot sauna, and there's no pool nearby. So, what's that about? And the beret, and the golf cap and the beanie and the newsboy cap and all the other hats you've been wearing since we got here. What's . . . their point?" Sensing he may have crossed some sort of line, Liam again assumed a sheepish look and shifted his eyes from Lee's face to a point just below the architect's knees.

"I mean, I was just sort of wondering, that's all. It seems a little . . . daft?"

Lee sniffed and affected a tight grin. Bent forward and anchored his elbows upon his thighs. "Well, Liam, you see it's . . . it's really just that . . . um . . ."

Suddenly, the world's most prominent architect felt as if he were in an elevator whose cables had just snapped and whose car was now plummeting to the basement. His chest tightened, his body chilled, and he began to chew his upper lip. He blew out several shallow breaths and gripped the edge of his seat to the point his knuckles turned beet red.

"It's just that um . . . I . . . uh . . . well, you see, Liam, it's the fact that I have, um . . . I have . . . a brain tumor. It's fairly small, I'm told, and we think we probably caught it in time but who the hell knows when it comes to a tumor, right, since it could start growing or metastasizing whenever it wants to and I really shouldn't be bothering you with all this because it's really my job to be taking care of all of you and focusing instead on finding and bringing back all of your loved ones but I think maybe I haven't been processing all of this as well as I should be and that I've been wearing all these hats because in some small way I think they'll protect me somehow, or stop the tumor from growing, or maybe if I keep the damn thing covered all the time it will shrivel up and die the way a plant does when it doesn't get enough sunlight, or something else stupid like that. And maybe it's bothering me because I've always had to rely on my brain to get by, on my intellect, and the possibility of losing my faculties, my one chief advantage, scares the hell out of me, more than the reality of dying does, and so you know, I haven't told anyone else about this, Liam, not even Lara, so I'd appreciate you not saying anything, not yet anyway, at least not until . . ."

His chest was heaving now, and he was bent forward at the waist, staring intently at the floor of the sauna. Slowly, he raised both hands to his head and cupped the back of the swim cap.

"Not until . . . we absolutely have to."

For several minutes he remained hunched over, head down, looking as if he were about to throw up. Over time, however, his breathing returned to normal, and he slowly slid his hands from the back of his head to a place just above his knees.

"When did you learn all this, Dalton?"

Lee chewed the inside of one cheek, pushed his head further toward the floor.

"I had an MRI done when we were in London," he said softly. "I'd been experiencing some . . . some symptoms . . . for a year or two, and so my physician back in the States recommended it. I really didn't think much would come of it, but then the results came back, and . . ."

Liam waited, then decided not to wait any longer.

"And you've been carrying this around inside of you ever since."

Lee moistened his lips and nodded, almost imperceptibly.

His young employee anchored his hands firmly against his upper legs and pushed himself to stand. Looked down at his boss for several seconds, then ambled over until he was standing just a few inches in front of him. Bent over, reached out with both arms and brought Lee firmly into his embrace. Not the passionate embrace of a lover, nor the perfunctory embrace offered by some distant relative at a holiday gathering. But a firm, controlled, commanding embrace that radiated commitment, reliability, resilience and resolve.

"We are there for you, Dalton, *no matter what*," he whispered into the architect's ear. "I promise you that we are with you now and we'll be with you and take care of you however you need us to."

He held Lee tightly for several second more, as if to emphasize those points. When he finally felt all the tension drain from the architect's body, Liam released his hug, straightened his torso, gave his boss a beneficent smile and placed a strong hand on Lee's right shoulder.

"She'll be right, mate," he reassured Lee. "No frets about that."

Lee looked up at the towering young Aussie.

"You're referring to Anisa."

Liam chuckled once and shook his head.

"No, Dalton," he answered. "I'm referring to you." He then backed toward the door, nudged it open with the lower half of his body and left Lee sitting by himself in the thin eucalyptus haze. The door to the cubicle came to a swift, definitive close.

When it did, the world's most prominent architect put his face into his hands.

And, at long last, allowed himself to weep.

41

His first inclination was to order dinner in. Or maybe, hide behind a newspaper in some discreet banquette in the hotel's four-star restaurant.

Instead, Dalton Lee decided to duck out of the hotel and stroll over to Chez Toulouse, which was fortunately just a few blocks away. He was happy to see that the establishment was quiet, almost empty. The gentle but steady mist outside, along with the fact it was early in the week, probably had deterred a lot of diners from coming out, he decided.

He was struck by a mix of stunning aromas the minute he stepped through the door. A mélange of rosemary, lavender and tarragon swirled around him, transporting him to a small café he had once patronized just outside the seaside town of Argelès-sur-Mer. He thought he might stay and have an entrecôte with merlot butter, or a simple roast duck accented with cassis. But he was not really here for the food. He was here to collect some data. So, it was more likely he'd just end up having a cheeseburger at the fast-food emporium around the corner.

A young woman, dressed all in black and wearing a large turquoise necklace, stepped around a partition and approached him.

"May I help you?" she asked. "Table for one or two?"

The architect ducked his head to one side. "Actually . . . I have a question to ask you," he replied. "I might dine here tonight, but right now, I'm more interested in a canceled reservation." He became briefly distracted by a server flying past with a tray crammed with extraordinary parfaits.

"Sorry. A cancellation, did you say?"

Lee turned his attention back to the woman who had greeted him.

"Um, yes. You see, I could have sworn I phoned here a couple of weeks ago and made a reservation. For two. My guest arrived and I never showed up thanks to a flat tire. Anyway, the greeter–it wasn't you, I want to be very clear that I am NOT blaming you–this greeter told my guest there wasn't a reservation on the books under my name. And I just can't believe that because I'm absolutely certain I made a reservation. Anyway, I was in the neighborhood tonight, so I thought I'd just drop in to see if we got our wires crossed or if I was just losing my mind."

The young woman fidgeted with her necklace some and looked confused, but nodded as if she were not. "Okay," she said, turning to a large tablet computer perched on the lectern beside her. "For which date did you make the reservation?"

Lee gulped once, looked to the ceiling, calculated in his head and delivered the date he hoped was the one he had seen in Jocelyn Cheng's appointment calendar. The greeter scrolled through several screens, giving him a cynical glance now and then as she did. Eventually, she came to the calendar devoted to the date he'd given her.

"And the name?" she said, brightening some.

Lee smiled back at her and nodded. "Cheng," he said. "It should be under Cheng. Maybe J. Cheng, or maybe just Cheng."

The young woman looked confused again but placed a finger at the bottom of the screen and slowly scrolled up through the list of names. Lee couldn't help but notice that her nail polish was a shade of green that clashed with her turquoise necklace, and that she appeared to bite her nails rather than trim them.

Just then, an older man ducked his head around the partition and uttered to her in Cantonese what sounded to Lee like some sort of ultimatum. She nodded at the elder, who retreated from wherever he came.

"I'm very sorry, can you wait just a moment?" she said with a weak grin. "I need to tend to an emergency. I will be right back. Again, I'm so very sorry. This should only take a moment."

"Of course. Take whatever time you need," Lee answered, raising up onto his toes then back down on his heels as she squeezed around the partition. Once the greeter was safely out of sight, however, he craned his neck to review the list of names on the screen in front of him. He first noted that, indeed, there was no reservation under the name of Cheng listed for that particular day. Then he saw there were a couple of reservations under family names he had encountered since he'd arrived in the region, but they were fairly common names, so he considered that par for the course.

After all, there are more than seven million people in Hong Kong, he reminded himself.

His reconnaissance mission had gone more smoothly than he expected it would. His objective achieved, he ran one finger around the brim of the brown felt Trilby he was wearing, did a quick one-eighty and dashed back out the front door before the greeter could return.

42

"So, you're prepared to confess to the murder of Jocelyn Cheng, is that right?"

Kip Silva was almost gleeful as he asked the question of Alexandra Wentworth. The Canadian woman wore a simple gray smock no doubt issued to her by the Macau Correctional Services along with sensible off-white sneakers. She had a look on her face that said, 'Here I am, once again, in a bleak interview room with a couple of investigators staring me down.'

But shortly after Silva finished his query, she furrowed her forehead some as she tried to decipher what he had just said. Then, she slammed both palms on the table in front of her.

"Wait, no!" she replied. "I told you, I didn't kill Jocelyn. I'm not confessing to that at all!"

Dalton Lee cocked his head to one side, and Kip Silva removed the lollipop from his mouth and tossed it into a nearby trash can. A portly guard with his hands crossed in front of him stepped forward and caught Silva's eye to see if his colleague wanted him to intervene. But Silva glanced up and shook his head once. The guard shuffled back then leaned casually against the cinder block wall behind him.

"So, what ARE you confessing to?" Silva asked her. Lee found it unusual that someone who had been sitting in a holding cell for almost a week looked more scrubbed and alert than she did when they last interviewed her.

"We have a deal, right?" was her reply. "I get to go free if I confess to . . . um . . . a lesser crime?"

This was all news to Lee, who had taken the first morning helicopter over from Hong Kong Island right after Silva had summoned him with a text that said: 'BETTER GET HERE QUICK.'

"What's the lesser crime?" Silva responded. "And do we understand that you are waiving your right to counsel here?" She nodded that she was.

Alexandra Wentworth rolled her eyes and sighed. "Hell, I don't really know what the legal term for my crime is. Embezzlement, I guess? Conspiracy to defraud. Something like that, I guess."

Lee cocked his head to the other side. He was playing nonchalant, so she'd be less suspicious of him recording the conversation on his phone. Which he was. He wanted to document what she said, word for word, so he could listen to it later on.

"Go on," Silva urged.

She dropped her head for a moment then brought it back up abruptly.

"All right. We've been skimming money from the Lucky Fortune Casino. Rigging the tables. Making it so the balls landed where they weren't supposed to or so the dice rolled differently than they were supposed to. We skimmed a reasonable amount of the profits for ourselves. Not millions but in the hundreds of thousands. Deposited the proceeds in a couple of bank accounts we'd set up in Switzerland and the Cayman Islands.

"I admit to that. All of that."

The confession dangled out there for several seconds. Alexandra Wentworth now wore an expression that was two parts defiant, one part relief.

"Whom, exactly, are you referring to when you say, 'we'?" Silva asked. Lee had a vague idea of the names she was about to utter, and she proved him right on all counts.

"The croupier at the roulette table, another two at the craps tables, and that ill-mannered server, Ramona, Roberta, something like that."

"Regina? You mean Regina Bauer." She nodded, glanced up at the ceiling.

"But to be clear, I wasn't the mastermind of it all. Jacquelyn was."

Lee thrust himself forward, couldn't stop himself. "Jacquelyn Cheng? Jocelyn's sister?" Silva glanced at him, a bit shocked by his outburst, but said nothing.

"Oh, yes, her dear, sweet, innocent little sister." She gave them an 'are you kidding me' look, then added, "NOT!" She stared at Kip Silva's tie for a minute or two before continuing. "She came up with this grand plan to get back at the sister she'd hated all of her life. Recruited the server and even coached her what to do in Jocelyn's suite when big sister was away. The server then got the croupier involved and the other croupiers worked behind the scenes to manipulate outcomes when they weren't actually staffing a table."

At this point, the blond who had traded a velvet pantsuit for a prison jumpsuit took on a smug expression. "I spotted a mark the minute I met Jocelyn on that cruise," she said. "I knew she was much too trusting and nowhere near the savvy executive she considered herself to be. Lucky for me, her sister felt the same way."

Silva and Lee exchanged looks. Then the head of the police force sat up straight and assumed a more magisterial air.

"So, you insist you didn't kill Jocelyn. Did one of the others? Did Jocelyn discover what was going on and threaten you or any of them in any way?" He paused dramatically, then added, "I could possibly get your sentence reduced if you had any information to that effect that you'd be willing to share with us."

She studied him for a few seconds then took on a sly, almost evil grin.

"If memory serves me right, Kip Silva" she sneered, "you're the detective here, not me."

***

A bright, hot, late-afternoon sun had burst through the clouds that had blanketed the region throughout the day. So, Lee was glad that

Julian had suggested a dark, cozy bar not far from the Macau police headquarters for their happy-hour rendezvous. He had been unnerved by Alexandra Wentworth's story. More concerning to him, though, was the fact that her revelation of the web of deceit that she, Regina Bauer, the croupiers and Jacquelyn Cheng had been engaged in had really brought them no closer to knowing who had slain Jocelyn Cheng. Or whether any of them (or all of them) were members of 'O.'

Or where O had stored its microwave arsenal.

"You look weary, Dalton, what do you want to drink?" Julian asked as the architect sunk onto the plush leather love seat across from him. The bar had just opened, so there was hardly anyone else in the establishment, save for a few die-hard regulars who occupied the tall stools at the bar across from them. "And like I said on the call, this is on me," the security consultant added. "I'm feeling badly for all the bum advice I've given you since you've been here."

Lee spent a few minutes filling Julian in on Alexandra Wentworth's confession and the details of the embezzlement scheme she and her cohorts had been engaged in. The security professional shook his head non-stop as Lee related the story; his eyes grew larger and larger, and his mouth grew rounder and rounder.

"That's just stunning," Julian exclaimed once Dalton's story had run its course. "Absolutely stunning." He paused, then turned a bit sad. "But it just confirms what I've been thinking, which is that I am completely out of my league these days. I mean, it never even dawned on me that sort of trickery might be taking place." He looked far away from their table and shook his head in bewilderment.

Lee sniffed once and smiled. "Julian, I've appreciated your counsel and companionship immensely," he countered. "If anything, you've been a great escape valve for me during this investigation."

Julian chuckled at that, but his tone quickly turned serious.

"Well, I'm pleased I've been able to keep you entertained," he said, "but no, really, all my miscues have only convinced me that it's probably time I hang things up for good. And I'm fine about it, truly I am. I'm not getting the new clients here I had hoped for and . . . well . . . let's just say my enthusiasm for investigation and security assessments has diminished considerably." His eyes trailed off again to some distant nook of the darkly lit room."

Lee let the comment suspend in the air for some time before asking, "So what will you do, Julian? Will you stay here?"

The security consultant quickly shook his head. "No, I don't think so. Jocelyn's murder, all the tension here in the region, it's all soured me on a place I used to adore." He chewed the inside of one cheek for a moment, then added, "But as for where I'll go, to be honest, I'm not really sure. Bora Bora, maybe. The Maldives, perhaps. The eastern seaboard of Thailand is nice." Lee nodded and dwelled on how enticing all those places sounded to him right now.

"And what about you, Dalton? I know you still have half your career left, but the time will come when you'll want to wind things down. Where do you want to settle?"

A male server in a dark vest, white dress shirt and gray plaid slacks arrived to take their orders. Lee asked for a Buffalo Trace bourbon neat, while Julian requested that the bartender surprise him with some form of mocktail made from a variety of tropical fruits. "Only not papaya," he cautioned. "I cannot abide papaya." Lee chuckled some, but once the server had departed, he became wistful.

"Oh, I guess I have my eye on a little corner of the Lake District," he replied with a sigh. "Who knows, maybe I'll become a shepherd or a park ranger."

Julian let out a quick guffaw, then became mellow as well. "Ah, the Lake District. Cumbria. A lot of tourists at times, but a lovely choice, I must say." He leaned toward his companion and gave him a sly wink. "I would certainly consider joining you there. If an invitation were extended."

Lee smiled broadly, leaned forward, patted the hand Julian had resting on his left knee, then pushed himself back into the love seat. "We would make quite a pair in our elder years, wouldn't we, my friend?"

They held a gaze for a few seconds before Lee broke the reverie by coughing into his right fist.

"So, the case, Julian. Any more ideas about it? About who murdered Jocelyn, or where the microwave equipment might be? To be honest, I don't think we've got much more time to spare."

The server returned with their drinks. Julian took a quick sip of his, brightened and gave the waiter a thumb up. Then he turned back to Lee, and his mood became morose.

"I'm sorry to disappoint you, Dalton, but I'm afraid I'm out of ideas. I mean, I strongly suspect the murderer is nested somewhere within that sorority of conspirators who were embezzling money from the casino. But I'm not confident even they are aware of the killer among them. O doesn't like the identity of its assassins being all that well-known, know what I mean?

Lee nodded, took a sip of his bourbon. "I do," he replied, lifting his glass as a signal of his agreement.

Julian lifted his mocktail in response, his expression turned grave. "Dearest Dalton, my best guess is that one of those four women is most certainly the person who murdered Jocelyn," he intoned.

"But as for which one administered the poison, I, at this point, haven't a clue."

43

"So, sir, do you want me to sing a little ditty, or dance a little jig?"

Dalton Lee was standing with his arms crossed in front of him, in one of the darkest corners inside Dragon Lodge. He looked the busker up and down, glanced toward the front entrance of Hong Kong's most haunted house.

"No," he said quietly but firmly. "I don't want you to do anything. No singing, no dancing, no playing of any instruments. We don't want to call attention to ourselves. That's why I had you wear that jumpsuit and hoodie outfit on the way over here. To keep all this under the radar. And, so no one might think you were the person who should be arriving here any moment now."

The musician fell quiet. Put weight first on one foot, then shifted it to the other. Studied the cracks in the ceiling and the shards of plaster that littered the floor around them. In some other room, a drip beat a steady cadence. And every so often, the stench of sulfur drifted past them. Dalton Lee almost wished there was some force of wind outside, for the complete and utter stillness beyond the mansion's walls just made their circumstance feel that much creepier.

"If I do say so myself," the busker whispered, "you sure chose a strange place for this transaction."

Lee sniffed once, kept his arms tight around him.

"You are right, my friend. Strange is most definitely the word for it. The first owner of this place went bankrupt. The next owner died here, close to where you're standing, I believe." At that, the musician did a little hop, which prompted a chuckle out of Lee given that particular detail was one he had made up on the spot. "They say Japanese soldiers decapitated a group of Catholic nuns here during World War II. And construction crews won't come near the place because they keep hearing the cries of a mournful child they never actually see.

"So, yes, I'd say strange would definitely be an accurate way to describe it."

The busker raised both eyebrows but said nothing, then slowly turned away from the architect and began to inspect the decaying interior even more closely.

Meanwhile, Lee peered out the window nearest him in hopes of seeing headlights or a rickshaw–*anything* that might be bringing their visitor to the lodge. He was ready for this to be over with, and he wasn't entirely confidant his plan was going to succeed.

At that moment, he heard some form of shuffling headed their way from one of the other rooms. He couldn't see anyone, but there was the distinct sound of someone padding or straggling toward them. The noise continued for several seconds. Then, Lee finally made out in the dimness a medium-sized porcupine waddling into the room from the foyer beyond.

"Well, would you look at that!" the busker exclaimed. "A *jiànzhū!* Who'd have thought you'd come upon one here?" At the busker's outburst, the animal stopped and turned its head in their direction. Lee worried the busker might coax the porcupine to come over to them or, worse yet, try to pet it.

"Don't move!" he barked, more sharply than he had intended. He lowered his volume by half and added, "We don't want to agitate him. Or her. Whatever its gender."

It was too late. The porcupine stiffened its quills and launched a pungent secretion of urine into the air around it. The pair were far enough away to avoid the ejaculation but were quickly assaulted by the fluid's fetid smell.

"Ugh," the musician moaned.

Lee just nodded back, as he thrust his forearms upward in a futile attempt to block the scent from entering his nostrils. They said nothing and did nothing for several moments, unsure as to whether they should remain in place to remain discreet or bolt the lodge in search of fresh air. To their relief, the animal slowly began to turn around, resembling in the process a bulky steamship trying to reverse course in an unusually narrow inlet. Finally, the rodent began to bob and weave a path in the opposite direction, making the same shuffling and scratching noises it had made when it had arrived.

Once the animal's aroma had abated, the musician turned to Lee. "I may need some additional combat pay for this assignment, sir." he said.

"Understood," was all the architect could muster from behind his forearms.

A shaft of moonlight suddenly entered a window on the opposite side of the room. The beam put a spotlight on a tattered mattress resting on one side next to a dresser that lacked any drawers. Graffiti in several languages blanketed the wall behind the furnishings; the drip (which the porcupine had made them forget) resumed its Chinese-water-torture rhythm.

"By the way, how am I dressed?" the busker asked. "Did I do right by your instructions?"

Lee smiled. "You did fine. Exactly what I requested. Under that jumpsuit, all in gray, no accessories of any kind, perfect actually." He paused to peer out the nearest window once more. "I only hope our guest followed my directions as well as you did and purchased the exact same items from the store I sent you to."

The drip stopped, was immediately replaced by a scuffing noise of shoes on gravel. The grating continued for a few seconds then went away when the shoes landed on solid flooring.

"Hello, Dalton. Nice place you've got here."

"Ah! You've arrived. Did you walk?"

"At my advanced age? You must be joking. No, I took a bus to the bottom of the hill. A nice but very nervous taxi driver brought me the rest of the way up. I guess I shouldn't have been surprised by his reluctance. Most drivers aren't too keen on bringing someone to a haunted mansion, I suppose."

"But I didn't see any headlights. Did they follow you?"

"Oh, I'm sure of it. And I instructed the driver to turn off the lights as he approached. Fortunately, he was driving an electric vehicle, so there was almost no engine noise whatsoever. Amazing, that technology." Lee's confidant stepped toward the pair, gave the busker the once-over.

"I have to say Dalton, the likeness is uncanny. The height, the hair color . . . how did you find such a doppelganger?"

Lee sniffed once. "It was kismet, I guess."

"Remarkable facsimile," the musician chimed in. "Truly remarkable it is."

The confidant breathed in deeply. "Well, can we get this little transfer over with? I'm eager to shake off these shackles that have confined me for so long."

"Not yet," Lee replied. "We need to make this look as authentic as possible. Whenever you and I have met, we've spent what, twenty , thirty minutes together? Maybe more?"

The confidant nodded. "Yes. Good point. If I left here too quickly, they might get suspicious. We most definitely need to be sure they think they see 'me' leave here. But only after an adequate amount of time, I suppose."

The three went quiet for some time. Their guest sniffed and made a sour face. "It smells like porcupine piss in here." The busker cackled once before Lee put a finger to his lips with the hope of preventing another outburst.

"Can we please talk about something else?" the architect implored.

"Like what?" the confidant asked.

"I brought my harmonica," the busker suggested.

Lee quickly raised his right palm. "No thank you! As I said, no instruments." The musician's expression sagged, and the harmonica returned to its place of hiding.

After a minute or two, Lee said, "Why don't we talk about microwave equipment. Yes, let's most definitely talk about microwave equipment. Where it's stored, how soon it's going to be put into use." He paused for dramatic effect then added, "Let's talk about those sorts of things, shall we?"

This time, it was the confidant who sniffed. "You're breaking our pact, Dalton, not that I'm all that surprised by that. I agreed to tell you anything you wanted to know . . . *except* the details of our . . . I mean, *their* . . . next initiative. I think we even linked pinkies on that, didn't we?"

There was a short pause, followed by, "Besides, I *can't* tell you that information because I don't know where they moved it or when they plan to start their little party. They don't share such specific details with me. All I know is that they've moved the systems to a very secure location. That the intensity of the microwaves they produce is very, very powerful. And that they are going to begin to use it to wreak havoc, very, very, *very* soon."

"Who's 'they'?" the busker asked. "What do you mean by 'havoc'? Are you saying I shouldn't be using my microwave to warm my meals?"

"Never mind," Lee replied. "What you don't know can't . . . destroy you."

Lee started tapping the heel of his right foot in agitation. "All right, then, just tell me this. Why did you, I mean, why did *they*, kill Jocelyn Cheng? What purpose did that serve?"

The confidant looked out the front window Lee had been gazing out of, then nodded definitively. "I suppose I can tell you that. The fact is, Dalton, she became a liability. She had been willing to host the equipment in that chamber we built onto her executive suite shortly after she joined the cause. In return, we laundered quite a bit of the cash the casino was generating, so it wouldn't have to be reported in their financial disclosures. It was a tidy arrangement for more than a year or so."

Those cash laundering escapades would probably be the 'activities' her former assistant somehow stumbled upon, Lee thought.

"Then, she changed her mind. Not so much about her commitment to the cause but about hosting all of the equipment. Claimed she'd feel more comfortable being just a financial supporter of ours rather than someone so intimately connected to the mechanics of what was to come. Then she became difficult when it came to our needing to access and remove the systems. She was either too consumed with work that

Murder Becomes Macau

week and couldn't be distracted, or she wasn't feeling well. There was always an excuse."

"We decided that we couldn't trust her. And that we couldn't wait much longer. So, we took the steps we always do whenever we need to remove an . . . obstacle . . . from our path."

"I see you're back to using the pronoun 'we,'" Lee noted. "Are you sure you're totally committed to this defection?"

The confidant appeared embarrassed by the comment. "Quite committed, Dalton. I couldn't be more so. My allegiance to the cause diminishes with each passing day. Each passing hour, actually. However, I am finding that it takes more effort than I thought it would to let go of the linguistics."

Lee nodded then let out a sigh, "Well, I hate to bring an end to our little chit chat, but I suppose it's time for *you* . . ." On that word, he turned and ducked his head in the direction of the busker. " . . . time for you, to go."

The entertainer raised one arm to the left shoulder, bowed and trudged toward the lodge's main entrance.

"Before you leave," Lee interjected, "you have the address of where our friend here is currently staying, correct?"

"I do, sir," the busker replied.

"And you're going to give that jumpsuit you wore over here to our friend, correct?

The musician put one finger in the air, then quickly unzipped the jumpsuit and stepped out of it. "Here you are, your majesty. For you to wear when you leave here with . . . 'my friend.'"

The confidant smiled. "Thank you. And you have the extra key to my flat that I had made for you, is that correct? And you know where to find the outfit you can change into once you're inside my flat? And the details on how to exit my building through a side door on the ground level. And the instructions on how to locate the car Dalton will have waiting for you a couple of blocks away, the car that will take you to wherever it is you want to go to continue living your busker life?"

"Thank you very much for all those details. Yes, I have them."

Lee and the confidant looked at one another, satisfied with the arrangement. "Well then, Godspeed," the confidant whispered. "And

245

don't forget that I limp slightly onto my right foot now and then."

Lee stole a look at his phone. "The cab I just called has arrived and is waiting for you at the bottom of the hill," Lee said to the busker. "Its license plate will have the numbers 5757 on it. Good luck."

The busker darted toward the door, stopped, turned back toward the pair, smiled meekly, then moved forward once more, limping this time on the appropriate foot.

Once the street entertainer was out of earshot, the confidant whispered, "I must say, Dalton, I feel rather optimistic about this. Our resemblance is impressive." Lee nodded his agreement but said nothing.

"Okay, let me put the jumpsuit on, and then we can go," his companion added.

As they trudged down the hill toward the car that awaited them, Lee took off his coat and draped it over his companion's shoulders so the limp would be less obvious. In case they were being shadowed and their deception was under scrutiny.

"Do you think Lara will forgive me, Dalton?" the confidant asked as the hired car came into view.

"I can't say for certain," he replied. "Perhaps, but perhaps not. Your retirement might usher in some new work you'll need to do on the personal front." As the world's most prominent architect opened the back passenger door, his long-time confidant patted him generously on the back.

"There's one thing I *can* say for certain, Dalton. And that is that I can't thank you enough for this. I now owe you everything." With that Lee's friend disappeared into the back seat of the car, which sped off into the ink-black night. As the sedan banked a curve at the bottom of the hill, the architect shoved his fists into the pockets of his slacks.

Well, he said to himself, *at least I've accomplished that.*

44

Late that night, clad in the sumptuous cashmere robe and slippers the hotel had provided him, Dalton Lee traipsed softly across the living room carpet toward the front door leading into his suite. He halted just a few inches from it, held his breath and listened intently.

He heard nothing.

Satisfied there was no one in the hallway, he raised his right hand and, as deftly as possible, turned the security lock so it bolted inside the jamb. Stopped, listened again, was pleased to still hear nothing except a soft whooshing sound through the hotel's air vents.

He then pivoted, tramped back into the living area and over to the window on the far side of the armchair. In one smooth move, he closed the drapes, wasting no time to see if there was anyone, or anything, either peculiar or arresting on the late-night sidewalks below. He then skittered behind the armchair, attended in the same way to the drapes on either side of the room's other street-facing window.

The room now shrouded from the outside, he shuffled over to the long worktable that was situated between the back of the armchair and the French doors leading to the suite's bedroom area. Like a sommelier handling an expensive goblet, he delicately lifted his tablet computer from one corner of the table and strode to the French doors on his right.

To some, this ritual may seem ridiculous, he noted. *But like the hats I've been wearing, it's a ritual I feel comfortable with. And, given the import of what I'm about to do, the more secretive I am about it, the better I'll feel about it.*

From there, the world's greatest architect and most reluctant detective nudged open with his hip one of the French doors. He edged his way into the bedroom, closed the door behind him, pressed one hand against it firmly to make certain it was secure.

He was satisfied that it was. Allowed himself to relax just a tad.

The sheers that graced the expansive window beyond his bed were drawn but the drapes were not. So, he rapidly brought those together as well and pivoted to dim the light emanating from the lamp on the nightstand closest to him.

Working solely by computer light might raise someone's suspicions, he thought.

He had some research to do, research brought on by the swirl of facts, sentiments, rules and relationships he had bumped up against over the past couple of weeks. He had an idea, but only a hint, a faint shadow, of one. It was time for him to shine a bright, perhaps even garish, light upon that idea. To see if what he sensed was a real true thing, or just the figment of one.

The lamplight was still too bright, he decided. So, he pulled the lamp cord toward him and dimmed the bulb even more by rotating with one thumb the serrated toggle wheel connected to it.

Perfect, he thought as he slid his legs beneath the bed's billowing duvet.

His phone buzzed, causing him to wince. It was Lara, asking if he wanted her to fetch him a grilled cheese sandwich from the hotel's lobby restaurant.

That's not really why she texted me, of course, he reminded himself. *The grilled cheese is a pretext to something else.* He paused, then added silently to himself, *A tempting pretext I must admit.*

He shot back a quick: 'No thank you. GOOD NIGHT, LARA,' then returned his attention to the computer. A sheaf of rain suddenly splattered across the nearby window, then stopped, then was followed by yet another, which landed harder than the first. He recalled hearing somewhere that a squall was to pass across the region during the evening. It wouldn't be severe and, he decided, it was actually a perfect soundtrack for the clandestine activity he was about to undertake.

First he logged onto a website that hosted people's work histories and places of employment over time. Spent a few minutes there and noticed a particular timeline he found interesting. But decided everything else he was curious about appeared to check out.

He reached for the pillow on the other side of the bed, plumped it, and shoved it behind his lower back to give him more support. Turned his attention back to the screen and launched an app on his desktop that enabled him to hack into the archived records of a variety of enterprises, from hotels, to restaurants, to casinos and more. It took several minutes for him to peruse all the data he had in front of him and for a time, it all roiled in front of him like a vast sea of meaningless nothing.

The vision of a perfectly executed grilled cheese sandwich started to gnaw on him, but he was too absorbed with his research to stop for a meal. He began to pound his keyboard like a pianist in the midst of a Rachmaninoff concerto, landing eventually on a private website that gave him entrance to a wealth of educational information. Who taught at what schools, who graduated from which universities, who had been the dean or president of most every academic institution, public or private. All across the world.

Fortunately, the site was expertly organized, and Lee had a very specific destination in mind. Almost out of breath, he navigated his way to the precise corner of the site he had in mind and started to scroll through all the text in front of him. First, through a list of schools and departments. Then, through certain years. Finally, he scanned the very long list of names that were in front of him.

He continued scrolling to the end of the list but did not see what he had come looking for. Scrolled rapidly back up through the list, but again had no success. He frowned, made himself work back through all the names one more time.

And then, he came upon it. Stumbled upon something he hadn't been expecting. Something he hadn't been expecting *at all*. He allowed his lower jaw to go slack at what appeared before him, read it three more times to make certain he understood it correctly. Slowly lifted his line of vision from the screen and then turned as another cloud of rain buffeted the bedroom window. Cupped his hands over his mouth, closed his eyes and fluttered his eyelashes some in order to compose himself.

Then he took one last, extended look at the evidence in front of him, the evidence that tied everything together for him into a neat, nefarious bow.

The evidence that, in his mind, clearly confirmed who it was that had murdered Jocelyn Cheng.

45

Dalton Lee was shaving when his phone began to shimmy and buzz with an almost ferocious intensity.

He frowned. He really needed to move quickly on what he had discovered during his research the night before. At the same time, he had just floated off into a delightful reverie, bewitched by the aroma of menthol that his shaving cream exuded and the melody of a childhood song that had just come to mind.

"The sun is like one big red flower, hanging on the edge of the Eastern sky," he murmured. *"He's shy in the red sky, a silent smile on his round face. But the sun goes back home when he is tired. Don't be afraid when you rest at night. The moon will set, and the sun will be back again tomorrow morning."*

He grabbed a facecloth, wiped off the excess lather from his hands and used one finger to both answer the call and put it on speaker.

"DALTON, where are you RIGHT NOW?" he heard the minute he pressed the answer prompt on his phone. "Wherever you are, turn on your television, NOW! It's starting!"

Julian's edge alarmed him.

"Okay," he barked. He ended the connection, dashed into his living quarters and punched the power button on the television remote.

The first image to appear was the broadcast of an animated show for children, so he jabbed the channel selector on the remote several times. Finally, a screen arrived, with a BREAKING NEWS banner in scarlet stretched along its lower third. A reporter with a worried expression was standing before the emergency entrance to a hospital and talking into his microphone in an agitated state.

Lee urgently increased the volume, then had to backtrack when the sound came on much too loud for the room.

"His condition is described as critical by the medical team here at Royal Britannia Hospital," the reporter announced, "which admitted him just about forty-five minutes ago."

The journalist paused to catch his breath, squinted, nodded in reaction to an instruction he had apparently just received over his earpiece, then barreled forward.

"Again, for those of you who are just joining us, the chief executive of the Macau Special Administrative Region, Tso Shi Ming, collapsed at home early this morning after complaining of severe nausea and vertigo along with an intense ringing in his ears. He was rushed here to Royal Britannia Hospital in an ambulance, where hospital officials report he is in a coma and non-responsive to doctors. They describe his condition . . ."

The reporter suddenly ducked his head and put the fingers of his right hand against his earpiece. His expression slid from serious to grave.

"I'm . . . I'm sorry," he said as he removed his hand from his ear. "I am very sorry to inform our viewers that I have just received word from the officials here at Royal Britannica Hospital that Macau's chief executive, Tso Shi Ming, passed away just about ten minutes ago."

Lee allowed his right arm to first go slack, then reach for the top of the armchair beside him. Once he found it, he gripped it tightly and pulled his upper lip over his upper row of teeth.

"Damn it!" he exclaimed, to everyone, and to no one in particular.

During the report, his phone had taken on the personality of a beehive, humming and quivering with a fierce intensity. He glanced at the log and saw he had text messages from Lara and Julian and a voice mail from Kip Silva.

From Lara: 'Let me know what you want me to do.'

From Julian: 'Call me when you can.'

He went into his voice mail to hear what Kip Silva had to say.

"Dalton, I assume you've heard the news about Tso Shi Ming," he began. "But I've also just gotten word that Taiwan's vice president has taken ill with many of the same symptoms. They've taken her to hospital as well." The timbre of Silva's voice was low, and it sounded as if his teeth were clenched. He added one more comment before ending the call.

"I can't believe it, but we may be too late."

Lee wasn't entirely sure why, but he had the urge to go to Liam's room. Perhaps, in the midst of chaos, he needed to feel the safe harbor he had felt when he had confessed his diagnosis to his youngest associate.

When Liam answered Lee's knock, his eyes grew large. "Oh, boss, come in, I'm sorry," he blurted. "I mean, the place is a wreck, as it usually is. I apologize." Lee put a palm up to calm the Australian, chose not to glance around the room.

"And, I'm sorry to bother you, Liam," he began. "it's just that O has launched their initiative." He pulled up, not sure what else to say. Then he did. "I guess I was thinking, hoping actually, that maybe you had ferreted out some sort of information, something, that might help us . . . stanch the bleeding, if you will. Anything?"

Liam looked at the carpet, scratched the back of his head. "I . . . I've really tried, Dalton," he replied. "But . . . " He looked up at his boss and shook his head.

Lee turned slowly toward the computer on his colleague's desk. Liam had been playing with the software he had been using to try to identify the locations of their loved ones. A few pulsating circles appeared here and there on the screen, like planes on an air controller's radar.

The architect's expression shifted from one of desperation to one of curiosity.

"Liam, how does that work?" he asked. "How does the software work?" The employee followed his boss's gaze toward the desk and frowned.

"Not as well as I had hoped," he said disconsolately.

"No," the architect said as he bounded toward the computer. "I didn't mean how *well* does it work. How does it work? Explain the engineering of it to me." Liam described how the software could pick up pings from different devices, particularly those whose technical specs he had programmed into the system.

Lee nodded. "Okay, but pings from what? What is it inside the devices exactly that's pinging the software."

"Well, every mobile device sends out little transmissions," Liam began. Mostly, transmissions of microwave activity."

His voice slowed as he pronounced the last two words of the sentence, and his mouth went slightly agape."

"Crikey, Dalton, are you thinking . . .?

Lee gave his associate a steely stare and raised both eyebrows.

"What I'm thinking, Liam, is that the first thing I need to do is get hold of Kip Silva to see if he has the technical specs for that equipment we found in Jocelyn Cheng's office suite.

He paused for just a moment, before adding, "The other thing I'm thinking is once we have that, you need to get to work."

46

By late that afternoon, three more Asian leaders had taken seriously ill. Two members of Hong Kong's legislative council were in critical condition at Prince of Wales Hospital. Before collapsing, both had complained to business associates or family members of severe vertigo and excruciating pain behind the eyes.

The third victim, Singapore's Deputy Prime Minister for Economic Policies, was found dead on the floor of his bedroom and therefore unable to express his symptoms to medical professionals. However, there was no indication the minister had experienced any form of respiratory or cardiac event, doctors said.

"Are you all right, Kip?" Lee barked into his phone. "How are *you* feeling right now?"

"I'm fine," Silva responded. "Thanks for your concern. I must say, everyone here–actually, everyone in Macau's government I've spoken to–is on high alert. I mean, I have no doubt they will ramp up their assault in the hours ahead."

Lee sighed heavily into the phone. "Well, I do have one of my associates doing everything possible to identify the location of the transmissions. I can't go into details, but he has this state-of-the-art software he's using. Is it at all possible we captured some of the technical specifications of those microwave systems in Jocelyn Cheng's suite?"

Silva sighed heavily. "You know we didn't, Dalton. It was gone before we had a chance to put our hands and eyes on it." Lee kicked at the carpet, until the superintendent-general eventually said, "Wait a minute. I don't have the technical specs, but I do remember seeing a brand name on the side of one of the servers. Terrecom 6500. One of the large antennas had the same logo. Can he work from that?"

"It's a start. I'll text it to him as soon as we're done."

The new lead didn't seem to buoy Silva's mood much. "There's something else, Dalton," he intoned.

Lee tilted his head and shut his eyes. "What is it?"

"It's not just the illnesses. I'm hearing rumors that some of the legislative bodies in the countries where people are falling ill are suddenly rushing to implement . . . well . . . changes to their constitutions. Enact amendments or other measures that will do such things as allow certain individuals–some of whom have been appointed to their positions not elected–to institute martial law. Impose widespread curfews. Form tribunals that can call up any citizen they want on any charge they dream up. It seems they've been planning this overthrow far longer than we realized, planting confederates into positions of power so when those they attack begin to fall . . ."

"Double damn it!" Lee exclaimed. A faint rap landed on his door. "I need to go, Kip. Will hit you back soon."

"WAIT! Before you go, Dalton . . ." The urgency in Kip's voice startled him. "Before you go . . . I have this hunch. It's totally out there, but . . ."

"Tell me."

"Do you have a pencil and paper?" Lee shuffled over to the hassock where he'd left the acrostic he'd been finishing up. He grabbed the pencil and tore off a corner of a page from inside the puzzle book.

"I do now. What do you have?"

He heard Silva take a breath in. "Ask your associate to see if he can pick up any unusual activity at a particular industrial estate over there on Hong Kong Island. It's in Tai Chik Sha."

"Okay, I will. But why there?"

Silva didn't say anything for a minute, held his breath long enough to cause Lee to worry.

"You still there, Kip?" he shouted. The rapping at the door resumed, more fervent than before.

"Yes, sorry, all's good. Ask him to explore the innovation park there. Its name is Tseung Kwan . . . O."

"I see. Okay, I will. Doesn't sound ridiculous at all." Lee jotted down the details Kip had given him and shoved them into his pants pocket. "And by coincidence, I have a hunch I need *you* to act on ASAP," he added. "I'll send it to you after we hang up. Gotta run, now. Someone needs me."

He clicked off the call then dashed to the door. When he opened it, he found Anisa's right fist elevated and in mid-knock. Liam stood just beside and behind her, wearing colorful board shorts and a purple singlet.

"Perfect. I'm glad you're here," he said to them. Liam and Anisa cast puzzling glances at each other, waited for Lee to continue. "Liam, we need you to research some microwave equipment that goes by the name Terrecom 6500. And then to check out this location." The architect snatched the jagged piece of paper from his pocket and thrust it toward the young Australian. "It's not in Macau, it's here in Hong Kong, on the mainland side."

Liam glanced at the paper then nodded several times. "Okay, I'm on it." He reached out and squeezed Anisa's arm. "You've got this," was all he said before turning and dashing down the hall toward his room.

Lee's face twisted into a mild scowl. "You've got what? What's Liam talking about?" He felt himself starting to flush with Anisa in the room, so he turned his back on her and moved as far to the other side of the room as possible. "What's been going on, Anisa? O is well into executing their plot and . . . well . . . sorry, but Warren thinks you might somehow be involved. Is that true? For god's sakes, if it's true, I need to know." He bit his lower lip, frustrated he had blurted out as much as he had.

"What? Wait, Warren thinks WHAT?"

Lee stayed quiet for a few beats. Decided he needed to defuse the situation. "Never mind," he said. "What did you need?"

Anisa's eyes bulged as she pondered whether to continue or storm out of the room. She decided to go with the first option.

"Okay, we'll deal with Warren and his outrageous accusations later," she began. She pressed her palms together, took a quick breath and stepped forward. Lee, noting her movement, took another couple of steps in the opposite direction. "Dalton do you remember my college friend from Berkeley, Kasuo? The one I recruited to take out the bomber when we were in London?"

Lee softened some. He had feared she had come to hear him offer his support for her romance with Liam.

"Yes. Of course, I remember him. What does he have to do with anything?"

"Well, let me put it this way. He received a package a couple of weeks ago. A package containing the foot of someone dear to him, someone with whom he played soccer with at Cal."

Lee lifted his head, felt a chill overtake the mild fever she had caused when she arrived. "And, let me guess, that close friend of his . . . has been taken hostage, I presume?"

Anisa was nodding but Lee didn't realize it given he was still turned away from her. "Is that right?" he asked, swiveling in her direction.

He was taken aback by the look on the face of his newest employee. Never had he seen beauty and vulnerability so majestically merged.

"Yes" she said. "So, he wants to join the team, Dalton. He *needs* to join the team. I've been telling him for weeks I didn't think it was the right time to broach the subject with you, or that you were even in the mood right now to take on another associate. But given how much he helped us in London, I was sort of hoping that . . . maybe . . ."

Lee scrunched his face. "I'm not entirely against the idea, Anisa. It's just . . . he's part of the diplomatic corps, isn't he? I understand his motivation for wanting to be a part of our *investigative* endeavors." He shook his head once. "But I'm not clear how he'd fit into our *architectural* endeavors."

A broad smile swept across Anisa's face. "He graduated summa cum laude from Cal's law and diplomacy program, Dalton. Who better to negotiate all the contracts for our commissions, hmm?"

Lee chuckled and shook his head, indicated with a nod of the head that she had a point.

"Can we let him join, Dalton? I've been keeping him dangling on this for about three weeks now."

"Yes, yes, of course Anisa. He can join. Put him in contact with Lara. She'll arrange all the details as she did with you." Lee outstretched his arms toward Anisa only a half-beat before she darted toward him and tumbled into his embrace.

"Thank you, Dalton," she whispered into his chest. "For that, and for accepting Liam and me and . . ."

"Don't push your luck," Lee interrupted, a tiny smirk on his lips.

She patted his chest with both palms, then pushed herself away from him and skipped toward the door. "I'm going to go see if I can help out Liam with that assignment you just gave him." She cocked both eyebrows, then added, "And probably have more than a few choice words with Warren." As the door was closing, she peeked through the narrowing crack and mouthed, "Thank you so very much."

When the door was shut, Lee stood in the center of the room, trying to maintain his balance.

"But of course, Anisa," he eventually said in the softest voice possible. "Whatever it takes to keep you on this team."

47

"So, how many people die so far?"

They sat on a bench beside the harbor, side by side, watching the sunset. With the Transformation underway, they couldn't risk meeting online. Yang Li, having completed her weaving project, played a word game on her phone. The others contemplated the solar phenomenon in front of them, as well as the answer to her question.

"Last I checked, about an hour ago, it was five or six," the American replied, his elbows on his knees and his chin in the palms of his hands. "But it's probably higher by now. Maybe up to ten."

"Not enough!" she spat, as her thumbs flew across the keyboard of her mobile phone.

The Brit sat erect on the bench, hands cupped on the back of his head, one ankle crossed over the other. "Now, Yang Li, I don't think it's appropriate to celebrate the deaths of these people. Don't forget, they have families, perhaps young children who will miss them. They aren't like our murder victims, who betrayed us somehow or interfered with our campaign.

"They didn't really choose their demise, the way those others did."

"Did so," she replied. "They chose to be part of the status quo. Chose to be persecutors. Chose to be supremacists. That make them just as bad as the others."

The Brit watched the sun sag closer to the horizon before responding to her comment.

"Now that I think about it, you're right, Yang Li," he said. "You're absolutely right. "In fact, they might actually deserve their torment even more than the others. They spent several years working to ascend to their authoritarian perches and have invested several more trying to hold onto them. No, you're dead on, Yang Li. They've accepted every opportunity to torture the working class, so why shouldn't they experience a little bit of torture themselves?" He uncrossed his ankles, then crossed them in the opposite direction. "Or maybe even, a lot of torture?"

The American sniffed, swept some dust off the top of his right shoe.

"There will be many more deaths, Yang Li, don't worry about that," he said softly. "At least another thirty or forty, if not more." He moved his attention to his left shoe for a time. Then added, "But the numbers don't really matter, because everyone who is dying a difficult death is being replaced almost immediately by someone else. Someone far more amenable to our way of thinking, of course. Someone more inclined to open up the floodgates that restrain the masses every single day from enjoying widespread, unadulterated freedom."

Yang Li stopped playing her game and peered down the bench at the American.

"Floodgates," she said with a nod. "Good word. I like that." She went back to her game, went back to fiddling with the keyboard on her phone.

"That word, and torture, too," she added.

48

Lee strolled into his bedroom, extracted his phone from his pants pocket and opened his messaging app: 'Julian. Are you okay? Checking in. Need to get away from all this, if only for an hour. Meet up in the morning?'

The security professional's reply was almost instantaneous: 'All good here. Yes, of course I can meet you! Where? When?'

Lee paused for a few seconds, then answered: 'How about a ride on the peak tram? The forecast calls for clear weather so our views should be awesome!'

There was no reply for almost a minute. Finally, one arrived: 'The Peak Tram it is! Meet you at the Central Terminus. Say about 9:00 a.m.?'

Lee agreed to Julian's time frame, then set his phone on the dresser nearby. Walked up to the bedroom's floor-to-ceiling window with its expansive view of the city and Victoria Harbor beyond. Tapped his thigh with the fingertips of his right hand.

Yes, getting some fresh air, and away from all the tension for an hour or so, would certainly do me a world of good, he said to himself. *Wouldn't that be nice?*

He then took the phone back out of his pocket and shot off to Kip

Silva the text he had promised during their call.

***

The forecasters had been spot-on. The sky was a luminescent blue and punctuated by only a smattering of fluffy white clouds. It was warm but not oppressively so. A trace of humidity hung in the air, but it was tempered by a genial breeze that floated in from the harbor. Even the streets seemed less tumultuous than usual, as if everyone in Hong Kong had gotten a memo saying the day was to be a day of nothing but calm and quiet.

In his reply to the text Lee had sent him the night before, Kip Silva relayed the fact that overnight, three more leaders in the region had taken ill. They included government officials in Vietnam and Cambodia, as well as a high-ranking industrialist in Guangzhou. The last of those took Lee by surprise.

That means O isn't even aligned with the Chinese government like I thought they might be, he told himself. *I guess their mindset really is, 'every nation for itself.'*

As Lee approached the tram's Central Terminus, a double-decker bus not unlike the one he had encountered several days earlier rumbled past him, then stopped. Like the first bus, it bore an advertisement on one side, but rather than the business's spokesperson being a cartoon character, this time it was a younger female of Chinese descent urging people to switch internet providers.

Lee braced himself for a conversation to begin. But instead of the woman uttering some critique of his clothing or gait, she nodded her head and discreetly winked at him. The bus then chugged forward, sending a few puffs of exhaust into the atmosphere as it departed.

The world's most prominent architect had a sneaking suspicion as to the meaning behind her understated communication. He decided that if he was correct, his interpretation gave him at least a modicum of comfort.

"Dalton, there you are!" Julian boomed from just outside the entrance to the station. The security professional was standing beside the *Eye of Infinity,* a contemporary sculpture he knew to have been created as a tribute to Hong Kong's 'spirit of ascent.'

Lee glanced at his phone. "Am I late?"

"No, no, not one bit," Julian replied, looping his left arm into the one on Lee's right. "I was worried you might have gotten here early and had gone inside. I rode over on the Maicoletta, and with it being early morning and all, I got here earlier than I expected."

The pair ambled through the station's street-level entrance. "I'll get our tickets," Julian said, dislodging himself from the architect. "Wait here. The queue is short, so it shouldn't take me more than a minute or so."

Those milling about represented a motley mix of tourists, students, executives and residents. Those with tickets on their phones plowed through the turnstiles and rushed toward the platform where a tram sat waiting. A few like Lee stood by patiently as a companion purchased their tickets at one of the machines in the foyer.

The architect was taken by how much the terminus had changed since the last time he had seen it. He calculated it had undergone at least two, and possibly three, upgrades since his most recent visit. Gone were the staircases that intimidated older patrons and thwarted those using a stroller or wheelchair. And the newest incarnation of the terminus paid tribute to its predecessors through a series of multimedia exhibits that showcased the tram's history from the Victorian Era to the present.

Once Julian escorted him through the turnstile, he found even more updates that surprised him. Next to the boarding area was a wraparound animated video that educated passengers on the wildlife they might encounter on Victoria Peak. And the tram cars themselves had morphed from the Chinese red that Lee remembered to a color that was closer to grass green. The cars had also increased in size to where one could now carry around 200 people.

"Isn't it fabulous?" Julian said as they settled onto their seats. "I heard they spent about HK$800 million on the refurbishing, and I think the results are fantastic."

The car was not quite full, so they were able to spread apart a bit. Nonetheless, Julian continually leaned over to clap a hand on Lee's shoulder or pat him on the back.

Soon they were on their way, making in just a few minutes a dizzying 396-meter ascent. Many in the tram soon began to rumble in awe, but Lee had prepared himself for The Peak Tram Illusion, an optical phenomenon that makes it appear as though the high-rises on one side of the tram are leaning at a harrowing angle. Lee was delighted that one of the most powerful memories of his childhood continued to entertain people some three decades later.

Julian leaned across once again and elbowed Lee in the side. "Look at how diverse the passengers are," he whispered. "Imagine what people who rode the tram in the early twentieth century would think, back when only British colonial officials and residents of the peak could sit in first class, and the non-residents and animals all had to stay in third class."

Lee smirked. "And a time when the first two seats in the tram were always reserved for the governor of Hong Kong and whoever accompanied him."

The tram pulled into the Kennedy Road station, lost a few riders and took on a few more. As the carriage started to continue its climb, Lee noticed a man in his thirties with a handlebar mustache staring at him from inside the station. The man dipped his head briefly; instead of react somehow to the man's gesture, Lee chose to turn away and stare out the opposite window.

"Oh, look. wild boars!" Julian exclaimed. He was pointing into the foliage located on his side of the tram. Lee could barely make out two medium-sized animals with dark coloring and pointed snouts rummaging through the greenery. "You know, I hear it's not that unusual these days to see a porcupine or two up here," Julian added.

"Thanks, but no porcupines, please," Lee insisted. Julian found the comment unusual but decided not to pursue it.

No one requested the tram stop at the MacDonnell Road station, so after slowing for a moment, the tram resumed its acceleration. But Lee noticed another male, this time in jockey attire, staring at him from the platform. The jockey raised his right hand in what came across as a half-hearted salute, then whirled around and walked toward the station's exit.

Once again, Lee chose to shift his attention to the scenery beyond the opposite window. Someone a few rows ahead of them coughed twice, then launched into a longer coughing spasm.

Julian studied his companion, took on a look of concern. "Are you okay, my friend? he asked. "You seem distracted. Even a little withdrawn. The stress of what's underway, I assume?"

Lee forced a smile and patted Julian on the knee.

"I'm fine, Julian. I think maybe I feel a little guilty that I'm here enjoying a beautiful sunny day on Victoria Peak when I should probably be busting my ass on the case."

Julian shook his head gently. "My friend, there's only so much we can do. But I understand how you feel. My heavens, Fan Chiu Chin, the vice president of Taiwan? I worked closely with her on a security project a few years ago. I'm told she likely won't survive what they did to her. Which is infuriating, because she has to be one of the most astute and visionary leaders I have ever collaborated with."

The tram whizzed through the May Road station. No one appeared to want the tram to stop at the Barker Road station, but as it neared the platform, Lee suddenly reached across his friend's torso and pressed the stop request button nearby. "Let's get off here, Julian," he suggested. "The peak will be much more crowded with tourists. It's glorious here, and we can speak more confidentially."

The pair were the only ones to disembark at the station, proving Lee's theory was correct. They sauntered along the concrete pathway that led from the quiet platform to the hairpin curve that redirected them back uphill. Their climb was heavily shaded by towering trees on both sides. But if they turned to their left, they could enjoy a bird's eye view of the majestic skyscrapers across Hong Kong Island. A retaining wall on their right narrowed the path some, and the sense of intimacy prompted Julian to grip Lee's arm once again.

"It's always good to be with you, Dalton," Julian said softly. "Even if the circumstances that have brought us together are less than ideal."

Lee peered through the trees at the silhouette of the sun, nodded, but did not respond.

They strolled for several meters more before the security professional nudged Lee in the ribs. "I hate to disrupt your reverie, but I'm curious. Any good news regarding the case? Any progress in identifying where *O* has installed the microwave equipment?"

Lee now looked at the pavement. "Perhaps," he answered. "Silva thinks it's most likely they moved it, overnight, to one of the industrial estates over here on Hong Kong Island. I'm not clear how they could have done that very easily–I'd think a convoy of trucks coming across the bridge at two in the morning would be somewhat suspect. But apparently not."

Julian stroked his chin. "My guess is he's thinking they've embedded it somewhere within Kwun Tong, San Po Kong or maybe Yuen Long. And, now that I think about it, that makes quite a bit of sense. All those zones have an abundance of empty warehouse space, and my understanding is they aren't as closely monitored as they'd like for you to believe. If *O* has installed an accomplice high up in the administration of whichever industrial zone they chose, that probably made the relocation of those assets go that much more smoothly."

Lee was nodding as Julian talked. He remained quiet for a few beats, then let out a soft sigh. "Well, I'm not really at liberty to share exactly where it is they think the systems got moved to." He waited, looked up at his companion and sent him a quick grin. "But what I can say, Julian, is that you may, or may not be, on the right track. No pun intended."

They reached the crest of the pathway, where it turned and spilled out onto Barker Road. From their location, their view in one direction of the cityscape and the harbor was almost entirely unobstructed. But the trees and the steep slope behind them mostly shielded them some from the occasional car or bicycle that traveled along the adjacent thoroughfare.

"Well, I wish I could be of more help, Dalton, but I'm afraid I am all out of hunches." He let out a long sigh and gazed out across the harbor. "And even if I had one, I wouldn't blame you at this point for heading off in the *opposite* direction."

Lee felt a pang of sympathy for someone who had tried so valiantly yet failed so miserably. He had an urge to pat his friend on the back but resisted it.

"Well, Julian, if we're able to shut down this campaign of theirs sooner rather than later, maybe we can share a celebratory glass of champagne once the situation has been all tidied up."

The security professional squinted at the sun and frowned.

"Sadly, I'm not confident I'll still be around then to join you, Dalton," he replied. "All the tumult of Jocelyn's murder, and O's horrible initiative here . . . it's done me in, my friend. I think I need a fresh start. Someplace different. Someplace exotic. In fact, I'm flying off to Honolulu next week to scope out some real estate on Maui. I'm thinking a more tropical climate might better suit my retirement."

"Really?" Lee said, poking the ground with the toe of his right shoe. He looked out to the street, where a motorcycle was whizzing by, then out to the harbor, where a flock of black kites were circling in the sky.

"Well, Julian, I hate to say this, but I'm afraid that's not going to happen."

"I'm sorry . . . what did you say?"

Lee continued to punch at the ground with his shoe, gouged a small divot with the intensity of his thrusts. "I said that's not going to happen, Julian. It's not going to happen, because you're about to be arrested for the murder of Jocelyn Cheng."

Julian erupted with a short, derisive laugh. "What on earth are you talking about? That's ridiculous. Of course I didn't kill Jocelyn. She was a dear friend of mine. You know that." The security professional tilted his head up to scan the sky and to survey the hillsides above them. "And what do you mean, I'm about to be arrested?"

Lee abruptly stopped digging at the ground, thrust both fists into his pockets.

"There are police now waiting for you up at the Peak Terminus, back down at the Central Terminus and at all of the four other stations in-between," Lee replied, glaring directly at Julian for the first time since they had exited the tram. "Not to mention just around the corner here." He softened his tone as he added. "It's no use, Julian. We know you murdered her. Now we just need you to help us stop O's plot by telling us where the microwave equipment is."

Julian scoffed once more, shook his head several times. But a slightly desperate tone began to dominate the timbre of his voice.

"Again, Dalton, this is absurd. What would possibly make you think I murdered Jocelyn?"

Lee pivoted his body so he could take in the extraordinary panorama in front of them. "I must say it took me some time to string together the beads," he said wistfully. "I thought it odd that someone who claimed to know Kip Silva so well kept referring to him as 'Ray,' the name he said no one who really knows him well actually uses. Then there were all of those hunches of yours that didn't turn out. Jocelyn's sorority friends and her former assistant. The microwave systems being moved to a storage site out on Macau. Even that printout of a conversation you claimed you overheard between two men at The Governor, which wasn't a real conversation at all, was it, but one you made up.

"None of those things were genuine but instead were feints, weren't they, meant to send us off in the wrong direction. To delay the investigation long enough for you and your cohorts to get your so-called transformation fully underway."

Julian continued to shake his head but said nothing.

"And then of course there was the notation on Jocelyn's appointment calendar for a lunch at Chez Toulouse with 'My sis, J.' That appointment wasn't with her biological sister, Jacquelyn, but with her soul sister, YOU–wasn't it, Julian? I dropped by Chez Toulouse a few nights ago and saw there never was a reservation made on that date under the name of Cheng, but there was one for someone named Lao, with a line drawn through it. I'm guessing you cancelled the reservation at the last minute and instead offered to bring lunch, as well as the spiked martini, to her suite. You were able to place the telltale note in her purse when she was distracted or left the room. Then, after the two of you had finished your meal, you left, took the empty martini glass–a martini glass from *your* bar set, not hers–and tossed it into the dumpster behind the casino. You understandably assumed sanitation would soon haul off that dumpster–along with the evidence that might incriminate you. But that didn't work out the way you hoped it would, did it, sanitation strike and all?

"And then there's all the furniture in her suite that had been repositioned to better hide the controls to the adjacent room. I couldn't understand why it was all so incongruous to how Jocelyn would have wanted it until I remembered the disdain you have for feng shui."

Julian now peered at Lee from beneath heavy eyelids.

"Oh, Dalton, that all sounds so very mystery theater," he intoned. "But you're overlooking one critical detail. You know very well the DNA they found on the glass indicated the murderer was female, not male."

Lee sniffed, then smiled, but quickly pulled the expression back in. "Ah, yes, that." He started again to poke at the ground with his shoe, then kicked a stone toward and over the slope just beyond Julian. "A few nights ago, I conducted a little sleuthing into the alumni records of some educational institutions in the region. Or, maybe I should say, one program at one educational institution in particular–the criminology program at the National University of Singapore you attended." Lee stopped to scratch behind one ear before continuing. "You know, it's funny, but their records didn't show any Julian Lao having graduated from there."

Julian cocked his head to the left. "Is that so?"

Lee nodded rapidly. "It is," he replied. "But they did show a *Julia* Lao having completed the program."

He waited a few breaths, then broadened his grin. "I assume it was during your assignment in Thailand that you began your transition? Maybe around the same time as that dancer friend of yours you introduced me to at Club Octavia?" He paused again before adding, "When you said you were *never* a man Jocelyn would be interested in, you meant that literally, didn't you?"

Julian shook his head gently from one side to the other but didn't respond for some time. Finally, he wet his lips and stared directly at Lee. "That's all very shrewd of you, Dalton. Quite shrewd, I must say, Only, you're nowhere near as shrewd as you think you are. The fact is, Jocelyn betrayed us. We had a contract, and she violated that contract. And she knew very well when she entered that alliance what the consequences might be if she interfered with, obstructed in any way, our plans. But really, she was just like all the rest of you. She smugly believed she was smarter than us. More powerful than us. *Superior* to us.

"My only regret is that I didn't get to be there the moment the rat poison took effect. I regret not being there to see her throat constrict, her body collapse, and her glamorous, oh-so-entitled life come to a horrifying, humiliating end."

Lee extracted his phone from his pants pocket and held it up between them. "And I don't regret at all recording that confession from you. Thanks for that. Now they can move forward with your arrest. For moving forward on that 'new project' you said just happened to materialize out of nowhere shortly after your plans to work with Jocelyn fell through. Just how much did 'O' pay you for betraying someone who had come to trust you so?"

Painstakingly, Julian reached into his pants pocket, slid out a revolver and directed it at Lee.

"Arrest me all you want to. That's not going to help you locate the microwave equipment or stop us from delivering to everyone in this region the ecstasy of knowing what completely unshackled freedom feels like."

Lee stiffened, took half a step back. "And killing me won't do you any favors, Julian. There's no way you can escape this hillside, given the number of officers that are crawling all over it right now. All you'll be doing is tacking onto your criminal record yet another charge of first-degree murder."

Julian stepped cautiously to one side, shoved the gun forward. His expression tensed, the hand holding the pistol quivered.

"Julian . . . don't do it! Think about everything you'll be giving up if you pull that trigger."

The security professional grimaced, took another step closer to his prey.

"I've already lost most everything I truly cared about. My career. Jocelyn." He ran the back of his free hand across the bridge of his nose. "Even you, Dalton." The firearm swayed from left to right, then back again. But suddenly Julian planted his feet against the pavement, steadied the pistol and aimed it directly at Dalton's chest.

The architect tensed, looked up, thrust both arms out in front of him.

"NO! WAIT! PLEASE! DON'T!

49

With four people occupying the small holding cell, it felt unusually cramped. In one corner, Kip Silva sucked on a strawberry Chupa Chup. In another, a wiry man in spectacles and a rumpled suit occupied a three-legged stool, his attorney's briefcase resting on his lap.

Julian Lao sat on a cot against the opposite wall. It was so low to the ground that his knees came up to his chin. His head was bowed as he massaged his forehead with the fingertips of both hands.

Silva cracked his knuckles and leaned away from the wall. "Your arraignment hearing will be the day after tomorrow, Mr. Lao," he said. "You took a nasty fall forward onto the pavement when our officer jumped you from behind, so we'll be sending you to the clinic here in a couple of hours to see if they can determine whether you suffered any internal injuries."

The security executive merely nodded and continued to knead the spot in the center of his forehead where a medium-sized lump had formed.

"When I kicked that rock off of the cliff, Kip, that was my signal to your cop below to capture him, not clobber him." Dalton Lee stood in the last remaining corner of the cell, his arms encircling the front of his torso, one ankle crossed in front of the other. He gazed down at the normally dapper, but now dowdy, terrorist with a look that straddled a spot somewhere between pity and heartache.

"Unfortunately, Dalton, we haven't quite perfected the art of taking a terrorist into custody," Silva replied.

"I thank you though for stationing all those officers along the tram route, and making sure they let me know they were ready to pounce when I needed them to," Lee acknowledged.

The attorney scribbled some notes onto a legal pad that rested on top of his briefcase, capped his pen and stood up. "Let me know, please, when all the charges have been drawn up," he announced, not looking at anyone I particular. With that, he marched toward the door of the cell, which a guard automatically swung open. The lawyer headed out the door, around a corner and out of sight.

The cubicle fell quiet for several moments. Eventually, Julian shifted his body on the cot and scowled as he did. "Ray . . . I mean . . . Mr. Silva. Are these handcuffs really necessary? I mean, I'm in a *cell* for God's sakes. Can't we remove these? They're chafing my wrists."

Lee glanced over at the head of the police force, who was moving the Chupa Chup from one side of his mouth to the other with just his tongue. The police officer eventually slid it out of his mouth and gave his prisoner a stern look.

"They are *very* necessary, and they are staying where they are . . . for the time being," He went to return the candy to its previous location, then changed his mind and dropped it beside him.

Julian groaned once more, looked up at the world's most prominent architect.

"I'm so sorry it's ending this way, Dalton. I've grown so fond of you. And I know you've grown fond of me, as well. I guess you understand now why you've had the feelings you've had for me. Pheromones being what they are, and all."

"Still, I really believe we have developed such a special . . . bond. One of those bonds that transcends continents and lifetimes. Do you understand what I'm saying?"

"Where's your little arsenal, Julian?" Lee demanded. "Is it in Tseung Kwan O? Somewhere else? You have no hope now of benefiting from any of the 'freedoms' you think will be brought on by this deaths of more business leaders and government officials.. Officials, I might remind you, who in most cases were freely elected to their positions by the people.

"Really, your only hope for not rotting in prison here is to cooperate and tell us where the equipment is."

Julian looked down at the floor for a few seconds, then raised his chin defiantly toward both Lee and Silva.

"I don't share secrets with those who assist the oppressor class," he spat out.

Lee's phone suddenly buzzed. It was a text from Liam: 'Epic amount of microwave activity around that industrial zone Kip Silva suggested. Seems to be increasing every thirty minutes or so.'

Lee leaned over, nudged Silva with his shoulder and showed him the text.

"Looks like Tseung Kwan O, it is," the police officer said, breaking out into a broad grin.

Julian's passive expression sagged into a frown. "Fuck," he grunted.

Kip Silva instantly swiveled to his right and headed for the cell door, beckoning Lee to follow him.

"DALTON!" Julian called out as the architect was departing. "We can at least stay good friends, can't we?"

Silva punched a few buttons on his phone as the pair raced toward the prison's main exit. While Silva was waiting for the call to connect, Lee nudged his colleague's shoulder once again.

"Maybe you can go a little easy on him?" he whispered. "He's not all that bad a person, really."

Silva shot Lee an irritated look and vigorously shook his head.

"No chance in hell," he said just as someone back at headquarters answered his call.

***

By the time Kip Silva had been able to mobilize a tactical team, three more government officials in the region had passed away. The president of the senate of the Philippines was discovered dead on the running track at the University of Makati. The CEO of Hong Kong's third largest bank died in the hospital he was admitted to after complaining of severe nausea, dizziness and vomiting.

The mayor of Fukuoka, on Japan's southern coast, leapt off a bridge into the Naka River. A note she left behind only said, "I cannot endure this physical torment any longer. I feel as though my mind and my body are at war."

Local officials insisted the mayor had had no prior history of mental illness or psychological distress.

"I sure hope your hunch, and Liam's software, are right," Lee said as Silva's police cruiser raced toward Tseung Kwan O. As they approached what was known locally as the Innopark, a phalanx of helicopters appeared overhead. Silva had ordered the perimeter of the park cordoned off; no one was being allowed to enter or leave the industrial zone.

Lee opened his phone and punched out a message: 'Liam have u been able to pinpoint where within the zone those microwave transmissions are coming from?'

The young Australian provided his superior a list of coordinates, which Lee passed on to Silva.

Meanwhile, reports had surfaced out of Canberra that the deputy prime minister of Australia had suddenly taken ill and was being rushed to a nearby hospital out of what was called an 'abundance of caution.'

Silva gave Lee an anxious look. "Anyone unusual being moved up to assume his duties in the interim?." The world's most prominent architect returned the question with a slow, solemn nod.

In a moment, Lee felt as if he were at the center of a Hollywood action film. At least six helicopters now hovered overhead, their propellers creating an almost deafening roar. A phalanx of vehicles, their sirens and lights blaring, screeched up to the scene from every possible direction. Lee could also make out what looked like an armada of patrol boats speeding across Junk Bay, toward the eastern edge of the industrial estate.

Silva opened his door, stepped out, then ducked his head back in.

"I'm ordering you to stay in this vehicle. You don't need to get yourself all wrapped up in this." He winked once, shot Lee a smile of confidence, then darted off toward the section of the industrial zone that Liam had identified.

The police assault was brief but victorious. Lee had jumped and grabbed for the door handle when two small explosions, one almost on top of the other, rocked the area. Soon after, he saw what appeared to be the remnants of tear gas, or some other chemical irritant, trailing up above some of the single-story warehouses about a half-mile away.

Then, as swiftly as the bombardment had begun, it stopped. The chaos–caused by sirens and helicopters and police watercraft–as well as tactical officers dashing through the streets with weapons drawn– subsided. The operation quickly morphed from a frantic and violent incursion into an organized restoration of peace and calm.

Lee waited patiently for Silva to return. The tactical teams filed past and behind the car, their rifles now pointed toward the street. The helicopters banked in the sky and drifted away. Whatever smoke the offensive had unleashed began to dissipate.

Lee's phone buzzed with a text from Silva: 'Mission accomplished. However, in my official capacity as superintendent-general of Macau, I still demand you remain in the car until I return. ☺

Lee smiled, pushed himself comfortably back into his seat, pulled a kerchief out of his jacket pocket to collect the sweat that had formed across his brow.

Then, the world's foremost architect noted out of the corner of his eye a curious and amazing sight. Padding casually down the sidewalk on the opposite side of the street was a Chinese woman he'd guess to be in her late forties or early fifties. She seemed carefree as could be and oblivious to all the bedlam she had just walked away from.

So content and composed the old woman was, she had no trouble staying focused on whatever handiwork project it was that she seemed so engrossed in . . .

50

"You wanted to see me, Dalton?"

"Yes, Lara, come in. Let me move my acrostic off that armchair. Take a seat there, please." The architect darted over to the chair, snatched the puzzle and pencil from the hassock in front of it and extended one arm. Lara ambled across the carpet, smoothed her skirt, descended into the chair and carefully folded her hands on her lap. Lee padded over to the chair opposite her and dropped himself onto its cushion.

"Just so I'm clear, Dalton, is this about The Lee Group or the murder case? Do I need to be taking notes?"

"No, no, you're fine. And to answer your question, my reason for asking you here doesn't really have anything to do with either of those things."

Lara moved her head forward, assumed a puzzled look. "Then, what . . ."

Her employer put up one palm. Took a couple of moments to choose his words. "Lara, there's been what you might call . . . an interesting development. By interesting, I mean that someone has made the decision to defect from 'O.' Or, as they prefer to describe it, retire."

Lara considered the revelation, then shrugged her shoulders. "Well,

I agree that is very interesting. But I don't see what that has to do with me."

"Right." Lee continued looking at Lara without saying anything for another couple of moments. Then he pressed both hands against the armrests of his chair and pushed himself up and out of it. He sauntered over to the French doors leading to his bedroom, opened them with a flourish, looked into the room and tilted his head back toward the living area.

A form emerged from the back area and as it did, Lara let out a gasp.

"MOTHER?" she cried.

The person who had served as Dalton Lee's clandestine confidant in Manhattan, Miami and Mayfair stepped carefully forward and hesitantly extended both arms toward her daughter.

"I'm so sorry, Lara. I'm sorry for deceiving you. I'm sorry for making you think I had died when I hadn't. But please try to understand I had to follow your father, to keep an eye on him. Take steps at time to keep him from assisting them more than he should. Be an emergency brake to his expertise.

"I'll understand perfectly if you want nothing to do with me. It was a terrible betrayal on my part, I know."

Lee's executive assistant staggered forward, fell into her mother's embrace.

"I forgive you," was all she said. Lee circled away from the pair and strolled over to a far back corner of the room.

The two women maintained their embrace for several minutes, with Lara's mother patting her daughter on the back repeatedly. Eventually, however, they released their grasp on each other. Lara wiped tears away with the back of her hand.

"I have to say, mother, it's hard for me to understand how you could have joined forces with those fanatics under any circumstances. But right now, I'm just so shocked and grateful that you are still alive."

"My relationship with them is . . . was . . . complicated, my dear. I'll do my best to explain it to you in due course. Until then, know that I have never stopped loving you and that I have actually been keeping close tabs on you all these years without your realizing it."

At that, she looked over her shoulder and tilted her head in Lee's direction.

The architect cleared his throat and crossed his arms in front of him.

"I think I'll leave you two here to catch up," he said. "Plus, I believe I need to drop a check in the mail to a certain street entertainer."

As Lee opened the door to leave, Lara interrupted him. "Dalton, I can't even begin to . . ."

Instantly, he put his right palm up in front of his face, smiled, shook his head once and then strode out through the door, closing it gently behind him.

***

Bree decided she needed to make one last shopping run before she returned to America.

She didn't really want anyone to know, but she was somewhat disappointed that they'd soon be heading home soon. She would never deprive Lara of the unexpected reunion she had enjoyed with her mother. And she certainly didn't want Dalton to think she was unhappy they had stopped O's rampage when they had.

Still, she felt melancholy. She believed that in pointing out to Lee how the feng shui of Jocelyn Cheng's office seemed awry, she had meaningfully contributed to O's plot being foiled. And, she had grown to admire the architecture and ambience of Macau and Hong Kong (if not its humidity).

So, one last trip to a mall was in order, she decided. To cheer herself up and to bring back at least one beautiful memento of their assignment in the region.

She chose Pacific Place, in Hong Kong's Admiralty section, as her destination. From the brochures in her room, it seemed to be the most luxurious and sophisticated option. And luxurious and sophisticated was definitely what she was in the mood for.

However, once she stepped inside the massive complex she didn't know where to start. She hadn't brought a shopping list per se, so the four floors featuring one high-end boutique after another overwhelmed her for a few moments. But it wasn't long before she had found two blouses, two pairs of slacks, a kimono-like wrap-around in red and black and a floral head scarf that all met with her satisfaction.

Luggage! she suddenly reminded herself. *I need to pick up another piece of luggage for everything I've bought since I've been here. Maybe two.*

It only took about fifteen minutes to find what she wanted in that category and arrange for the bags to be delivered to the hotel later that day.

She had one more stop she wanted to make, at a designer boutique on the mall's top level. She felt a little ashamed, given that the shop's namesake was Italian, not Asian. She knew she could probably find the same shop at one of the premier shopping centers back home. Still, she was here, and this was now. And, she really needed to be back at the hotel in about an hour to start packing for the flight.

The boutique seemed oddly serene. There were few customers milling about and, it seemed, even fewer salespeople, either on the floor or behind the few counters that dotted the establishment. She appreciated that she was not being pestered while she shopped, but the absence of any noise–save for what vaguely sounded like elevator music–felt more than a little bizarre.

She sauntered from one rounder to another, finding a few items that piqued her curiosity–until she glanced at the price tags. This boutique was definitely more expensive than its counterparts back home, she decided, and that caused her to consider heading back to the hotel before she had intended.

Then she spotted a fragrance counter nearby and chose to wander over to explore their offerings. She tried a couple of samples and decided she could not live without one that blended the scents of bergamot and nutmeg.

She didn't think anyone was staffing the counter, which was long, oval and open in the center. Its centerpiece was another, smaller counter bearing glass shelves that displayed a variety of perfumes, colognes and hand creams. Out of nowhere, she heard a thump on the other side of the center counter and then saw someone rising from near the floor.

"I am so sorry ma'am," the young salesgirl said as she stood up and used both her hands to brush lint from her black skirt. "I was stocking the lowest drawer, so I did not see or hear you come up. How may I help you?"

The young woman raised her face to look at her customer, and both she and Bree froze.

The salesclerk was a young woman around twenty years old with painstakingly applied makeup and an inviting smile.

A young woman with sandy-brown hair expertly coiled into a tightly knotted chignon.

A young woman with impeccable cheekbones and almond-shaped eyes projecting a piercing glare in brilliant, robins-egg blue.

A young woman of Eurasian descent that Bree was absolutely certain she had seen, more than once, crouching beneath the vestibules in the street markets of Kowloon.

Bree opened her mouth to say something, but as she did, the clerk became anxious, glanced over her left shoulder, swiveled quickly and dashed to the back of the store and through a dark curtain.

Never to return.

51

"So, if I could have one wish granted," Warren said, "it would be that it was Dalton's mother being released."

Bree pushed an errant strand of hair off her forehead and tucked it behind one ear. "I agree," she replied. "After all he's done for us. Saving you and the kids from that assassin in Manhattan. Securing the release of Roberto's little sister in London." She scanned the horizon for the helicopter that was scheduled to arrive at any moment with a hostage secured thanks to information Kip Silva had extracted from Julian Lao. "The generous advance he gave me while we've been here."

Warren pivoted toward the firm's other senior architect. "Wait, he gave you a hefty advance?"

Bree smiled coyly. "An *advance*, Warren. I just said *an advance*, not a *hefty* advance." She turned toward him, nudged his shoulder gently. "And don't worry, I made sure it went to a worthy cause." But the minute the phrase left her lips, her smile dipped. "At least, I thought I did, anyway.

The comment elicited a puzzled look from Warren. But he quickly shrugged it off and returned his focus to the world's most prominent architect.

"Something's up with Dalton," he murmured. "The hats. The way he keeps deflecting the conversation whenever we bring them up." Once again, Bree nodded in agreement.

"I know. I've felt it too. And I can't figure out what it is either." She sighed, turned to watch the sinuous path across the sky being taken by a purple balloon that a child next to them on the helipad had just set free.

Whether the child had released the balloon by accident or on purpose she couldn't be sure.

"Maybe he just wants to look nice," she offered. She watched the balloon trail away into the bright blue sky. "No, it can't be that. Looking dapper has always been part of Dalton's brand."

They both chuckled, and after they did, Warren sniffed the air a couple of times. "Why do I smell coconut?" he announced. "Suddenly I have a craving for coconut chicken soup."

Bree inhaled a couple of times. "I'm not smelling it. All I smell is exhaust. Besides, I'm not fond of coconut. You can have it. The soup, that is."

They retreated to their own thoughts for a while. Wondered whether it was their loved one, or the loved one of the person standing beside them, who was about to be returned. All they had been told, all the federal agency had revealed to them, was that the returnee was a woman whose location had been extracted from Julian Bao in exchange for his sentence being reduced.

"You know, it could be Liam's sister," Bree blurted out.

"Yes, it could be," Warren acknowledged. "And that would be terrific."

Bree tapped her right food nervously. "Still, Dalton sent the two of us to greet the hostage," she countered, clearly articulating the strong likelihood that the person on the helicopter was someone either she, or Warren, knew very well. His long-lost wife, or her mentor who had introduced her to feminism and activism.

She waited a few beats before adding, "If it is your wife they're bringing back, will you leave the firm? Return to Canada?"

He nodded a couple of times. "Probably," he replied. "After all this, I'd need some serious normal back in my life. If getting back to normal is even possible after all of this." He looked at his colleague, "And you?

Back to Arizona? Back to the ranch?"

Her expression of doubt surprised him. "Not so sure about that," she answered. "There's not really anyone close to me there anymore. And, I have to say that all of our international assignments have caused me to think about the bigger universe out there beyond saddles and stables."

Warren cocked his head to the left. "I think, maybe, I hear something." Sure enough, the distinct sound made by an approaching chopper intensified. After a few seconds, a speck in the sky appeared in front of them. Bree shielded her eyes to view the aircraft and was able to confirm it was not an airplane but a helicopter.

"Well, here we go," she pronounced as the whirlybird loomed larger in front of them. Warren, Bree and the family to their right retreated several steps as the pilot hovered the craft above the pad, then set it down as if he were placing an heirloom teacup onto an expensive saucer.

Warren felt his pulse throbbing; unconsciously, Bree balled both of her hands into tight, rigid fists.

Several excruciating moments elapsed before the copter's hatch finally opened. Two crew members stepped out, then turned to help a passenger depart the craft. It was a man in his early sixties, apparently a beloved patriarch of the family they were sharing the helipad with. The child who had lost the balloon, and a sibling, clambered around the pants legs of the silver-haired man, who tousled their hair and hugged their parents as they all trotted away from the helicopter.

For one long stretch, nothing else happened. Finally, another form appeared in the dimly lit doorway, then emerged into the bright sunlight.

"It's your wife, Warren," Bree announced. "It's her."

She released her left fist and went to place her palm on Warren's back, but he was already halfway across the helipad. His wife had a noticeable limp but hobbled toward her husband nonetheless, her arms extended toward him.

It was a long embrace, a tight and unyielding embrace, a silent embrace that nevertheless spoke volumes. An embrace everyone watched with admiration, an embrace no one on the helipad wanted to see come to an end.

As she watched the couple reunite, Bree found herself vacillating between feelings of disappointment and gratitude. She worried about Carole's welfare but could not help but be thankful that Warren's two children would soon see their mother again. After years of longing for her. After years of missed recitals and soccer games and oft-repeated bedtime stories. She knew that if Warren returned home as he had indicated he likely would, she would become the firm's most senior architect, a role she now felt better equipped to step into.

Her thoughts drifted from Carole to the young woman she had come upon first in the marketplace and then at the fragrance counter, to Lara and her long-lost mother and then to Warren and his wife.

Never before had she felt so connected to the grandeur of life, to all the precious cords that connect us to one another.

52

"Can anyone tell me why Dalton asked us to meet up all the way over here before the car takes us to the airport?"

Lara was standing behind Liam, who was absorbed in a slot machine that was not accommodating his wish to hit the jackpot. The executive assistant wore an exasperated look and kept glancing at her watch when she wasn't studying the reels as they spun then stopped, spun again then stopped again.

Anisa was leaning over one side of the machine, her head close to Liam's. "Come on, jackpot," she whispered. "Bring it home to mama." Warren, who was standing behind her, turned toward Lara on his left and bulged his eyes at his younger colleague's comment. On his right, Warren's wife used a forearm to stifle a laugh.

"Well, Lara, I think he just wanted us to visit the scene of the crime again before we went home," Warren said without much enthusiasm. "But the scene of the crime was over *there* by the roulette tables, not over here at the slot machines, so I'm not really sure what's going on . . ."

"Well, that's all well and good, but he asked us all to convene here and yet he's nowhere in sight," she muttered.

A squeaking of wheels began to compete with the sounds from

the slot machine. Everyone, Liam included, turned to see what was causing the commotion.

"Blimey, Bree, have you gone completely *troppo?*" he blurted.

The senior architect was striding toward them, a valet beside her. He was pushing a large bellman's cart teeming with suitcases–the four suitcases she had brought over from the States . . . and three more she had picked up earlier that day for all her recent purchases.

The smile on Warren's face straddled amazement and hilarity. "Bree, do you have any idea how much you're going to have to pay in excess baggage fees?" he said between laughs. "What do you have in there, all the furniture from your hotel room?"

"That's none of your business," she replied. "Besides, I'm confident Liam here is going to win a really big jackpot and pay those exorbitant fees for me."

"No, I won't," he replied as he pushed a button on the screen in front of him to launch another spin of the reels.

Bree shook her head, then tipped the valet, who bowed his head in thanks for the generous amount she had handed him. "And that reminds me, Warren, when did you become such a snoop into other people's affairs?" she added. Anisa let out a snort at the comment and looked over her shoulder at the target of Bree's barb.

Warren sent a genuine look of remorse her way. "I'm so sorry I pegged you for a terrorist," he said, shaking his head. "Really I am. It's just . . ."

"It's okay, Warren, it is. I mean, if I wanted to, I could–as the Aussies say–arc up and insist you only assumed I was a terrorist because I'm from the Middle East." She flashed a wide, somewhat fake grin in his direction, then added, "But I won't."

"And I thank you for that," he replied. He shook his head and put his arm around the shoulders of his wife. The couple stared into one another's eyes for several moments before the world's most prominent architect broke the reverie unceremoniously.

"Here I am," he announced as he walked up to the group from behind, bedecked in his black denim jacket. "And here you all are, I see." He tossed a quick look at the cart beside Bree. "Bringing all your ex-boyfriends with you on the trip back, I presume?"

Lara stepped in to defuse the situation. "Well, Dalton, we can all tell you're wearing an abundant amount of deodorant this morning," she began. "But you're not wearing any sort of hat. This must be the first day since we've been here that you haven't had something covering your head."

"Well," he began, catching Liam's eye in the process, "I guess I no longer feel like I have the need for one."

The young Aussie winked once at his superior then spun back around in his chair to try the slot machine one more time. And one more time, the machine disappointed him.

Anisa broke from her crouch and turned toward her employer. "I have a question, Dalton. Jocelyn Cheng's sister, and the others who were skimming money from the casino, what's going to happen to them?"

Just then Kip Silva strode up to the group alongside a woman of Filipino descent who appeared to be in her late fifties. Bree pulled in when she noticed Kip had his arm around the woman's waist. And that he was wearing the red and green tie she had intended to buy for him in the market.

"I can answer that," he said with a grin. "But before I do, let me introduce you to my partner, Ophelia. She's a senior vice president at the Banco Nacional Nuevo here. So, you'll understand it when I say we were 'sweating bullets' when O's initiative started taking down financial executives in the region."

As Ophelia exchanged pleasantries with the group, Bree ducked her head toward Lara's ear. "Well, there you have it," she whispered. "I thought maybe he wasn't interested in me was because he was gay. Turns out it's because he's a gigolo." Lara scowled back at her associate, then tempered it with a quick smile and a swat at Bree's nearest shoulder.

"Anyway, back to your question, Anisa," Silva continued. "You'll be happy to know that Regina Bauer has lost her Macau work visa and will be returning to the United States in the next couple of weeks. So, should she ask any of you whether she can go now, the correct answer is that she most certainly can and should."

The team all laughed at the joke. Silva, however, put one finger in the air.

"But wait, there's more. Both Alex Wentworth and Jacqueline Cheng will face charges for their roles in the conspiracy against the casino, so they'll be staying here, under confinement, until either their trials take place, or they strike some sort of plea deal. Confronted with Alex Wentworth's confession, the others caved in fairly quickly, although I must say Regina Bauer stuck to her guns much longer than we expected her to. Only when we presented her with an audio feed from the elevator bank, in which you can hear Jocelyn Cheng calling her 'Regina,' did she admit that it was her we saw in the videos."

"I knew it either had to be her or Kim Kardashian," Warren joked, "so I'm glad she cleared that up for us."

Everyone laughed heartily and then did so even more when Warren's wife piped up, "You used to say you couldn't tell Kim Kardashian and *me* apart."

Warren reached around his wife and punched his boss on the upper arm.

"And do we assume those multi=million-dollar payments Jocelyn Cheng received from those bogus companies were rent checks for her continuing to watch over their microwave equipment? And that, when they murdered her, they withdrew the money as quickly as they could?"

"We do," Lee answered. "One of the downsides of allowing external firms to have complete access to your accounts. Those automatic deposits are convenient, but the automatic withdrawals can hurt like hell."

Everyone chuckled again, only in a more low-key way, as the significance of the architect's comment sunk in.

Lee surveyed his team and was pleased to see everyone in a jovial mood. Everyone except Liam, who continued to be frustrated by the slot machine he'd been playing for almost twenty minutes.

"That's it! I'm done!" he announced, jumping up from the seat. "Now I know why it's called a bandit. Your turn, Dalton?"

The architect put both palms up in the air. "No, no, I've never been a gambling man," he said quietly.

"Come on, Dalton!" Warren urged. "We still have another ten

minutes before the car taking us to the airport arrives. Let yourself have some fun. You can afford to lose a couple of dollars at least."

Lee kept shaking his head, but steadily moved toward the seat vacated by Liam. Once he was situated comfortably, he took a deep breath and squinted at all the lights and numbers and symbols in front of him.

"I have no idea how to work this thing," he admitted, jutting his head forward to get a better look at the display.

"Here, boss, let me show you." Liam leaned over Lee's shoulder, quickly explained how the slot machine operated, then pushed himself upright.

"Dalton, you only have time for one play," Lara interjected. "I just got a text saying our car has already arrived."

"Okay, here goes nothing," Lee said as he pressed the button setting his machine's reels off on a spin. He was mesmerized by the multimedia extravaganza that appeared in front of him. The team leaned in toward him and chanted 'Go Dalton, go!' over and over again.

And then, he hit the jackpot. A one-million-dollar jackpot.

Lara pivoted toward Bree and threw her hands in the air. "I don't believe it!" she muttered.

"What happened? Did I break the machine?" Dalton looked first in front of him, then back over both his shoulders, as the cacophony being created by the machine itself, and his colleagues behind him, swelled into an aural roar.

"No, you won, Dalton!" Anisa exulted. "You won A LOT OF MONEY!"

The beeping and clanging and sirens and shrieks almost drowned out the reply from the world's most prominent architect.

"Oh, good," Lee said as his team ruffled his hair and clapped him enthusiastically on his back. "Because, I'm going to need a lot of money to get all of you back to the United States safe and sound!"

***

The chiming of her cellphone irritated the Chinese woman who was resting on a chaise longue following her having received the best foot massage of her life.

"Hello. Is this Yang Li?"

"*Shi de.*"

"How are you, doing? We hear you were able to escape the takeover of our assets in Hong Kong."

She hesitated. Thought to ask who it was. But didn't because she knew who it was.

"Yes, I escaped. What do you want?"

"Although our initiative in Macau did not produce the objective we hoped it would, we like to reward our most loyal compatriots."

"Go on. And hurry. I get a chamomile facial in fifteen minutes."

"Yes, well, do we understand correctly that you speak French as well as Cantonese."

"*Mais oui.* And Italian and Cantonese and Mandarin and English and Russian. But no Japanese. It too hard."

"I see. Well, if you speak French fluently, Yang Li, let's just say we think we may have another assignment for you soon . . ."

Foreshadowing

The terrorist organization *O* may have been stopped for the time being. But it hasn't given up on its main strategy of helping people live flawless lives in a flawed world.

Dalton Lee and the rest of The Lee Group will realize that soon enough, when they are summoned to one of North America's most colorful cities and discover that Murder Becomes Mardi Gras, as well.

***

Please post a review of "Murder Becomes Macau"

We would be grateful if you would write an honest review of this book on the website of the bookseller you purchased it from. If you participate on Goodreads, we'd appreciate a review of it there as well. Your review can help other mystery lovers find this book and dive into it the way you did.

***

Get the Backstory

This is not the only time The Lee Group has solved a mysterious murder and deduced how the victim interfered with a takeover scheme planned by O/The Organization.

Learn more about the architect-detectives who make up The Lee Group, as well as the cult they are shadowing, in:

Murder Becomes Manhattan

Murder Becomes Miami

Murder Becomes Mayfair

murderbecomes.com

Connect with Jeffrey Eaton via:

Facebook
facebook.com/daltonleemysteries

Twitter
twitter.com/murderbecomes

Instagram
instagram.com/murderbecomes

Get the inside scoop about the next *Murder Becomes* mystery thriller, and the other upcoming works of Jeffrey Eaton, by signing up for the Jeffrey Eaton email newsletter:

murderbecomes.com/subscribe.html

About the Publisher

The Cornet Group LLC was established in 2014 to bring forward intriguing perspectives and intelligent writing presented through the genre of fiction.

Learn more at:

CORNET

thecornetgroup.com

Milton Keynes UK
Ingram Content Group UK Ltd.
UKHW012159200923
429086UK00013B/153/J

9 781735 209227